ASHLEY FARLEY

Cover design: damonza.com

Editor: Patricia Peters at A Word Affair LLC

Leisure Time Books, a division of AHF Publishing

also by ashley farley

Marsh Point

Long Journey Home

Echoes of the Past

Songbird's Second Chance

Heart of Lowcountry

After the Storm

Scent of Magnolia

Virginia Vineyards

Love Child

Blind Love

Forbidden Love

Love and War

Palmetto Island

Muddy Bottom

Change of Tides

Lowcountry on My Mind

Sail Away

Hope Springs Series

Dream Big, Stella!

Show Me the Way

Mistletoe and Wedding Bells

Matters of the Heart

Road to New Beginnings

Stand Alone

On My Terms

Tangled in Ivy

Lies that Bind

Life on Loan

Only One Life

Home for Wounded Hearts

Nell and Lady

Sweet Tea Tuesdays

Saving Ben

Sweeney Sisters Series

Saturdays at Sweeney's

Tangle of Strings

Boots and Bedlam

Lowcountry Stranger

Her Sister's Shoes

Magnolia Series

Beyond the Garden

Magnolia Nights

Scottie's Adventures

Breaking the Story

Merry Mary

one

. . .

Isabelle spent the morning reading a Pat Conroy novel in the hammock, strung between two palmetto trees near the pool. While she'd read all the celebrated author's novels many times, *South of Broad* was among her favorites. She could never get enough of Conroy's vivid descriptions of her beloved Lowcountry. His portrayal of dysfunctional characters made her feel like her family's problems weren't so bad after all.

Isabelle seldom indulged in the luxury of a morning spent lounging. She had little free time between social obligations and keeping her home spit-polished clean. But with the court case tomorrow, her nerves were on edge and she needed the distraction.

When a shadow crossed the page, Isabelle shielded her eyes from the sun as she looked up at the middle-aged woman looming over her. She sat bolt upright, throwing her legs over the side of the hammock. "Who are you? And what are you doing on my property?"

"My name is Pearl Lee, and I've come for my ten o'clock appointment."

Isabelle's mind raced. She didn't remember scheduling an appointment, but her memory had been slipping lately. She gave the frumpy woman a once-over. Dressed in a black cobbler apron with her gray hair fastened into a tight bun, she was certainly no one Isabelle would ever socialize with. "I'm afraid I don't know what appointment you're referring to."

"The job interview. About the housekeeping position you posted on JobQuest."

"You must be mistaken. I've never heard of JobQust," Isabelle said, struggling to get out of the hammock.

The woman offered a hand, hauling Isabelle to her feet. She retrieved her phone from her black patent purse and tapped on the screen. "Says here that Pritchard St. Clair posted the announcement. Is he your husband?"

"No. My husband's dead. Pritchard is my son. Excuse me a moment while I call him." Isabelle crossed the pool deck to the house. When the woman tried to follow her inside, she instructed her to wait on the terrace.

Isabelle sat down at her Queen Anne desk in the living room and dialed her son's number on the landline. When he answered, she barked out, "Pritchard! There's a woman here about a housekeeping job. She says you posted about the job on some website."

From his end of the line came the sound of rustling paper. "Yes, Mother. That would be Pearl. Three others will follow in forty-five-minute intervals. Their names are Florence, Doris, and Hilda."

"I don't understand, Pritchard. I already have a cleaning service."

"A weekly service. When you open for business on Friday, you'll need a daily staff to clean the guest rooms."

Isabelle brought her fist down on the desk. "This isn't an inn, Pritchard. This is my home. I will win my court case tomorrow and end this nonsense."

"You're right. It's not an inn. It's a bed and breakfast." Pritchard exhaled an aggravated sigh. "Dad's will is iron tight,

Mother. You won't win tomorrow. Then who's going to clean your guest rooms? You?"

"Heavens, no!" But what if Isabelle didn't win? She wouldn't be caught dead cleaning up after strangers. "Fine, Pritchard. I'll take care of it."

Rising from her desk, Isabelle smoothed out her linen capri slacks and tucked her gray shoulder-length hair behind her ear. She opened the French door to let the woman in. "My son has confirmed the appointment. Come with me and I'll show you around."

Pearl walked swiftly and quietly behind Isabelle up the sweeping staircase. "This place is humongous. Is it a hotel or something?"

"Currently, it's my home. But my husband is determined to turn it into a bed and breakfast."

"I thought you said your husband was dead."

"He is. It's a long story." Isabelle retrieved a stack of clean white bedsheets from the hall linen closet and entered one of the guest rooms with Pearl on her heels. Pulling back the bedspread, she stripped the linens and handed the clean set to Pearl. "Let's see how well you can make a bed."

Isabelle peered over the woman's shoulder as Pearl stretched the bottom sheet taut enough to bounce a quarter. She created neat hospital corners with the flat sheet at the foot of the bed and spread the cotton blanket on top, folding the top edge of the sheet over the blanket. After adding the coverlet, she stuffed the pillows into the cases, arranged them neatly on the bed, and then added the decorative shams.

Isabelle straightened one of the shams and smoothed out a wrinkle in the bedspread. "That'll suffice."

Pearl gathered the sheets Isabelle had stripped off the bed. "Having starched sheets makes all the difference. Do you send them to the cleaners?"

"Never! They put too much starch in them. I iron them myself. I have high standards for my home."

Pearl handed the sheets to Isabelle. "I can see that. I'm surprised you don't have full-time help."

"I did when I was younger, when we frequently entertained out-of-town guests. It isn't easy to find good help these days. No one seems willing to do things the way I want them done."

"I'm a quick learner, Mrs. St. Clair. You'll only need to show me once."

"I'll keep that in mind." Isabelle deposited the balled-up sheets on the bed to deal with later and showed Pearl the rest of the upstairs. "We have seven bedrooms in the main house and five in the pool and garden houses."

Pearl went to a window and peeked out at the ocean view. "How many staffers will you hire for your bed and breakfast?"

"Only one to start."

Pearl gawked at her. "Only one?" She spread her arms wide. With all these beds to make and this big house to keep tidy? With all due respect, this is entirely too much work for one person. I typically work five days a week. I'm willing to work six *if* I'm being paid overtime, but I need at least one day off to reset."

Isabelle scrutinized the woman, wondering if her tight bun hurt her brain. "Reset? Why doesn't anyone just say *rest* anymore?"

Pearl hunched her shoulders to her ears. "Good question," she said, and they both laughed.

Continuing down the stairs, they moved through the living room and Edward's study to the dining room. From there, they circled back through the butler's pantry to Isabelle's favorite room —the kitchen.

Isabelle asked Pearl about the type of brass polish she preferred and what setting she used when vacuuming Oriental rugs. While her answers satisfied Isabelle, she wasn't yet ready to hire her.

They stepped out the front door into the stone courtyard. Isabelle pointed ahead to the pool house and to the right toward the garden house, both built in styles similar to the main house.

Together, the three residences formed an inverted U-shape with a manicured garden filling the center of the U and stretching down to the courtyard.

"This place is amazing," Pearl said in wonder. "And your view. Does the property occupy the entire southern tip of Sandy Island?"

A sad smile crept across Isabelle's lips. "Yes, it does. My husband used to call Magnolia Shores the end of the world."

"Did you and your husband build all this?"

Isabelle looked at the woman as though she'd lost her mind. "The compound is over a hundred years old. My husband's grandparents built the estate in the early nineteenth century. He was a tobacco farmer from North Carolina, and Magnolia Shores was his summer residence." She motioned the woman to the beat-up Toyota parked in the driveway. "I've taken up enough of your time. Have a good day. I'll be in touch about the maid position."

"Housekeeper, ma'am."

Isabelle raised an eyebrow. "I beg your pardon."

"I prefer to be called a housekeeper."

Isabelle gave Pearl a curt nod. "I stand corrected."

Another jalopy of a car arrived as Pearl was pulling out, and for the next two hours, Isabelle repeated the interview process three more times. While Pearl was the most qualified of the four candidates, Isabelle preferred Hilda, a quiet and efficient young Brazilian woman who spoke no English. Isabelle saw no reason to hire any of them until Judge Buchanan announced his decision tomorrow.

Isabelle had no sooner closed the door on the last housekeeper when the doorbell rang again. Seeing the attractive man on her stoop brought a smile to Isabelle's face. "May I help you?" she asked.

"I'm here about the bellman job."

Isabelle's smile faded. "That position has been filled," she said and slammed the door in his face.

She returned to her desk in the living room and pulled out the file containing her husband's will, a labyrinth of conditions and demands. Upon his death from pancreatic cancer ten months ago, Edward left token gifts to their children and placed the bulk of his estate in a trust for the upkeep of Magnolia Shores. The will further stipulated that Isabelle was to fulfill his long-held dream of converting their home into a bed and breakfast. Should she refuse, she would receive only a meager monthly stipend for living expenses—an amount insufficient to cover her current clothing allowance, much less the rent for a cottage or apartment to the standard she was accustomed to. Pritchard would then get first dibs on running the inn, and if he opted out, her daughter, Kate, would have her chance. If neither chose to become the innkeeper, the property would be turned over to the state and converted into a park.

Isabelle saw no way out unless the judge ruled in her favor tomorrow.

two

. . .

Shelby finally landed a job interview—not that she'd been trying very hard to get one. She'd been living at home since graduating two years ago from Texas A&M. Her parents were fed up with her staying out late and sleeping until noon. They kept telling Shelby to grow up but offered no guidance on how to do that.

Flipping through her hanging clothes, Shelby chose her favorite teal swing dress, which Luke said matched the color of her eyes. Twisting her strawberry-blonde hair into a messy knot, she dabbed concealer onto her freckles and stepped back to admire her reflection. Despite her efforts, nothing seemed to hide the freckles completely.

She slipped her feet into her most sensible shoes—cork wedge sandals—and headed downstairs to the kitchen.

Her mother stood by the window, talking quietly on the phone, and her sister sat at the round breakfast table. On her way to get coffee, Shelby glanced at the colorful fabric swatches covering the table. "What's all this?"

Grace's head jerked up. "What does it look like, Shelby? I'm picking out a color for my bridesmaid's dresses."

"Oh. For a moment there, I thought you'd barfed up confetti."

"Ha ha. Aren't you the comedian?"

Shelby removed a K-cup and popped it into the Keurig. "I thought your bridesmaids were wearing black."

"You're just jealous because you're not in the wedding."

"Hardly. I'm busy that weekend anyway." Shelby pressed the Keurig button and watched hot brew stream into her to-go cup. "Who's Mom talking to?"

"Izzy. About her court case tomorrow." Grace left the table and moved over to the island. "I'm surprised to see you awake before noon. Are you going somewhere?"

"I have a job interview. Not that it's any of your business."

Their mother, overhearing mention of her job interview, ended the call with their grandmother. "Shelby? Did you just say you have an interview?"

"Yep," Shelby said, adding three spoonfuls of sugar and a long pour of creamer to her coffee.

Kate placed a hand on Shelby's shoulder. "That's wonderful, sweetheart. Who are you interviewing with?"

Shelby took a sip of coffee. "A bougie boutique hotel downtown. I don't want to jinx my chances by telling you which one."

Grace eyed her dress, her nose turned up in distaste. "Couldn't you find something more appropriate to wear? You don't stand a chance dressed like that." Grace was a sophisticated young professional in a dark gray business suit with a white silk blouse. Her honey-blonde hair complemented her flawless complexion, which was unmarred by freckles.

Kate ran her hand over the sleeve, feeling the pilling fabric from too much wear. "This dress has seen better days. Why don't you wear the gray pantsuit I bought you?"

Shelby brushed her mother's hand away. "This dress is fine. I'm applying for a job in a hotel, not at a bank," she said, slinging her purse over her shoulder and heading for the door.

Tears stung Shelby's eyes as she backed her convertible out of the driveway. Three years that felt like a lifetime separated Shelby and her sister. Although Shelby had sparked the latest argument with her confetti comment, it was usually Grace who initiated their fights with her endless criticism and condescension. Truth be told, Shelby was still reeling from being excluded from the wedding party. As Grace's only sister, she had expected to be the maid of honor. Bare minimum, a bridesmaid. She's the only sister in the history of the universe not included in her own sister's wedding.

Grace had set the bar high. In high school, she was an all-state tennis player and valedictorian of her senior class. In college at UVA, she was president of her sorority, made the dean's list every semester, and graduated magna cum laude from the McIntire School of Commerce. Grace and her fiancé, Wyatt, earned a gazillion dollars a year in high-tech jobs Shelby couldn't begin to understand. They were the quintessential power couple, both gorgeous and social and athletic. Grace's wedding, scheduled for late April of next spring, would be Austin's social event of the year. And everyone in attendance would wonder why Shelby wasn't a bridesmaid.

Unlike her sister, Shelby was a natural-born underachiever—a total loser with a face full of freckles.

Shelby entered the hotel's posh lobby with feigned confidence, chin up and head held high. Approaching the front desk, she gave the clerk her name and asked to see the hotel's manager.

"His office is right over there." The clerk motioned her behind the desk to an office where Darian Gilbert, a cheesy-looking man with slicked-back hair and polyester clothes, greeted her at the door.

Shelby declined his offer of a beverage and sat down opposite him at his desk.

"Well then." Darian opened a file in front of him. "I reviewed your resume, such as it is." He looked up at her. "Have you ever held a job, Miss Kinder?"

"No, sir. I've been in school."

He arched a bushy eyebrow. "Not even a summer internship?"

Shelby's face warmed. "No, sir. But I have a degree in hospitality management from Texas A&M."

He tapped on her resume. "Which you received over two years ago. What have you been doing since graduation?"

"I was taking a gap year," she said with a fake laugh.

He pressed his lips thin. "I see. While you're unqualified for the reservations manager position you applied for, we have an opening for a desk clerk. Is that something you might be interested in?"

Shelby remembered her argument with her parents two nights ago when her father threatened to take away her credit cards and kick her out of the house. "Potentially. Can you tell me more?"

"It's the night shift. You'd be working from eleven until seven."

Shelby's jaw dropped and her eyes grew large. "Including weekends?"

"Of course. It's an entry-level position, and weekends are our busiest time." When he told her the weekly salary, Shelby barked out a laugh. She routinely spent more than that on dinner in five-star restaurants.

He closed the file folder and placed his hands on top. "I'm sorry, Miss Kinder, but you're not the right fit for our staff. We're an upscale boutique hotel, catering to pampered guests like yourself." He rose from his desk, indicating the interview was over. Have a nice day."

"Thank you for your time," Shelby mumbled on her way out.

She made it to her car before bursting into tears. Growing up would have to wait another day. Taking a few minutes to compose herself, she cruised around town aimlessly for over an hour before parking in front of the house next door to Luke's. He also lived at home with his parents, only he was making a fortune managing other people's money. Shelby often staked out his house during his lunch breaks. She didn't care if he saw her. She'd been unabashedly stalking him for over a year.

Her phone buzzed in her lap with a text from her best friend.

Where are you? The pool opened today, but no one is here. Get over here fast. We have the place all to ourselves.

Nobody's there because they are all at work. Shelby texted Emily back.

Sorry. Not today. Maybe tomorrow.

When she looked up from her phone, Luke was standing beside her car. She rolled down her window. "Hey," she said, flashing him her most brilliant smile.

"Shelby, you have to stop coming over here like this. Our relationship is over. You need to accept that I'm with Alexis now."

Her throat thickened. "I know that, Luke. But I can't help it. I miss our friendship."

Luke hung his head. "I do too, Shelby. But Alexis isn't comfortable with me being friends with you."

"Wow. She really has her claws in you. You're making a terrible mistake, Luke. Don't count on me being around when you realize it." Rolling up her window, she turned on her engine and peeled away from the curb.

Shelby made idle threats like that all the time. But of course, she would still be around when he grew tired of Alexis. She'd been with Luke since middle school. He was the first boy she kissed and the only one she'd ever slept with. They were inseparable throughout high school and college. She couldn't remember her life pre-Luke. He'd promised her the country club lifestyle with a big house and lots of kids. He was driven and determined to be the next Warren Buffet, whoever that was. Shelby had never intended to work. She'd majored in hospitality management because she thought it would make her a better wife, equipping her with skills to manage a home efficiently. And now he was planning that happily ever after with someone else.

three

. . .

"I demand a retrial," Isabelle said from the back seat of her son's car on the way home from the courthouse.

Pritchard locked eyes with her through the rearview mirror. "Really, Mother? Based on what grounds?"

"Discrimination. Judge Merrick was your father's fishing buddy. Naturally, he would be biased toward Edward's will. Where was Judge Buchanan anyway? What was so important to keep him out of court today?"

"Apparently, he had a family emergency," Savannah said from the passenger seat.

"I'm aware of that, Savannah. I want to know what kind of family emergency is more important than court." Isabelle stuck her tongue out at the back of her daughter-in-law's head. She resented the young woman's intrusion into their lives. She rarely had time alone with her son since they married a few months ago.

Pritchard shot Isabelle a warning look over his shoulder. "That's none of your business, Mother. And there's no need to get snippy with Savannah."

Isabelle settled back in her seat. "Couldn't they have delayed the case until Judge Buchanan returned from his family emergency?"

"We needed a decision today with the bed and breakfast scheduled to open on Friday."

"We should've delayed the opening too," Isabelle said, riding the rest of the way home in silence. Her life was about to take a drastic turn for the worse.

When they arrived, Isabelle exited the car and hurried to the front door, rummaging in her purse for her keys. Hearing the car door slam behind her, she spun around to face Pritchard and Savannah. "Now is not a good time for a visit. In case you haven't noticed, I'm terribly upset and need to be alone right now."

"We aren't here for a social visit. We need to discuss opening the inn." Pritchard took the keys from Isabelle and unlocked the door.

She followed him into the living room with Savannah on her heels. "What's there to discuss, Pritchard?"

He shrugged off his navy linen blazer and tossed it onto a nearby chair. "For starters, how many reservations have you accepted?"

"A bunch." Isabelle lifted a file folder off the desk and handed it to him.

He thumbed through the disarray of scrap paper where she had jotted down names and dates. "This is a mess. You need to come up with a better filing system."

"She needs a website," Savannah volunteered.

Isabelle glared at her. "I don't do computers, Savannah. I have all of the reservations written in my daytimer," she lied.

The phone on the desk rang, and Isabelle snatched up the receiver. "Hello," she answered in a gruff voice.

The woman on the other inn coughed into the phone. "Excuse me. I may have the wrong number. I'm trying to reach Magnolia Shores Bed and Breakfast."

"You have the right number. But if you're calling about a reservation, we're booked solid through the summer," Isabelle said and slammed down the receiver.

"Mother! Why on earth did you do that?"

"Why do you think? I need a drink." Isabelle entered her husband's adjacent study and poured a splash of vodka into a cut crystal glass.

Pritchard followed her, taking the glass from her before she could drink it. "It's too early for this. You told me you had everything under control."

Isabelle let out a humph. "And you believed me? What do I know about managing a bed and breakfast? I haven't held a job since before you were born."

"Maybe you don't have real job experience, but you've hosted dozens of beach weekends for your out-of-town friends. This is only slightly different than that."

"Have you lost your mind? This is vastly different than that. These people are strangers. And they are coming to stay in my home. They will be sleeping in my bed." Isabelle crumpled into a nearby chair. "I was certain I would win in court today. How could Edward do this to me?"

Savannah lowered herself to the arm of the chair. "Look at the bright side, Izzy. You have an opportunity to make his dream come true."

Isabelle glared at her. "Edward's dream is my worst nightmare."

Prichard held out his hand to her. "Let's go to the kitchen. We'll fix some lunch and come up with a plan."

"Fine." She accepted his hand, and he pulled her to her feet, leaning on him as he walked her down the hall to the kitchen.

Savannah made lunch while Pritchard and Isabelle sat at the antique oak farm table with a pitcher of sweet tea and a legal pad.

"What staff have you hired?" Pritchard asked with pen in hand, poised to write.

"None yet. I guess I'll hire two of the maids I interviewed yesterday. Hilda and Pearl were the best."

"Good! That's a start." He scribbled on the legal pad. "And we already have a bellman."

Isabelle held her tongue. Her son wouldn't be happy to learn she'd sent his bellman packing.

Pritchard chewed on the end of the pen. "What other staff should we hire? Do we need a lifeguard?"

From across the island, Savannah suggested, "Why don't you determine your needs before you hire any more staff?"

Pritchard smiled lovingly at her. "That's probably smart."

Isabelle rolled her eyes. Her son would approve if his wife suggested they hire a belly dancer to greet their guests.

"Are you set up to accept credit cards?" Pritchard asked.

"Nope. That's not necessary."

Pritchard's mouth dropped open. "How do you plan for your guests to pay?"

Isabelle tapped on the bottom of his chin. "Close your mouth, son, before you catch a fly. The guests can pay by check."

Pritchard narrowed his blue eyes. "When's the last time you paid by check at a hotel?"

She leveled her gaze on him. "When's the last time I stayed in a hotel?"

He considered this a minute before nodding. "Fair point. Have you done *anything* to prepare?"

Isabelle shook her head. "I already told you. I was certain Judge Buchanan would save me from this predicament your father left me in."

Pritchard tossed his pen on the pad and fell back in his chair. "Since you're adamantly opposed to all this, let's discuss your choices. I'm your only other option since Kate's life is in Texas. Unless you're willing to turn our family's legacy over to the state."

Isabelle felt a stabbing pain in her chest. Was she having a heart attack? Or was this what guilt felt like? "Never."

"Not that I know more about running a bed and breakfast than you." Pritchard glanced over at his wife. "What do you say, sweetheart? Do you fancy yourself an innkeeper?"

Savannah smiled at him. "I know a thing or two about hospitality."

Isabelle held her tongue at the mention of her daughter-in-law's menial profession. While Savanah had recently been promoted to manager of the most popular tavern in town, she'd worked for thirty years as a bartender in Washington State. "What will happen to me? I'll be forced to live in the poor house on the paltry allowance your father left me."

When Pritchard placed his hand on hers, the world fell away, and Savannah disappeared from the room. They were mother and son, having one of the many heart-to-hearts talks they'd had at this table over the years. "You can do this, Mother. You set the bar high when it comes to entertaining. You welcome guests into your home with grace, no matter the size of the party. You'll be the town's envy, the elegant Isabelle St. Clair, mistress of the five-star Magnolia Shores Bed and Breakfast."

Savannah interrupted them by delivering their lunch—an assortment of sandwich halves and a bowl of kettle chips—to the table. Isabelle fell silent while they ate. She watched her son and his bride interact as they added items to the to-do list. Isabelle was once as lovely and vibrant as Savannah. Pritchard looked at Savannah with the same love in his eyes that Edward showed Isabelle every day of their lives together. Not once during all their married years did she question Edward's love for her. Until now. She was furious at her husband for putting her in this situation. He'd pulled the rug right out from under her beautiful life.

Isabelle sat up straighter in her chair. She would get through this. She'd survived much worse before. She would suffer through the first round of guests this weekend, but first thing Monday morning, she would meet with her attorney to begin the process of appealing Judge Merrick's decision.

"You're a million miles away. What's on your mind?" Savannah asked Pritchard in the car on the way home from Magnolia Shores.

"My mother." He glanced over at her. "I'm tired of her being so hostile toward you."

"She resents my sudden presence in your life. She's used to having you all to herself."

Pritchard returned his attention to the road. "Maybe so, but that doesn't excuse her rude behavior. She's in over her head with this bed and breakfast. She's not even trying."

"Do you blame her? She's seventy-five years old. Without her knowledge, your father imposed a drastic change on the comfortable life she's been living for decades. Why did he wait until he was dead to fulfill his dream?"

Pritchard sighed. "Because he ran out of time. Shortly after Dad retired from his law firm at age sixty-five, he was diagnosed with prostate cancer. He had one health issue after another until the pancreatic cancer killed him."

"I'm sorry, Pritch. I didn't realize he'd been sick with other illnesses for so long. That's a valuable lesson about not putting things off until tomorrow."

"Right? I give my mother credit. Despite her many faults, she took excellent care of him. And now, when she's finally unburdened of those duties, he saddles her with a bed and breakfast."

Pritchard pulled into the driveway and turned off the engine. He'd been thrilled when the small cottage on the inland side of the island came on the market. He enjoyed having a dock for his boat and watching the boat traffic in Catawba Sound. He and Savannah had completed the restoration themselves, opting for an interior of mostly white—walls, floors, and furnishings—with accents of ocean blues. She claimed the clean palette reminded her to focus on the future and leave her baggage in the past.

Savannah walked her fingers up his arm. "I don't have to be at work for a while. Can I interest you in a little hanky panky?"

"Hmm. I like the sound of that." Pritchard checked the dashboard clock for the time. "I have an hour before my call."

Giggling like children, they raced each other inside to their bedroom, stripped off their clothes, and fell into bed. They'd been married for two months and living together for almost a year, but their honeymoon was far from over. After thirty years of being apart, they had a lot of making up to do.

Thirty minutes later, they lay spent in each other's arms. "I'm sorry if I was grumpy earlier. I just want us to be a big happy family," Pritchard said.

"Your vision of the ideal family is unrealistic, Pritch. All families have issues. We have more than our share on both sides. Although my siblings are getting along better than we ever have."

"Thanks to you. You were the glue that brought them back together." Pritchard nuzzled her neck. "But you're right. My expectations are unrealistic. I'm grateful to have you and Harper back in my life."

Savannah splayed her fingers on his bare chest. "And Harper will marry Cody, and we will soon have grandchildren."

The thought of not sharing his grandchildren with his mother saddened him. But he would have no choice but to distance himself from his mother, Izzy, if her attitude toward Savannah and Harper didn't improve.

four

. . .

Shelby waited until the house grew quiet, when she was certain her mom had left for work, before emerging from her bedroom. She stopped short in the kitchen doorway at the sight of Kate working on her laptop. "Mom! What're you doing here? Won't you be late for work?"

Kate looked up from her computer. "Morning, sunshine. I'm working from home today. I was hoping to see you last night before you went out. How did your interview go?"

To avoid her mother's inquisition, Shelby had gone to dinner with friends before hitting the clubs. "The interview was great. Unfortunately, I don't have enough experience for the position. But don't worry, I'm tracking down some more leads."

"Good. Keep at it. You'll find something." Kate eyed her swimsuit cover-up. "Is the pool open already?"

"Yep. Today's the second day." Shelby eyed the Keurig. While she desperately needed coffee, if she lingered, her mom would undoubtedly question her about other employment opportunities, which Shelby would have to answer with more lies. She lifted her hand in a wave. "Gotta run, Mom. See you later."

A cloudless periwinkle sky and temperatures in the low seventies greeted her outside—a perfect day for sunning by the pool. A little color on her cheeks always made her feel better about herself, even if that color made her freckles more pronounced.

On the short drive to the club, Shelby thought about her mom's job with the most prominent lighting distributor in Texas. The company sold seriously cool fixtures if that sort of thing drew your attention. Shelby never understood why her mother worked when her father made a fortune as a cardiac surgeon. When Shelby won Luke back, they would get married, and she would never have to worry about finding a job again.

The pool was surprisingly crowded, and Shelby had to circle the parking lot three times before locating a space. Fortunately, Emily had saved her a lounge chair.

"I wasn't expecting anyone to be here," Shelby said. "Aren't they supposed to be at work?"

Emily hunched a bony shoulder. "IDK. I overheard some people talking. Today is Alexis's twenty-fifth birthday. Everyone took off work to help her celebrate."

Shelby's face fell. "Oh."

"I'm sorry, girlfriend. We can leave if you want."

"Nope." Shelby pulled her sun hat out of her pool bag, tugging it low on her head. "As club members, we have as much right to be here as they do."

She slathered on sunscreen and settled back on her lounge chair. When she looked at her friend, Emily was peering over her Krewe sunglasses at the crowd. "What're you looking at, Em?" She followed her gaze to Luke, who was standing at the end of the diving board. "What's he doing?"

Emily shook her head. "I'm not sure, but I'm getting a weird vibe right now. Something's going on."

Luke clapped his hands to get everyone's attention. "Hey! Everyone, listen up for a minute."

"This isn't cool. We should go," Emily said, gathering up her belongings.

Shelby's hand shot out, grabbing her friend's arm to prevent her from getting up. "No way! We're not leaving."

Luke gestured at Alexis on the pool deck near the diving board. She was gorgeous, her toned body in a red bikini and her thick mahogany hair pulled high in a perky ponytail. "As you all know, today is Alexis's birthday."

The crowd broke into a chorus of "Happy Birthday."

When the singing ended, Luke jumped off the diving board to the pool deck. "And I'm the luckiest man alive. Alexis has agreed to be my wife."

"It's true," Alexis called out, raising her left hand and wiggling her fingers.

Even from a distance, Shelby could see the sparkling diamond engagement ring. "This can't be happening. That was supposed to be me. That's my ring."

Emily swung her legs over the side of the lounge chair. "Come on, Shelby. You don't need to be here right now."

"What I *need* right now is a drink. Go get me a rum punch."

"That's a bad idea, Shelby."

"I don't care." Shelby stared at her lap, the tears blurring the cover of her new Colleen Hoover novel. "Please, Emily. It'll be too obvious if we leave right now. I can save face if I act like I don't care."

"You have a point." Emily jumped to her feet. "One rum punch coming right up."

There was no line at the bar, and Emily returned within minutes with her drink. "I'm sorry, Shelby. But I have to go home. Mom just texted me. She's not feeling well. She's having a party tonight and needs me to help her prepare. Why don't you come with me? We can grab some lunch and talk. You shouldn't stay here alone."

"Nope. I'll be fine." Shelby waved her novel. "I'm gonna soak up some rays and read my book."

"Suit yourself." Emily packed her things in her tote bag. "Be careful with that drink. The bartender poured you a strong one.

The last thing you want is to get drunk and make a fool of yourself."

"Don't worry. I won't," Shelby said, sipping the sweet punch through the straw.

Emily kissed the tips of her fingers and touched them to Shelby's cheek. "Stay in touch. I'll be at home if you need me."

Shelby waited until Emily was out of sight before guzzling the drink and ordering another from a passing server. She couldn't take her eyes off Luke and Alexis, who were surrounded by their friends, basking in the glory of their engagement. Shelby never stood a chance of competing against Alexis. Not only was she beautiful and smart—currently in her third year of law school—but she was also the daughter of a wealthy oil tycoon.

Shelby finished the second drink and stumbled to the bar for a third. The familiar voice in her ear sent a chill down her spine. "I'm sorry, Shelby. I didn't know you'd be here today. I hope you're not upset about the engagement."

Shelby spun around to face Luke, sloshing some rum punch on his white T-shirt. "Why would I be upset, Luke? You just gave everything you promised me to someone else."

When she stormed off, much to her disappointment, he didn't follow her. The third drink sent her from tipsy to hammered in a flash. She felt trapped on her lounge chair, surrounded by all of Luke's and Alexis's friends. She yearned to escape and order an Uber to drive her home, but she was afraid to get up. Closing her eyes, she passed out and woke hours later, her skin painfully crisp from sunburn.

She straightened her chair and took in her surroundings. The crowd had thinned out, but the few who remained were well on their way to being drunk. Alexis and Luke were floating on an oversized raft in the pool, their bodies pressed together with one of her long legs thrown over his.

Shelby gathered her stuff and left the club. She assured herself she was okay to drive. She hadn't had anything to drink in hours. She was rounding the corner, turning onto her street, when Lily, the little girl next door, came out of nowhere on her pink bicycle. Shelby jerked the steering wheel, and her car swerved, barely missing the child. Lily, seeming unfazed, waved at Shelby and continued down the road.

Shelby parked in her driveway and rested her head against the steering wheel. She'd come so close to running the child over. She knew better than to drive under the influence. She always took Ubers when she'd had more than one drink. But today, she'd been so distraught over Luke's engagement that she'd made a near-fatal error in judgment.

Shelby realized she was in trouble when her mom greeted her at the door. "How was the pool? Did you have a nice time? You're pink. I hope you didn't get too much sun."

Shelby stared at the floor, afraid to meet her mom's gaze. "The pool was okay."

Kate sniffed. "Have you been drinking?" When Shelby didn't answer, Kate lifted her chin. "Shelby?"

Shelby pressed her lips tight, hoping to minimize the smell of alcohol on her breath as she spoke. "I had a rum punch hours ago."

Kate looked past her through the open door into the driveaway. "Please tell me you didn't drive yourself home?"

Shelby swatted her mother's hand away from her chin. "I'm fine, Mom."

"You're in big trouble, young lady. I'm at my wit's end with you." Kate tossed a thumb over her shoulder. "Go to your room. And don't you dare leave this house until your father comes home."

Tripping up the stairs to her room, Shelby crawled into bed, buried her face in her pillow, and cried herself to sleep. When she woke, dusk had settled over the room. Rolling onto her back, she stared at the ceiling as the afternoon's events flooded her mind. Luke's engagement. Three rum punches. The near miss with Lily. Her eyes danced around, landing on the suitcase parked beside her bedroom door—the huge one, not her carry-on, but the one she had taken to Europe for her high school graduation trip.

What the heck? Shelby detangled herself from the sheets and got out of bed.

The sound of her parents' angry voices in a distant part of the house drew her to the door. They were probably in the kitchen, where most of their arguments occurred. Pressing her ear to the door, she couldn't make out what they were saying, but she was sure they were fighting about her.

Shelby plodded barefoot down the stairs. As she approached the kitchen, she heard her father say, "Why do we have to send her away? Why don't we just ground her?"

From the doorway, Shelby asked in a meek voice, "Where are you sending me?"

Her mom released a lungful of air as she turned to face Shelby. "To South Carolina." Kate retrieved a computer printout from the table and handed it to Shelby. "Here is your flight itinerary."

Shelby scanned the one-way itinerary. She was booked on American Airlines departing Austin tomorrow morning at seven, connecting in Charlotte, and arriving in Charleston just after noon.

While Shelby hated the idea of moving away from Austin, of leaving Luke, she could see herself working at one of the boutique hotels in Charleston's historic district. She looked up at her parents. "I don't understand. Am I moving to Charleston?"

Mom shook her head. "Not Charleston. Magnolia Shores. You're going to live with your grandmother. Izzy needs help opening the bed and breakfast."

Shelby let go of the printout, and the itinerary floated to the floor. "Magnolia Shores! Are you crazy? Izzy lives at the end of the earth."

"We've tolerated your destructive behavior long enough," Kate said. "You go out every night, sleep until noon every day, and you've done nothing about finding a job."

"I'm sorry. I'll try harder," Shelby pleaded.

Kate gripped Shelby's arm. "This is about more than a job, sweetheart. What you did today was unacceptable. You drove home drunk from the club. You could've killed someone. Or yourself."

The image of Lily on her bicycle flashed before Shelby. "I know. And I'm sorry. But Luke and Alexis got engaged and I was upset."

Dad's face tightened. "Luke broke up with you over a year ago, Shelby. Have some pride for crying out loud. You've wallowed in self-pity long enough. You need to move on with your life." He dragged a hand down his face. "Maybe your mom is right. Maybe you do need to get away for a while."

"How long is a while?" Shelby asked and braced herself for the answer.

"That's entirely up to you. Izzy will pay you a salary. If you don't like working at the bed and breakfast, you can save money and move to Charleston. But I've canceled your credit cards, and you're now on your own."

Shelby's jaw hit the floor. "You canceled my cards. How am I supposed to live?"

Kate handed her a wad of folded twenty-dollar bills. "This will hold you over until your first paycheck. I booked a driver to meet you in Charleston and take you to Magnolia Shores. His fare and tip are prepaid."

Shelby stared at her mom. Pain etched the lines on Kate's face. This was as hard on Kate as it was on Shelby. "But I'll need a car. How am I supposed to get around?"

"You won't," Mom said. "Not for a while. I'll let Izzy decide when to loan you her car to go to town."

"This is so unfair." Shelby fled the kitchen, dashed back up the stairs to her room, and slammed the door so hard that her framed poster of Taylor Swift fell off the wall. Her parents were sending her to Magnolia Shores Prison. By the time she was released, Luke and Alexis would be married.

Locating her phone in the twisted bedding, she texted Emily and waited five minutes for her friend's response.

Bummer. I'll miss you. 😢 But this could end up being a good thing. As the saying goes, absence makes the heart grow fonder. Luke will miss you and realize what he's lost.

Yeah, right! While he's planning his wedding to Alexis.

five

. . .

Isabelle was removing her hanging clothes from her closet when her daughter called in the early afternoon on Thursday. "I can't talk right now, Kate. I'm in the middle of something."

"This can't wait, Mom. But I'll be brief."

Her daughter's serious tone got her attention, and she lowered herself to the edge of her bed. "What's wrong, honey?"

"Nothing's *wrong*. I'm hoping this will be a good thing. Shelby should be arriving at Magnolia Shores any minute. She needs a job, and you need help running the B&B."

"In other words, you're exiling her. What did she do to deserve such harsh punishment?"

Kate hesitated. "She's going through a difficult time. The change of scenery will be good for her while she sorts out her life."

Isabelle pressed her lips into a thin line. "Mm-hmm. So, there *is* something wrong. I don't have time to babysit your wayward child. And I certainly can't afford to pay her." Isabelle set the phone on speaker and placed it on her bedside table while she dumped the contents of her dresser drawers into canvas tote bags.

"You won't have to pay her. The B&B will cover her salary. I've already worked it out with Pritchard."

"I'm a seventy-five-year-old woman. What do I know about parenting a twenty-four-year-old girl?"

"Don't parent her, Mom. Just be her grandmother. Try to get through to her if you can. After all, you two are an awful lot alike."

Isabelle slammed a dresser drawer. "Oh really? In what way?"

"You're both stubborn and headstrong, and you both have chips on your shoulders. Keep an eye on her, and don't let her drive—at least for a while."

The sound of someone clearing their throat made Isabelle turn toward the door. "She's here now. I'll call you later."

Ending the call, Isabelle crossed the room to her granddaughter and gave her a stiff hug. "Welcome, Shelby. I was just speaking with your mother."

"I heard." Shelby pushed her away. "You can buy me an airline ticket back to Austin and put us both out of misery."

Isabelle's heart went out to her granddaughter. The poor girl's eyes were bloodshot and swollen from crying. "And risk the wrath of Kate? No thank you. Besides, our first guests are arriving tomorrow, and I could use your help."

"Help with what?" Shelby asked in a skeptical tone.

"Clearing out this room for starters," Isabelle said, making a sweeping gesture at the clothes on the bed.

Shelby glanced at the clothes and back at Isabelle. "I don't understand. Why are you kicking yourself out of your own room?"

Isabelle resisted the urge to snap at the child. Why did Shelby think Isabelle was vacating her room? "Because I need it for the guests."

"But where will you sleep?"

A sense of dread overcame Isabelle when she realized she and Shelby would be roommates. "With you in the caretaker's cottage. I'll show you." Isabelle scooped up an armful of hanging clothes. "Bring your suitcase and follow me."

With her suitcase bumping along behind her, Shelby followed

Isabelle down the stairs and out the front door. They were crossing the courtyard when Shelby stopped short. "Wait! Can't I stay in the pool house like I normally do?"

Isabelle kept walking, calling over her shoulder. "Sorry. Every room on this property is booked for the next three months." She was exaggerating, but not by much.

Shelby caught up to her, nearly plowing her down with her suitcase. "This is the caretaker's cottage? I always thought it was a garden shed."

"Don't expect much. This is the only building on the property I haven't maintained," Isabelle said, struggling to open the door with her hands full of clothes. "At least it's clean. I had the new maids scrub it top to bottom this morning."

Shelby's face lit up. "Cool! We have maid service."

"Only that one time. From now on, we'll have to clean up after ourselves."

"Okay, I guess." Shelby brushed past her as she inspected the outdated room—kitchen circa 1970 and furniture upholstered in a scratchy green plaid fabric. "This is bad. Are you sure you won't buy that plane ticket for me?"

"Positive. You're stuck here for the time being." Isabelle nodded at the far corner door. "Your room is over there." She had staked claim to the queen-bedded room, leaving the one with twin beds for Shelby.

Isabelle took her armload to her bedroom, hanging the clothes in the tiny closet.

Through the Jack and Jill bath connecting the two rooms, she heard Shelby let out a squeal. "Ew, you mean we have to share a bathroom?"

"I'm afraid so. But don't worry, the fan works." Isabelle smiled to herself. She might enjoy having someone around to tease.

Isabelle and Shelby spent the next three hours moving her belongings from the main house to the cottage. By the time they finished, hanging clothes covered every surface.

"You have too many clothes, Izzy. Where will you put all this stuff?" Shelby asked, spreading her arms wide.

Isabelle tapped her chin, pondering the dilemma. "Good question," she said. "I may have to store some clothes in the attic." Then, with a sigh, she thought, *Good heavens. I've become one of those women who brings her clothes out of storage every season.*

With nowhere to sit, Shelby lay down on the floor, fanning herself with an old *National Geographic* magazine from the coffee table. "I'd forgotten how hot it is in the Lowcountry."

"No hotter than Texas," Isabelle said as she refolded a stack of colorful cotton T-shirts.

"Sure feels like it. What time are these guests coming tomorrow?"

"Check-in starts at four o'clock."

"Oh, good. I can spend most of the day by the pool, working on my tan," Shelby said, examining the skin on her arms.

"After we return from the grocery store."

Shelby crossed her arms over her chest, staring up at the ceiling. "If you give me your list, I can shop for you."

Isabelle chuckled. "Good try, but no chance. Your mother left strict instructions that you're not to drive. Did you get pulled over for driving under the influence?"

Shelby sat up straight. "No! I had a couple of drinks by the pool at the club. *Hours* later, I drove myself home. Unfortunately, Mom could still smell the rum on my breath."

With the flick of her wrist, Isabelle waved away the seriousness of her granddaughter's crime. "That's no big deal. I do it all the time."

"Because your club is at the end of your driveway, Izzy. I admit I made a mistake. But the punishment seems rather harsh, don't you think?"

Isabelle ignored the question. She would not take sides in a dispute between her daughter and granddaughter. "Speaking of clubs, why don't we get cleaned up and go to the Sandy Island

Club for dinner? This might be our last chance to dine out for a while."

"Why not? Since there's nothing else to do around here." Shelby got to her feet, retrieved her suitcase, and disappeared into her bedroom.

The atmosphere in the Sandy Island Club's grill room was festive with large groups of members celebrating the arrival of Memorial Day weekend tomorrow. Shelby watched with envy as several kids her age laughed and carried on at a nearby table. She felt like a loser eating dinner alone with her grandmother. While Izzy wasn't the bubbly type, she was usually fun to be around. But tonight, her grandmother's sullen mood mirrored her own. The gloomy twosome stood out like a sore thumb in the cheerful crowd.

When one of her friends stopped by the table to inquire about the progress of the B&B, Izzy told her to mind her own business.

Shelby waited until the woman left to call her out. "Why were you so mean to that poor woman? She was just being friendly."

"Ethel wasn't being friendly. She was being nosy. Everyone in this town is talking about me behind my back. Poor Isabelle St. Clair's husband left her penniless, and now she has to turn her home into a boarding house."

Shelby didn't get that vibe from Ethel, but what did she know about old people? Kids in her generation didn't bother pretending. They were brutally honest with one another. "Is that what really happened? Are you broke?"

"Of course not, Shelby," Izzy snapped. "Your grandfather had a burning desire to share his beloved property with the world. Unfortunately, he died before he could make that dream a reality. So now he's dumped that responsibility in my lap. Am I happy about it? Definitely not." A flush crept up her neck. "In fact, I'm downright furious with him."

"Geez. Sorry I asked." Shelby turned her attention to eating her crabcakes, but she looked up when she felt her grandmother's eyes on her. "What?"

"Nothing. I'm still wondering why your mama sent you here. How is Luke? You're not pregnant, are you?"

Shelby's face warmed. "Izzy! Gosh."

"If you are, you should marry him. You're old enough, and he comes from a fine family."

Shelby tuned out her grandmother as she blabbered on about how wonderful Luke was. For many years, he had accompanied Shelby to the Lowcountry for her summer visits. He and Izzy had become fast friends.

With Isabelle's loud snores shaking the tiny cottage, Shelby slept little on her first night at Magnolia Shores. She placed a mountain of pillows over her head and stuffed cotton balls in her ears. But even listening to soft music on her earbuds didn't drown out the sound of the freight train in the next room.

As she tossed and turned, Shelby considered her options for getting out of this jail. She came up with only one viable option—she would convince Emily to loan her the money for an airline ticket. Unfortunately, once she was back in Austin, she would have no place to stay and no money to live on. Shelby's and Emily's moms were close friends. Loraine would never defy Kate's wishes by allowing Shelby to live with Emily.

Like it or not, Shelby was stuck in Water's Edge for now. But she would never survive without a social life. Over the years, during her summer vacations, she'd met some local kids while visiting her grandmother. But she didn't know them enough to reach out on social media. She had met her uncle Pritchard's new wife, Savannah, at their wedding two months ago. Savannah seemed okay, and her daughter, Harper, was seriously cool. Even better, Harper was only a few years older than Shelby.

Her mom explained that Pritchard and Savannah had dated in high school and that Savannah had gotten pregnant and had the baby. Shelby was still unclear why the baby was put up for adoption or why Savannah had disappeared to Washington State for thirty years. Even more mystifying was how Savannah and Harper simultaneously reappeared in Water's Edge last summer. There were missing pieces to this story, and Shelby was determined to find out what they were. At least it would give her something to do while she figured out a way out of this mess.

six

. . .

Grocery shopping with Izzy on Friday morning was exhausting. Her grandmother had no clue what was in store for her. They would need more than two dozen eggs and a pound of bacon to feed thirty people breakfast for the three-day weekend.

When Shelby suggested they set up an account with a food wholesaler, Izzy scoffed. "That's preposterous, Shelby. Why on earth would we purchase from a food wholesaler when we can get everything we need at the grocery store?"

"So you won't have to run to the market every day. So you will have a wider variety of choices available to you."

Izzy silenced her with a glare. "We'll be fine. I know what I'm doing. I entertain for groups of guests all the time."

After hauling ten cases of bottled water and six bags of groceries from the car into the kitchen, Shelby was drenched in sweat. Once everything was put away, she made a ham sandwich and escaped to the pool before her grandmother found more work for her to do. She devoured the sandwich, and then stretched out on a lounge chair for a nap, which she desperately needed after her sleepless night. She'd no sooner dozed off when her uncle Pritchard nudged her awake.

She shielded her eyes from the sun to look at him. She didn't remember him being so handsome. He appeared younger. His salt-and-pepper hair was longer, curling at the base of his neck, and his gray-blue eyes sparkled. Was marital bliss responsible for this transformation?

"Welcome to the team, Shelby!" he said in a cheerful tone.

Some team, Shelby thought. The group consisted of her grandmother, two housekeepers, and herself—a real team of misfits. *Be nice, Shelby. Remember, he's your boss.* She smiled and said, "Thanks! I'm grateful for the opportunity."

"You look so peaceful, I hate to disturb you, but can you spare a few minutes to review this weekend's reservations?"

"Sure!" Shelby said in a feigned tone of enthusiasm.

She slipped on her cover-up, and they walked together across the terrace.

"I came over with the locksmith," Pritchard explained. "He's upstairs now installing knobs with key locks on the bedrooms."

"Cool! What reservation system are we using? I worked with several different programs in college."

"As of now, we don't have one. We are currently using Izzy's system, which will require some patient deciphering on your part. I'm meeting with a web designer this week. Unfortunately, the process will take a couple of months. Do the best you can until we get it up and running."

Shelby paused to consider this. "I'll do some research, but I'm pretty sure we won't need a website to use a reservation system."

Pritchard held the French door open for her. "That would certainly make things easier for you."

Her grandmother was seated on the sofa, absorbed in a home interior magazine, and she didn't look up when they entered the living room.

Pritchard retrieved a file folder off Izzy's desk. "I assume you have a laptop. Since Izzy doesn't have a computer, I was hoping you could use yours until I buy a desktop."

"That works. I brought my laptop with me."

He handed the file to Shelby. "I suggest starting with an Excel spreadsheet."

Shelby scrunched up her nose. "A what?"

Pritchard laughed. "Microsoft Excel is a spreadsheet editor. There's no sense in downloading Excel to your laptop if you don't already have it. I'll make getting that desktop a priority."

Shelby sat at the desk, opened the file, and flipped through the hodgepodge of reservations. One was written on a cocktail napkin and another on the back of a grocery receipt. "Sorting out this mess will take me a week."

Izzy looked up from her magazine. "Look in the top drawer. The reservations are recorded in my daytimer."

Locating the daytimer, Shelby flipped to today's date but could hardly make out her grandmother's elaborate cursive writing. "A whiteboard calendar would help. Do we have an Amazon account I can use to buy one?"

"A whiteboard is an excellent idea. We can use my personal Amazon account until I can set one up for the business." Pritchard narrowed his blue eyes. "Although, I bet Coastal Hardware carries whiteboards. And maybe computers as well."

"Seriously? You can buy a computer at a hardware store?"

"Yep. Believe it or not, Coastal Hardware sells everything."

A man dressed in overalls with a red baseball cap bearing the Carolina Locksmith logo entered the living room. "My assistant is installing your knobs. Here are the keys." He dumped a handful of brass keys on the desk. "We assigned each room a number, starting with one and counting from north to south. The numbers are etched on the keys." The man tipped his hat at Shelby and departed the room.

Shelby picked up a brass key and turned it over in her palm. "It'll be easier to keep track of these if we use colorful plastic tags or stretchy wristband rings."

"Another brilliant idea, Shelby. I'm sure they have those at Coastal Hardware too. I'll run over there now."

He left the room, and Shelby called after him, "While you're there, see if they have a board to organize the keys."

Shelby stared down at the odd assortment of reservations in the file. So much for her afternoon by the pool. She set about organizing the slips of paper into stacks, making sure the dates matched what Izzy had written in her daytimer.

She was still working at three thirty when an attractive young couple with an angelic-looking little boy entered the house through the front door.

"Hi," the woman said, flashing Shelby a wave. "We're the O'Connells. I realize we're early, but we misjudged our travel time. If our room isn't ready, we can hang out by the pool until it is."

Shelby glanced over at Izzy, who was now reading a Pat Conroy novel and seemingly oblivious to the newcomers. These were their first-ever guests. Shouldn't they celebrate with a glass of Champagne or a signature beverage?

Shelby remembered the name O'Connell. She'd assigned them to room three. The locksmith had finished upstairs and moved out to the pool house. She saw no reason to make them wait. "You're in luck. Your room is ready now."

"Excellent." Mr. O'Connell tugged his wallet out of his back pocket. "What do you need from me other than my credit card?"

Shelby's heart raced. Pritchard hadn't told her the room rates or instructed her on the check-in process. She doubted they even had one. But Shelby, who had traveled extensively with her parents, knew the drill.

She took the credit card from him. "Our systems are down right now. If it's okay with you, I'll take your credit card information and process the charge later."

"That's fine." He handed her the card, and she jotted down the number.

Mrs. O'Connell fanned her face. "It's boiling outside and I'm parched. Any chance I could get a bottled water?"

"There are cups in the rooms. You can get water from the tap," Izzy snapped, her eyes remaining glued to her book.

Shelby smiled apologetically at the woman. "Sorry. I'll grab a bottled water for you from the kitchen." She handed Mr. O'Connell his room key and walked him to the foyer. "You're number three at the top of the stairs."

Shelby was heading down the hallway to the kitchen for the bottled water when Mr. O'Connell called out to her. "Hey! Can someone help us with our luggage?"

Shelby did an about-face. "Coming."

Mr. O'Connell didn't want someone to *help* him with their luggage. He intended for someone to carry their suitcases *for* him. In the absence of a bellman, that someone was Shelby. It took multiple trips to haul their ten-plus bags up the stairs to the second floor. Why do three people need so much stuff for a three-night stay? Especially when one of those people is a little boy who wears tiny clothes.

Neither of the O'Connells offered a thank you, let alone a tip.

Mrs. O'Connell gave the haggard Shelby an exasperated look. "Can I have that bottled water now?"

"There's a cup in the bathroom. Use the tap," Shelby said and fled the room.

As she descended the stairs, she saw the line of guests in the hallway waiting to check in. Pritchard, who had returned from the hardware store, jumped in to assist her, and for the next two hours, they wrote down credit card numbers and helped guests to their rooms.

Pritchard read down the list of names for today's reservations. "Everyone has arrived except . . ." He squinted. "This can't be right. *Blossom* with no last name."

"That's all the information she gave me," Izzy said from the sofa.

"I remember the reservation," Shelby said. "She booked a room in the garden house for the entire summer."

"Sounds like a prank to me. We'll see if she shows up,"

Pritchard said as he crossed the room and loomed over Izzy. "What happened to the bellman I sent over here earlier in the week?"

Izzy inserted a bookmark and closed the novel. "I decided not to hire him."

Pritchard's blue eyes bugged out. "You what? Silas wasn't here for an interview. I hired him. He wanted to introduce himself and talk to you about his hours."

Izzy stood to face her son. "You should've told me, Pritchard. I'm not a mind reader."

Pritchard pulled out his phone. "All right. I'll call him and explain." He glanced over at Shelby, eyeing her cover-up. "Why don't you go change, and we'll have a much-needed organizational meeting in the kitchen."

"Yes, sir," Shelby said and beelined it out of the room to the caretaker's cottage.

She hadn't showered since leaving Texas more than twenty-four hours ago, and she took her time organizing her products in the bathroom. After a long hot shower, she tied her damp hair into a ponytail and dressed in white shorts and a gray Texas A&M T-shirt.

Returning to the main house, she followed the muffled voices down the hall to the kitchen. Pritchard and Izzy were seated at the table together. He was scribbling on a notepad, and Izzy wore a bored expression, her arms crossed over her chest as she watched him.

Pritchard appeared relieved to see Shelby. "There you are. I need to cut this short. One of my clients is in a jam and needs my help."

"I understand," Shelby said, wondering which of the country music stars he repped needed his attention.

"I apologize for our rocky start today." He cut his eyes at Izzy. "Izzy gave me the impression she had things under control."

Izzy stuck her tongue out at him. "I wasn't supposed to lose the will contest, thank you very much."

Pritchard chuckled at his mother's childish gesture. "Shelby, as the reservations manager, your job is to organize reservations and make room assignments. I bought everything you need, including a computer, at Coastal Hardware. If you create a list of potential reservation systems, we'll pick the one that makes the most sense."

Shelby gave him a curt nod. "I can do that."

"You'll also be responsible for assisting guests during arrival and departure."

Shelby's muscles still ached from *assisting* the O'Connells with their luggage. "You mentioned hiring a bellman?"

"I got ahold of Silas, and he's agreed to start tomorrow. He's more than a bellman. He'll be in charge of general maintenance and help with security issues. If the guests have any altercations, he'll intervene. Hopefully, there won't be many." Pritchard shifted his gaze to Izzy. "Mother, you're in charge of breakfast. Do you think you can handle that?" he asked in a snarky tone.

Izzy's face became indignant. "Indeed. You're the one who said I set the bar high when it comes to entertaining. The dining room is already set for tomorrow morning."

"I don't believe it," Pritchard said, pushing back from the table.

The threesome passed in single file through the butler's pantry to the dining room. Pritchard gawked at the table, which Izzy had set with her finest china, crystal, and linens. "Only twelve people will fit at the table. What do you plan on doing with the other twenty?"

Izzy furrowed her brow. She clearly hadn't thought of this. "I guess they'll have to eat in shifts."

Pritchard fingered a linen placemat. "Are you planning to reset this elaborate table after every shift? You won't have enough china. All this stuff has to be washed by hand."

Izzy planted her hands on her hips. "Then what do you suggest, genius?"

"Set up a buffet. Put your chafing dishes to use." Pritchard entered the butler's pantry and returned with a stack of glass dessert plates. "These smaller plates will prevent the guests from eating so much." He deposited the plates on the buffet and opened the middle drawer, removing a package of pink paper placemats. Use disposable goods like these. You can still make it look homey."

Izzy glared down her nose at him. "I don't do homey, son."

"You know what I mean, Mother. I trust you to make it elegant. Coincidentally, I've opened an account with Waterside Wholesale Food Distributors. The representative will contact you early next week. From now on, we'll order all our food from them. And they deliver, saving you from constantly running to the store."

"That's a marvelous idea, Pritchard," Izzy said, despite having dismissed Shelby's earlier suggestion about the wholesale distributor.

While her uncle and grandmother discussed breakfast food items, Shelby slipped out of the dining room onto the terrace. They were the blind leading the blind on a train wreck in the making.

seven

. . .

Izzy was cracking eggs in the kitchen on Saturday morning, watching the sun rise over the ocean through the window, when she heard the front door click shut and someone call out, "Yoo hoo."

As she cracked one last egg, Izzy listened more intently. *What was that sound? That clicking noise?* She crossed the kitchen to the doorway, peering down the hallway.

A little tricolor dog with long, floppy ears and short legs scampered toward her. A plump woman with flawless caramel skin followed the dog. She wore a long, flowy red dress patterned with pink hibiscus, and her mop of silver coils was fastened on top of her head in a halo of matching hibiscus blooms. On closer inspection, Isabelle realized the flowers were real.

"Morning, ma'am. I'm Blossom. I apologize for my late arrival. I managed to get behind a terrible interstate pileup in Tennessee."

The dog ran circles around Isabelle's feet. "Dogs are not allowed at Magnolia Shores."

Blossom scooped up her dog. "Your website didn't mention a no-pet policy."

The lines in Isabelle's forehead deepened. "We don't have a website."

Blossom wagged her finger at Isabelle. "Then I suggest you get one if you plan to enforce such strict rules."

"I beg your pardon," Isabelle said in an indignant tone. "*No pets* is not a strict rule. Lots of places don't allow them."

The dog licked Blossom's face. "Not in this day and age. Nearly everyone owns a dog, and they take them everywhere they go. Now, if you don't mind showing me to my room, I'd like to freshen up before breakfast."

"I'm sorry, but you'll have to wait. Check-in isn't until four o'clock."

"Ma'am! I've just driven over seven hundred miles, and I've already paid for my room for last night."

Isabelle gestured at the mixing bowl and egg cartons on the counter. "As you can see, I'm in the middle of making breakfast."

"Your eggs are scrambled and ready for the pan. Just cover the bowl and place it in the refrigerator."

"What're you talking about?" Isabelle returned to the counter to find both cartons empty, and all the eggs scrambled. "I don't understand . . . How . . . Never mind," she said, shaking her head. She was getting more forgetful by the day.

She covered the bowl in plastic wrap and placed it in the refrigerator. She rummaged through the meat drawer. "Where'd it go?" she said to herself.

Blossom peered over her shoulder, the dog licking at Isabelle's ear. "Can I help you find something?"

Isabelle slammed the refrigerator door and opened the freezer drawer below. "The bacon and sausage I bought from the store yesterday. I specifically remember putting them in the meat drawer." She closed the freezer drawer. "They're not in there either."

"Maybe you already cooked them?" Blossom suggested.

"I'm sure I would remember cooking three pounds of bacon and sausage." Opening the warming drawer, she discovered a platter of cooked breakfast meat inside. Isabelle pressed her fingers to her temples. *This is bad. I'm losing my mind. And it's no wonder, considering the pressure I'm under.*

Isabelle closed the warming drawer and straightened. "Well then, let's see about checking you in. Come with me."

Isabelle led Blossom back down the hallway to the living room. Sitting at her desk, she studied Shelby's tidy print on the whiteboard. "You're booked for the summer in room three in the garden house. I'll need your credit card information." She opened the center drawer for a pad and pen. "And what's your last name?"

"I don't have one," Blossom said with a deep chuckle. "I've been married so many times I stopped counting husbands. I got tired of changing my name, so I just dropped it. Not having a surname is surprisingly liberating."

"How does one go through life without a last name?" Isabelle's hand shot out. "Never mind. I don't want to know."

Isabelle came from behind the desk and handed Blossom her room key. "I'll make an exception to the rule about the dog as long as you pick up after him and he doesn't disturb the other guests."

"Thank you. And it's a she. Her name is Jolene."

Isabelle arched an eyebrow. "As in Dolly Parton's Jolene?"

"Nope. Jolene Van Vugt. She's a motorcycle racer."

"Never heard of her." Isabelle walked Blossom to the front door. "The garden house is across the courtyard on your right. I trust you can find it. If you'll excuse me, I need to get back to the kitchen."

"Can you help with my luggage first?" Blossom opened the front door to reveal a pale-blue miniature school bus.

Isabelle blinked hard. "What on earth is that?"

"My home. I've lived in so many different places, and I got tired of changing my address—"

"Let me guess. Not owning a home is liberating."

Blossom jabbed an elbow into Isabelle's ribs. "You're a quick learner."

A man appeared from behind Blossom's bus. Squinting, Isabelle realized he was the bellman Pritchard had hired, the man she had slammed the door on the other day.

"Morning, ladies. I'm Silas, your bellman."

Isabelle gave him a once-over. He had a large build and broad shoulders and wore his sandy hair in a crew cut. His muscles bulged beneath the sleeve of his white polo shirt, and his forearms were tatted up with an intricate design Isabelle couldn't decipher. "Where'd you get a name like Silas?"

Silas pressed his hand against his heart. "My mama got it from the Bible. Silas was a prominent figure who accompanied Paul on his missionary journeys. He is first introduced in Acts—"

"I know who Silas is," Isabelle said through clenched teeth. "Now, please stop talking and help this guest with her bags." Spinning on her heels, she went back inside to the kitchen.

Isabelle wasn't yet ready when the guests began arriving for breakfast around seven thirty. What happened to sleeping in on vacation? Pearl helped by retrieving the old percolator she once used for bridge parties from the attic and setting up a coffee station on the small buffet in the kitchen.

Pearl's arms were elbow-deep in soapy water when a flustered Hilda came down from upstairs. Gesturing wildly with her arms, she talked so rapidly to Pearl that Isabelle wouldn't have been able to make out what she said if she'd been speaking in English.

Pearl rinsed her hands and dried them on a paper towel. She squeezed Hilda's shoulder and spoke to her calmly in Portuguese.

Hilda inhaled a shaky breath, nodded, and left the kitchen.

"What's wrong?" Isabelle asked Pearl. "Did something get broken in one of the upstairs rooms?"

"The O'Connell's son vomited something red on the carpet. Probably fruit punch. But don't worry. I'm an expert at carpet stains. Can you hold down the fort while I assist Hilda?"

"Of course. We're done here. You can tend to your other duties. Thank you, Hilda."

She waited for the housekeeper to leave before casting her gaze heavenward. *Edward, what on earth have you gotten me into?*

By the time everyone had been fed and the dishes were done, Isabelle's head throbbed and her feet ached. Popping two ibuprofen, she went in search of a quiet place to rest. Her guests had taken over her home. They occupied nearly every available place to sit in the living room and on the terrace. She even discovered a young couple making out in Edward's study.

Retracing her steps to the kitchen, she exited through the back door and leaned against the terrace railing to gaze over her garden. Manicured boxwoods outlined the rectangular garden's perimeter, while around the small koi pond at the center, an attractive assortment of annuals and perennials burst with colorful blooms.

Isabelle noticed a clump of her prized zinnias fly through the air. *What in heaven's name?* Gripping the railing for support, she descended the steps and marched across the courtyard. She watched in horror as Blossom's dog dug a tunnel in the dirt.

"Get out of my flowers, you little beast." Isabelle kicked at the dog, missed, lost her balance, and stumbled into a prickly rose bush.

Blossom emerged from the garden house. "Jolene, what have you done?" She snatched up the dirty dog. "I gave her a bone. She likes to hide them in the bushes."

Isabelle jabbed a red manicured nail at the destroyed flowers. "These aren't bushes. They're my zinnias."

Shelby, who was crossing the driveway from the cottage to the main house, spotted the dog and rushed over to them. "Aww. She's so cute. What's her name?"

"Jolene." Blossom cupped the dog's muzzle. "Your granny claims Jolene destroyed her flowers."

Isabelle expelled a breath of indignation. "I am nobody's *granny.*"

"Her grandchildren call her Izzy," Shelby explained. She

looked past Isabelle at the flower bed. "Your flowers look fine to me."

Isabelle's head spun around toward the garden. To her utter disbelief, the dirt tunnel was gone, and the zinnias were intact.

"When's the last time you watered your garden?" Blossom asked.

Isabelle looked more closely at her drooping plantings. She'd been so preoccupied with her court case and opening the B&B that she'd forgotten to water. "Lord, have mercy," she said, smoothing the hair off her forehead. I've had enough of this day, and it's not yet noon. I'll be in my room if you need me."

As she strode to the cottage, she mumbled, "I am not imagining things. I know what I saw. That blasted dog ruined my flowers and dug a tunnel in my garden."

Inside the cottage, Isabelle collapsed onto a mound of her hanging clothes on the sofa and called her attorney. "Alice, I'm sorry to bother you on the weekend, but this is an emergency. I've been invaded by strangers. My husband has turned our home into an amusement park. You must do something! And soon!"

Alice let out an audible sigh. "I was going to wait until after the weekend to tell you the bad news. Judge Buchanan has denied your petition for a retrial."

Shelby watched her grandmother's elegant frame retreat into the caretaker's cottage before turning her attention to the guest standing beside her. On closer inspection, the woman was the most exotic creature Shelby had ever met with silver hair and sparkling emerald eyes. "Hi! I'm Shelby."

"And I'm Blossom," she said, placing the dog on the ground and extending her hand.

Recognition crossed Shelby's face. "So, *you're* Blossom. Welcome. When did you arrive?" She gestured at the main house. "If you come inside with me, I can check you in."

"Izzy already did that. I've been here for a couple of hours. I was in my room unpacking when all the commotion started."

Shelby dropped down to the sidewalk, pulling the dog onto her lap. "She's so little. Is she a miniature basset hound? Is there even such a thing?"

"There is, and she is, although they are rare." Blossom's hand disappeared inside the pocket of her dress, producing a round rubber ball. "Here! She loves this."

"Thanks," Shelby said, wondering what else Blossom had hidden inside the deep pockets of her flowery maxi dress.

"I should water Izzy's garden before everything dies." Locating a faucet on the side of the garden house, Blossom dragged the hose across the sidewalk and sprayed a fan of water on the withering plants. "You're a sweet girl to help your grandmother get the bed and breakfast up and running."

"I'm not doing it out of the kindness of my heart," Shelby grumbled. "My parents sent me here."

Blossom glanced over at her. "Uh-oh. That doesn't sound good. What happened?"

Shelby rolled the ball on the sidewalk for Jolene to fetch. "I broke up with my boyfriend. We've been dating since middle school. I was going to marry Luke. Now he's marrying someone else."

"I'm sorry, sugar. How long ago did you two break up?"

"A year. My parents were tired of me going out every night, but I couldn't help myself. I was desperate to see Luke, even if he was usually with Alexis, his fiancée." Shelby's shoulders slumped. "I kept meaning to find a job, but it was easier to stay in bed all day."

"Sounds to me like you were depressed," Blossom said, moving the hose to a new section of the garden.

"I haven't thought about it, but you're probably right." Shelby drew her legs in, resting her chin on her knees. "I'm not sure why I'm telling you all this when I don't even know you."

"Sometimes it's easier to talk to a stranger." Blossom finished watering. "There. All better."

Shelby got up from the sidewalk and went to inspect Blossom's work. The entire garden had been revitalized, the greenery lush and the colorful blooms perky. "Whoa. That's amazing. Did you sprinkle magic on them or something?"

Blossom's emerald eyes sparkled, and a smirk tugged at the corner of her lips. "Something." She coiled the hose beside the spigot where she found it and motioned for Shelby to follow her. "Let's go explore."

Jolene ran beside them as they walked down the dirt path to the beach on the Catawba Sound side of the property. To their right was the long pier where Shelby's grandfather once docked his fleet of boats. Way off in the distance to the left was another of the Lowcountry's barrier islands. Shelby couldn't remember which one.

As they walked in the sand along the surf, Shelby said, "My best friend back home thinks my absence will make Luke's heart grow fonder. Do you think that will happen?" Even if she was a total stranger, Blossom had a genuine air about her that made Shelby feel comfortable asking her such a personal question.

"I don't have a crystal ball, child. But I wouldn't hold your breath. Luke is engaged to another woman now. You need to find a way to let go of the past."

Shelby's eyes filled with tears. "I've been trying. It's not that easy."

When they reached the ocean, they turned with their backs to the water and stared across the dunes at the magnificent sprawling Lowcountry estate.

"You may not see it this way now, but your parents have given you a gift by sending you here. I can think of worse places to be exiled," Blossom said with a chuckle. "Parents love their children. They never intentionally hurt them, although they are sometimes forced to make difficult decisions they believe are in their best interest."

Shelby nodded. "Tough love."

"Exactly. You're at a crossroads, where one life ends and another begins. Concentrate on the new Shelby, the post-Luke you. What do you want out of life? Find your burning passion, that thing that lights your fire."

"I thought Luke was my passion," Shelby said in a small voice.

"Passion comes in many forms. Absence often makes the heart grow fonder but also helps us forget. You've traveled twelve hundred miles to get here, and Luke is in your rearview mirror." Blossom hooked an arm around Shelby's waist and drew her in. "Look at the bright side, baby girl. Maybe your absence will make Grace's heart grow fonder for you."

Shelby's jaw dropped. How did Blossom know her sister's name? Who told this woman about their strained relationship? But before she could interrogate Blossom, Mrs. O'Connell appeared over the dunes, waving and running toward her.

Out of breath, Mrs. O'Connell said, "There you are! I've been looking all over for someone to fix me a Bloody Mary. Do you have a bartender around here?"

"No, ma'am. I'm sorry. As a bed and breakfast, we're only responsible for providing a light morning meal. All other food and drink are your responsibility."

A deep *v* appeared between the woman's eyes. "But where are we supposed to eat lunch and dinner?"

"There are many charming restaurants in town," Shelby said, making a mental note to create a printed list for the guests.

"This is absurd. I'm paying a fortune for my room, and I can't even get a cocktail around here," Mrs. O'Connell said with a huff and stormed off.

When Shelby glanced behind her, Blossom and Jolene had vanished. She replayed her exchange with the eccentric woman as she made her way up to the pool. Blossom knowing about Shelby's relationship with her sister was only part of it. Izzy claimed Jolene had dug up her flowers, yet Shelby had seen no evidence of destruction in the garden. Moreover, Blossom hadn't denied it when Shelby had jokingly suggested she'd used magic to revitalize the garden.

Who was Blossom, and where had she come from? Had someone sent her here to rescue Shelby? Was Blossom Shelby's fairy godmother?

eight

. . .

Isabelle spent much of Saturday afternoon searching for a new home. She toured at least a dozen available apartments, cottages, and condos. A garage apartment at a seedy rancher in the middle of the boondocks five miles outside of town was the only one she could afford. And Isabelle drew the line at living in a place with rat droppings, roaches, and rotted floorboards.

She stopped by the cemetery to visit her husband on her return trip home. She had some things to get off her chest, and she was grateful no one else was around. She knelt in the grass beside his grave. "Why did you do this to me, Edward? You've upended my life with this circus of strangers currently occupying our home. You wanted this, not me. I can see you now, holding court in your study, sharing your expensive scotch, and telling your rapt audience about your extensive rare book collection." She ran her fingers across his name, etched in the granite headstone. "If only you hadn't gotten sick, you could've fulfilled this dream and left me out of it."

Isabelle plucked the weeds from the dirt surrounding his headstone. "You were such a fine man, Edward, a dear person, a much kinder human than me. You would've given the shirt off your back to a stranger in need. I'm a selfish old bitty, too stuck in my ways for such a drastic change. That iron-clad will of yours is holding me hostage. The only way out for me is the road to the poor house. And I can't be poor. Not at my age. So, I'm stuck being the mistress of Magnolia Shores B&B.

Isabelle slowly rose to her feet. "I won't be the one who denies you your dying wish. I came from nothing, and you gave me everything. I'll honor your memory by fulfilling your dream as repayment for the beautiful life you provided me. But how? We've gotten off to a rocky start, and I could really use some guidance. Lord knows I should have paid more attention when you were rambling on about your elaborate plan. If only you had written your ideas down. Understanding your vision better would help me find my way."

Shelby faced a barrage of emergencies on Saturday afternoon. Three toilets overflowed, one of which happened when the O'Connell kid tried to flush his stuffed turtle. A guest ignored the property's no-smoking policy and caught an outside trash can on fire with a cigarette butt. And Silas had to intervene in a couple's argument when the wife threatened to poke her husband's eyes out with her knitting needles. Shelby went beyond the call of duty to help one poor guest book an airline ticket to Utah when her elderly mother died unexpectedly.

In addition to putting out fires, Shelby managed a constant stream of requests from guests throughout the day. They needed everything from sunscreen and pool floats to beach chairs, towels, sandwiches, snacks, and alcoholic beverages. The sweltering heat also drove a constant demand for bottled water. Shelby diligently added these items to her growing list and promised to discuss the requests with management.

Meanwhile, the phone rang off the hook with inquiries about future reservations. During her few free moments, Shelby set up the new computer and researched reservation systems. By the time Pritchard stopped by with Savannah and Harper around four o'clock, she was utterly unhinged, her nerves frayed. Judging by their bathing suits and cover-ups, Shelby realized they had spent a relaxing day on the water in their boat while she had been holding down the fort here alone. If Pritchard expected her to be the manager, he needed to pay her accordingly.

A stranger might mistake the threesome as friends instead of mother, father, and daughter. Harper was prettier than Shelby remembered from the wedding. She was a real head-turner with white-blonde curly hair, sun-kissed cheeks, and sparkling blue eyes. Shelby experienced a pang of envy at the glimpse of Harper's yellow bikini and toned muscles through her crocheted coverup. Shelby was thin with curves in the right places, but she would kill to have such well-defined muscles.

"How're things going?" Pritchard asked. "I see you got the computer running."

"So far today, we've had a trash fire, multiple overflowing toilets, and an argument between two of our guests," Shelby said, ticking the problems off her fingers. "We were not prepared to open this weekend, and you're not paying me enough to do all this alone."

Pritchard frowned. "No one expects you to do this alone, Shelby. Where's your grandmother?"

Shelby tossed up her hands. "I have no idea. Her car's gone. I haven't seen her since this morning. She probably ran away. I would, too, if I had wheels. At this point, I'd settle for a golf cart or a bicycle."

Savannah drew her in for a hug. "You poor thing. No wonder you're frazzled. Why didn't you call us?"

Over Savannah's shoulder, Shelby, noticing Harper eyeing her with pity, choked back tears and willed herself not to cry in front of her cousin. "Because this isn't your responsibility. It's mine." She pushed Savannah away and turned to Pritchard. "I can handle the job. I just need the authority to make decisions and a business credit card for purchases." She nodded at the legal pad on her desk. "I made a list of today's requests."

Harper picked up the legal pad and scanned the items. "Pool floats and beach chairs. Wine. Beer. Mimosas. What you need is a bar."

"And a cafe, snack shop, spa, and fitness center," Shelby added.

Harper dropped the legal pad on the desk. "Not having a bar seems like a missed opportunity to make a fortune. And I know just where you should put it."

Shelby, Savannah, and Pritchard followed her into the adjacent paneled library.

Harper ran her fingers across her grandfather's giant mahogany desk. "Replace this behemoth with a custom-made bar." She knocked on the wall behind his desk. "The powder room is on the other side of this wall. You could tap into the plumbing for your sink. Clear off a few shelves for the liquor bottles, add a couple of small tables and some chairs, and you've got yourself a lounge."

"How do you know so much about this stuff?" Shelby asked Harper.

"I'm an interior designer. I have my own firm."

Shelby's eyes grew wide. "Really? That's amazing." She walked over to the French doors. "You might be onto something. We already have plenty of seating on the terrace. Our guests would love to have cocktails served outside. We would have to hire a bartender though. Pouring margarita mix out of a bottle is the extent of my bartending skills."

Harper placed a hand on Savannah's shoulder. "Lucky for us, we have a bartender in the family."

Savannah shook her head. "No way! I already have a job."

Izzy appeared in the doorway. "Are y'all talking about me behind my back?"

Prichard stiffened in alarm. "What? No, Mother! Geez."

"We were discussing turning Edward's study into a bar,"

Harper said with a mischievous grin that made Shelby wonder if her new cousin was intentionally trying to make their grandmother angry.

"Don't you dare!" Isabelle said. "My husband would roll over in his grave."

Shelby approached her grandmother. "Where have you been? You can't just leave me here all alone."

Izzy's face beamed red. "Don't use that tone with me, young lady. For your information, I was out looking for somewhere to live. I'm sure you'd all like to get rid of me, but unfortunately, I didn't find anything I could afford with the pennies Edward left me. On my way home, I stopped by the cemetery and had a few words with your dear old grandfather. He didn't respond, of course. But I'm hoping he heard me," she said, gazing heavenward.

Shelby scrunched up her face in concern. The pressure was starting to get to Izzy. She'd been a straight-up bitch since Shelby arrived. "I called you a gazillion times. Why didn't you pick up?"

"I'm no good with my phone. I don't even know where it is." Rummaging through her purse, Izzy located her phone and scrolled through her missed calls. "Not quite a gazillion. Why were you calling me anyway? My responsibility to this godforsaken B&B ended at breakfast. It's Silas's job to help you."

Shelby's insides churned in anger. "And Silas was a huge help. An extra set of hands would've been nice. I was under the impression you were more than the cook. Who is running this business? We need some leadership around here. My sorority house operated better than this place."

Izzy's hazel eyes grew wide. "If you're not careful, I will ship you home to your mother."

Shelby stuck out her palm. "Do it! Please! Give me the money, and I'll be out of your hair as quick as I can pack my suitcase and call an Uber." She withdrew her hand. "Never mind. I forgot you don't have any money."

Izzy drew herself to her full height. "How dare you speak to me like that? I am your grandmother."

The two women faced off with nostrils flaring and teeth clenched.

"Shh! Lower your voices. We have guests in the house," Pritchard said, closing the folding doors separating the library from the living room.

"I never asked to be put in this position," Izzy said.

Shelby puffed out her chest. "And neither did I."

Pritchard stepped between them. "You should be ashamed of yourself, Mother. You're acting like a petulant child. If you can't take responsibility for this bed and breakfast, you need to step aside and let me run it."

Savannah sighed. "The truth is, none of you can manage the B&B alone. You're booked solid through the summer. Working together as a team is the only way. With your coordinated efforts, you'll have things running smoothly in no time."

Izzy shot her an icy glare. "Oh, be quiet, Savannah. Save your mumbo jumbo for the staff at that dive restaurant you manage."

Horror filled Pritchard's face. "Mother! You are way out of line. Savannah is only trying to help."

"I don't need her help. I don't need anyone's help." Izzy spun on her heels and stormed out of the house.

Four sets of eyes watched the door slam behind her.

"Should I go after her?" Shelby asked in a tone of uncertainty.

Savannah shook her head. "Indulging her temper tantrums will only add fuel to the fire."

Pritchard placed a hand on the small of his wife's back. "I agree with Savannah. We should let her cool off. She's going through a lot right now, and we should try to be patient. Her life, as she's known it for more than four decades, is over. If she decides that running the B&B is too much for her, I'll set her up in a comfortable oceanfront cottage. But she must give this an honest try first."

"Who knows? Maybe she'll come around," Shelby said, although she had doubts.

Pritchard gave Shelby a half hug. "Regardless of what happens, I'm grateful to have you. I'm sorry you're in the hot seat, but you're doing an excellent job. And I will compensate you for it."

"Thank you, Pritchard. I'm trying." As the words left her mouth, Shelby realized she could be trying harder and complaining less.

"We have much to discuss," Pritchard said. "I'll text you in the morning, and we'll figure out a time to meet tomorrow afternoon."

"That would be great," Shelby said. I've been researching reservation systems, and I can share that information with you."

"We should discuss those options with our web designer. I've already had a couple of discussions with Claire. I'll loop you into those video conferences. Coincidentally, she suggested we take some photographs of the property to use on the website. I realize you don't have time for it this weekend, but maybe you can snap a few images during the week, if you're interested."

Shelby flashed him a broad smile. "I would love that. I took a digital photography class in college."

"That sounds like fun. Dad purchased a high-end Nikon before his diagnosis." Pritchard swept an arm at the cabinets below the bookshelves. "It's in here somewhere if you can find it."

Shelby nodded, her ponytail dancing about her shoulders. "Thanks!"

Savannah gave her a parting hug. "Hang in there, kiddo. Things will get easier. You can always call one of us if you need anything."

Harper hooked an arm around Shelby's waist. "Good to see you again, cuz. I'll stop by tomorrow and check on you. If you're free, we can go for a walk."

"I'd love that. Thanks, Harper."

For the first time since arriving in Water's Edge, hope

blossomed inside Shelby. If she was being honest with herself, this was the first time she felt truly good about anything since Luke broke up with her.

Pritchard maneuvered the boat away from the dock. He'd never felt prouder with his wife on the leaning post to his right and his daughter standing beside him on his left. If only his mother weren't such a pill. Izzy was raining on his parade when she should be waving to the crowd from the leading float.

Harper gripped the console's railing, steadying herself as they crossed the wake from a sportfishing boat returning from the ocean. "Poor, Shelby. I feel bad for her being stuck here with Izzy." She gave Pritchard a sympathetic look. "I'm sorry for always dissing your mom. I wish I had something positive to say about her."

"No need to apologize, sweetheart. Izzy brought this on herself." While Pritchard didn't blame Harper for her negative feelings toward Izzy, hearing her speak so harshly about his mother, her grandmother, hurt his heart. "I admit, I'm not a fan of this new Izzy. She's changed since . . ." His voice trailed off.

"Since Harper and I came back into your life," Savannah said, finishing his sentence.

His shoulders slumped. "Unfortunately, your presence is a constant reminder of her crime. Shelby spent a lot of time here during the summers growing up. She and Izzy shared an amiable relationship. Maybe Shelby will help improve her mood."

"Or maybe Izzy will ruin that relationship as well," Savannah mumbled loud enough for him to hear.

Harper's phone pinged, and she read the text. "Cody just got off work. He wants us to pick him up from the city dock."

Pritchard winked at Savannah. *Right on cue.* They'd been helping Cody plan the surprise for weeks. Keeping it a secret hadn't been easy.

As they drew near the dock, Harper shielded her eyes from the sun for a better look. "Who's on the dock with him? Looks like a crowd of people in black robes. Is that a choir?"

Pritchard shrugged, unable to hide his mischievous grin. The people in black robes were members of the Southern Harmony Gospel Choir from the local Grace Baptist Church. His wife, a musically gifted songwriter, had worked with the choir director to create a chorale-appropriate arrangement of Randy Travis's "Forever and Ever, Amen" for the occasion. When Savannah expressed concern about Harper not recognizing the song, Cody assured her that her daughter was a huge fan of classic country.

As Cody helped Harper off the boat, the choir belted out the lyrics with rich, resonant voices that filled the air. Savannah lifted her phone, capturing the moment Cody dropped to one knee and opened a black velvet box to reveal the sparkling engagement ring.

Cody waited for the choir to end the song before saying, "I'm gonna love you forever and ever, Harper. Will you marry me?"

Harper knelt to his level. "And I'm gonna love you forever and ever as well. Yes, I will marry you."

He pulled her up and carefully slipped the ring on her finger. The crowd that had gathered at the railing cheered loudly as the choir began singing again.

Savannah rested her head on his shoulder. "Our small family is growing."

Pritchard smiled. "And I couldn't have hand-picked a better son-in-law."

nine

. . .

Isabelle was hurrying across the courtyard when Blossom called out to her. "Yoo-hoo! Wait up, Izzy!"

Isabelle spun around to face her. "My name is Isabelle. Only my family is allowed to call me Izzy."

"That's a shame. Izzy suits you." Blossom shoved a brown leather journal at her. "I found this. I believe it belongs to you."

Isabelle took the journal and ran her finger over the three-digit locking mechanism. "Where'd you get this?" she asked accusingly. "My late husband was a criminal attorney. He often used these journals to record his private thoughts on his more complex cases."

"I found a copy of Pat Conroy's *The Prince of Tides* on his desk. But when I opened it, there were no pages, only a hollowed-out space used as a safe. This journal was hidden inside."

Isabelle frowned. "That's odd. I never knew Edward to hide his journals." She looked up at Blossom. "By *library,* if you're referring to my husband's study, those books are private property and not for the use of our guests."

"Then you should put up a sign."

"And you should refrain from snooping around in my personal belongings." When Isabelle started toward the cottage with the journal, Blossom's little dog ran after her, nipping at her heels. Feeling a sharp pain, she kicked at the dog. The dog let out a loud yelp and scurried back to Blossom. "Ouch! Your dog bit me."

Blossom picked up her dog. "Jolene is very protective. She gets defensive when people act aggressively toward me."

"You haven't seen aggressive, lady." Isabelle hiked up her pants leg. "Look! I'm bleeding."

"Let me see." Gripping her dog under her arm, Blossom bent over to examine Isabelle's ankle. "It's only a little scrape. She barely grazed the skin." She straightened. "But don't worry, she's up to date on her rabies shot."

Isabelle tensed. "Rabies! Good lord. I'm warning you, Blossom, either keep that dog away from me, or I'll have to ask you to leave," she said and entered the cottage, slamming the door behind her.

She washed the scrape with soap and water in the bathroom sink and located an old roll of gauze and a tube of antibiotic ointment in the medicine cabinet. After bandaging her wound, even though it was still daylight out and she hadn't eaten dinner, she changed into her pajamas and climbed into bed.

Isabelle entered Edward's birthdate in the combination lock. When that didn't work, she tried 3-1-2, their numeric address on Beach Drive. The lock clicked and she opened the journal. On the first page, in her husband's tidy cursive, was written *My vision for Magnolia Shores Resort.*

Isabelle had sat at his desk many times since his death, but she'd never seen *The Prince of Tides* book safe Blossom had mentioned. And she definitely would have noticed it. Edward was also a fan of Pat Conroy, and they'd often discussed the tormented characters in his novels. They agreed that, of all Conroy's works, *The Prince of Tides* offered the deepest dive into family dysfunction. She stared up at the ceiling. "Oh, Edward. You heard me at the cemetery, didn't you? That's how this diary found its way into that strange woman's hands."

Isabelle turned the page and began reading. What she learned from her late husband's words stunned her. The bed and breakfast was merely the first stage of a very elaborate scheme to turn their hundred-acre property into a full-blown resort. He dreamed of building a three-story boutique hotel on the large vacant lot beside the main house. He referred to it repeatedly as The Sanctuary. In addition to a large lobby with a check-in area, the first floor would feature a spa with a fitness center, a dining room, a cocktail lounge, and an upscale gift shop. With thirty new guest suites on the second and third floors, the main house would then revert to being home for the St. Clair family.

Isabelle read the entire journal, each page filled with inventive ideas for Magnolia Shores. Edward planned to offer fishing excursions and sunset cruises on Catawba Sound. He envisioned paddleboard and kayak rentals and a fleet of bicycles available to guests on a first-come, first-served basis. In addition to the three meals offered in the dining room, a less formal lunch would be served at a cafe by a new and larger pool.

When she finally finished reading, Isabelle closed the diary and hugged it to her chest. This venture was way over her head. Even reading Edward's ideas exhausted her. She knew her husband well and was sure of his intent—to create a future for the younger St. Clair generations. But why rope Isabelle into running the bed and breakfast? Why not simply provide her with ample money to live on and pass the property to Pritchard and Kate to manage?

Shelby waited until the last guest left for dinner in town before going to the kitchen for a sandwich. She was seated at the table, scrolling through Luke's social media posts, when Silas entered the room.

"Things are pretty quiet around here," he said. "If you don't mind, I'm gonna take off. If anything happens, call me. I live nearby and can be here in a matter of minutes."

"Okay, sounds good." She gestured at her pimento cheese sandwich. "Would you like a sandwich before you go?"

"Thanks, but I'm grilling a tuna steak at home. I wouldn't mind some water for the road though." He removed a bottle of water from the refrigerator and leaned against the counter. "I saw your granny enter the cottage. I assume she's in for the night."

Shelby's eyebrows shot up. "You'd better not let Izzy hear you call her that."

Silas chuckled. "Don't worry. I value my job. And my life."

"Where did you work before here?" Shelby asked and crammed the last bite of her sandwich in her mouth.

"In the laundry. At Ridgeland Correctional Institution."

Shelby's teal eyes popped. "You were in *jail*?"

A pained expression crossed Silas's face. "Ten years ago, when my ex-wife's boyfriend beat her to a pulp, she accused me of aggravated assault to protect him. I was convicted and sentenced to twenty-five years." He paused, his voice heavy. "She eventually admitted she had lied about the incident, and I was released from prison. Two weeks after her confession, that same boyfriend—who had become her husband by then—murdered her."

Shelby's jaw hit the table. "Goodness. That's some story. I'm sorry, Silas. I can't imagine going to prison for a crime I didn't commit."

Silas stared down at the floor. "I probably shouldn't have told you. I'm not good at lying. Can I trust you to keep my secret? I don't think Izzy would approve of me working here if she knew about my past."

"You're right about that. She'd fire you on the spot. But don't worry. I promise not to say anything." Shelby got up from the table and took her plate to the dishwasher. "I can tell you're a good man, Silas. Having you around makes me feel safer."

After seeing Silas out, Shelby searched her grandfather's study for his Nikon. She found it in the cabinet behind his desk. Once the guests had returned from town, she took the camera and her laptop upstairs to the room vacated earlier by the woman whose mother had passed away. She stayed up late watching YouTube instructional videos to better understand the features of this particular Nikon camera model.

Waking before dawn on Sunday, she took the camera out to the dock and photographed the main house with the pink rays of the rising sun in the background. Hearing the soft rumble of an outboard motor, she turned to see a center-console fishing boat approaching from behind. When the engine quieted, she assumed the boat had passed by. But a few minutes later, the boat's bow inched up beside her, and a casting net splashed into the water.

"Morning, ma'am," said the guy pulling in the casting net. "I hope I'm not disturbing you."

"Not at all." She waved her camera. "I already captured the magic moment."

The guy emptied his net in the live bait well at the back of the boat and returned to the bow for another cast. He posed a serene figure in the glorious morning sunlight, too intent on his task in the quiet surroundings to notice when she snapped a few photos of him wrestling his net into the boat.

After plucking all the minnows from the net, he dipped it in the water to rinse off the mud and dropped it in the boat. Starting his engine, he eased over to the dock.

He flashed Shelby a kilowatt smile. "Thanks for letting me fish your waters."

Shelby laughed at his joke. Everyone knew Catawba Sound was public property. "Any time."

"Are you a guest at the new bed and breakfast?"

"Actually, I'm working here for my grandmother, Isabelle St. Clair. I'm taking some pics for our new website."

"Cool! I knew your grandfather. Edward was a really good dude."

"Thanks. He was a good dude. We all miss him." Shelby held up the Nikon. "This was his camera."

"So, you're Edward's daughter's daughter. The one from Texas."

"Right. I'm Shelby Kinder, Kate's daughter."

"Nice to meet you, Shelby. I'm Matt Hitchcock. Are you just here for the summer?"

Shelby shrugged. "I'm not sure yet. If I like the job, I may stay for a while."

"Maybe we can go out sometime."

Out of habit, the words tumbled from her mouth, "I have a boyfriend."

He appeared disappointed. "Lucky guy," Matt said, putting the boat in reverse. "I've gotta run. My old man is waiting for me to go offshore. Have a good day."

Shelby lifted her hand in a wave. "Bye."

She strolled up the dock, enjoying the peacefulness of the early hour. Most of their guests were still sleeping, and the wildlife was beginning to stir. She couldn't remember the last time she'd awakened before sunrise. Come to think of it, she wasn't sure she'd ever willingly gotten up so early. In her new life, she was discovering many things about herself, and not all of them were bad.

When she reached the cottage, she was relieved to find her grandmother had already left for the main house. She packed some clothes and toiletries in a tote bag and returned to the room where she'd spent the night. Based on her rudimentary reservation system, the room was free until Thursday. She'd sleep in a tent, if necessary, to avoid her grumpy grandmother.

While showering, she noticed the absence of individually wrapped soap bars and trial-size shampoo bottles, conditioner, and shower gel. She made a mental note to add these items to her expanding to-do list.

Shelby slipped on a yellow floral sundress. If she ever received a paycheck, she'd bum a ride to town to shop for more appropriate work attire. She took her camera downstairs to her desk and uploaded the sunrise images to the photo editing software. The photographs were stunning. While she'd learned some digital photography from her college class, she gave her grandfather's camera and God all the credit.

She studied the images of Matt. His yellow-green eyes mirrored the expanse of marsh grass rustling in the breeze behind him. His sandy hair, tousled and spiked at the front by the wind, underscored his rugged charm. The gray T-shirt he wore clung to his broad chest and bulging biceps, accentuating his toned body. During their brief exchange, she'd sensed a gentleness about him, and his genuine smile had warmed her heart.

Why had she told him she had a boyfriend? Dozens of guys had hit on her since her breakup with Luke, and she'd given them the same answer. Telling them she was in a relationship seemed less cruel than saying she wasn't interested. And no one had interested her, until now.

ten

. . .

Isabelle's attempt at making blueberry pancakes—a breakfast food staple in their household when the children were little—was a disaster. She undercooked her first batch and had to start over from scratch. Panic set in. She was far from being prepared for her first guests, who would appear at any moment. She was spooning pancake batter onto her electric griddle when she heard the back door open, followed by dog nails on hardwood floors.

"Good morning, Izzy!"

Isabelle's skin crawled at the use of her family's nickname. She craned her neck to look behind her at Blossom. "Keep that dog away from me. If it bites me again, I'm calling the pound."

Blossom picked up the dog, holding her close. "I can't believe you would consider subjecting an innocent animal to such cruelty. How is your foot, by the way?" Coming around the island, she looked down at her foot and back up at Izzy. "You wrapped your foot in gauze? Seriously, it was only a tiny scrape."

"I didn't have a Band-Aid, thank you very much." Isabelle waved her spatula at Blossom. "I'm warning you. Get that dog away from me."

The dog growled at Isabelle.

"See! She's going to bite me again."

"She feels threatened because you're waving a spatula at her." Blossom's gaze shifted to the griddle on the counter behind her. "Oops. Looks like you burned your pancakes."

Isabelle's head swiveled around, and she stared in horror at what were now black hockey pucks on the griddle. "How did they burn when I haven't even flipped them?"

"Maybe the pancakes don't like you either," Blossom said and disappeared into the dining room.

Isabelle dumped the burned pancakes down the disposal and ladled fresh batter onto the griddle for a third time. At this rate, she would be serving her guests pancakes for dinner.

Blossom returned with a cup of coffee and sat down at the table with the dog in her lap. "That's quite the elaborate feast you have on display. You realize you're going about this all wrong?"

Isabelle grunted. "I don't remember asking for your opinion."

"Then you're in luck. I've never been good at keeping my thoughts to myself. Why not offer a simple buffet with mini muffins, bagels, and items you can freeze? Or foods you can prepare the night before, like fresh fruit? Containers of yogurt and bowls of granola are excellent options, as are small boxes of cereal."

Isabelle let out a humph. "I will not serve boxed cereal to my guests." She transferred the pancakes from the griddle to one side of a chafing dish tray, filling the empty space with sausage and bacon. She carried the tray into the dining room. When she returned to the kitchen, Blossom had her face glued to some catalog.

She peered at Isabelle over the top of the catalog. "How about ordering frozen chicken sausage patties and bite-size frittatas? You would thaw them the night before, warm them in the morning, and you've got yourself a meal."

Isabelle went to stand beside her. "What're you looking at?"

Blossom showed her the catalog's front cover. "A brochure from Waterside Wholesale Food Distributors." She nodded at an envelope on the table. "A handwritten note and business card were attached to the front. Marilyn Daily says she'll stop by on Tuesday to discuss your first order."

"So now you're reading my mail?" Isabelle snatched the catalog from Blossom's hands. "Where'd you get this?"

Blossom pointed at a spot on the table. "It was right there when I sat down with my coffee."

Lines appeared on Isabelle's forehead. "I wiped the table down before starting on the pancakes, and I'm certain the catalog was not there."

Blossom held up her hands. "Some things you just can't explain."

Since Blossom's arrival, many unexplained things had occurred, including burned pancakes and rejuvenated plants. And it was no accident that Blossom had found the journal containing Edward's ideas for the bed and breakfast—ideas she had asked him about that very afternoon during her visit to the cemetery. There were two possible explanations. Either Blossom had magical powers, or the stress was getting to Isabelle and she was losing her mind.

Isabelle returned to the stove, where her pan of sausage patties had begun to boil.

From the table, Blossom, as though reading Isabelle's mind, asked, "Were you able to unlock your husband's journal?"

Isabelle spun around, long meat fork in hand. "That's none of your business, Blossom. Why are you wasting a perfectly lovely morning when you could be walking your beast on the beach?" She brandished her fork at the door. "Get out! Please! I need to focus on cooking, and you're distracting me."

"Great day in the morning! Isabelle St. Clair, you are one grouchy woman." Blossom rose from the table. "Come on, Jolene. We know when we're not wanted." She opened the back door, and the little dog ran outside ahead of her.

Isabelle fielded complaints and requests throughout the breakfast hours. Some guests were vegan, and others were gluten free. A few named diets she'd never even heard of. They wanted poached eggs and eggs cooked sunny-side up. They asked for fruit, smoothies, and yogurt parfaits. One woman claimed to have found an eggshell in her pancakes. One man said his sausage was raw. And one young woman called Isabelle over to her table to show her the rash on her arm.

"I'm allergic to dairy," the woman said. "Did you use real milk in the pancake batter?"

Isabelle glared at her. "Of course. What else would I use?"

The woman rolled her eyes. "Dairy-free. Duh. Either soy or almond. Real milk is so last century. Then again, considering your age, I wouldn't expect you to know that."

Isabelle grabbed the woman's arm and inspected the rash. "Looks like sunburn to me."

The woman snatched her arm back. "Are you out of your mind? No ray of sunshine has touched my skin in a decade."

Isabelle studied the woman's pale complexion. "That explains why you're so gaunt looking. A little color on your cheeks might improve your disposition." She felt the woman stare daggers at her back as she disappeared into the butler's pantry.

Sneaking a peek down the hallway, Isabelle was relieved to see Shelby at the reception desk. After their unpleasant exchange yesterday afternoon, she had been worried when her granddaughter hadn't returned to the cottage last night. She must have found somewhere else to sleep, which was just as well. The girl had an attitude, and Isabelle was too preoccupied with her own troubles.

On Sunday morning, numerous guests complained about Shelby's grandmother, citing a long list of grievances about breakfast food and Izzy's rude behavior. It was only a matter of time before one of these disgruntled guests would voice their irritation on a travel review, which could mean the endgame for Magnolia Shores B&B.

A smiling Pritchard appeared on time for their one o'clock meeting.

"You seem happy," Shelby said. "Did you win the lottery?"

He started to say something but then changed his mind. "I'll let Harper tell you the news when she stops by later."

Shelby narrowed her eyes. "Now I'm curious. I know she's been dating the same guy for a while. Did they get engaged?"

Pritchard drew an imaginary zipper across his lips.

"Ugh, okay. I hate to burst your happy bubble, but we've had several complaints about Izzy this morning," she said, handing him the list.

Pritchard sighed as he scanned the list. "This isn't good. I'll talk to Mom."

"We have our reputation to think about, Pritchard. One bad review on Yelp, and we're doomed."

Pritchard furrowed his brow as though he hadn't thought of this. "That's a valid point."

Seated together at the desk, Pritchard and Shelby discussed options for central reservation systems, identified their preference, and sent the information to the web designer for approval.

"As soon as Claire gets back to us, we'll purchase the software so you can start using it," he said.

"I took some photographs of the main house at sunrise this morning. Here, I'll show you," Shelby said, accessing the pics on her computer.

Pritchard peered at the computer screen. "These are excellent, Shelby. You've inherited your grandfather's keen eye for photography. Keep up the good work."

Shelby beamed. "Thanks." She turned away from the computer to face him. "I'm still unclear about my hours and responsibilities. Am I supposed to be stationed at this desk all day long?"

"Not at all. Only during peak check-in and check-out hours. Let Silas know how he can reach you when you're away from the desk, and return all calls as soon as possible when you get back. Does that work for you?"

"Yes! That sounds perfect!"

They were finishing their meeting when Harper arrived, wearing her bathing suit and cover-up. Shelby's eyes traveled to the small diamond ring on her left hand. "You got engaged! Pritchard said you had news. I thought it might be this. Congratulations!"

Harper admired her ring. "Thanks! I'm beyond thrilled. Wait until I tell you how he proposed. Are you free to take that walk now?"

Shelby looked uncertainly at Prichard. "Do you think it's okay?"

"Of course. I'll be here for a while. I can cover for you. I need to have that little talk with Mom anyway."

"Let me go change. I'll be back in a second." Dashing up the stairs, Shelby quickly changed into her bikini and coated herself with sunscreen. Returning to the living room, she took her cousin by the arm and dragged her through the French doors. "Come on. I can't wait to hear about the proposal."

As they crossed the terrace toward the dunes, Harper told Shelby about the gospel choir Cody had hired to sing one of her favorite classic country songs.

Shelby placed her folded hands on her chest. "Aww. That is so romantic. When's the wedding?"

Harper laughed. "Good question! We only got engaged last night, but we're thinking sometime next spring."

Shelby walked ahead of Harper down the path to the beach. Over her shoulder, she said, "Will you please make it April nineteenth? If you get married the same day as my sister, I will have a legitimate reason not to attend her wedding."

"That would make things complicated for family members who would like to attend both. Why would you want to miss your sister's wedding?"

Shelby kicked at the sand. "We don't get along. She didn't even ask me to be a bridesmaid."

When they reached the beach, they walked side by side, heading north. "I'm sorry, Shelby. As an only child, I don't pretend to know what that feels like. I always wished I had a sibling."

"And I always wished I was an only child. You'd understand if you knew Grace. I'd rather have Cruella de Vil for a sister." Shelby inhaled a deep breath of salty air. "It feels good to be outside. I'm not used to being stuck inside all day."

Harper laughed. "Adjusting to the working world takes time. I was a paralegal before moving to Water's Edge. Being cooped up in an office is difficult. At least your office is swanky. And you have incredible views from every window."

"True," Shelby said with a chuckle. "Tell me about your fiancé. I don't even know his name."

"His name is Cody Porter, and he's an officer with the local police force."

Shelby thought his occupation sounded dreadful, and she didn't think police officers made much money. "How'd you meet?"

A dreamy expression settled over Harper's face. "Cody was the first friend I made when I moved to Water's Edge. I was working at a women's boutique at the time, and he showed up one Sunday morning to help me give the shop a minimakeover. I'd just lost my mother, and I wasn't interested in romance, but he waited patiently until I was."

"That's so sweet. I'm so happy for you, cuz."

Harper shoulder-bumped her. "What about you, cuz? Do you have a significant other back home in Texas?"

"We broke up. He started dating someone else right away and now they're engaged. I keep hoping he'll come around." Shelby grew silent for a minute, thinking about Luke. "Do you think absence makes the heart grow fonder?"

"Sometimes. It also makes you forget."

Shelby's heart sank. "That's what Blossom said."

Harper made a funny face. "Interesting name. Who is she?"

"Some woman who is staying here for the summer. I get the feeling she's more than a guest."

Harper tilted her head. "What do you mean?"

"Like maybe she's here on a mission. She appears to have magical powers." Shelby told her about the odd things that had happened in Blossom's presence. "Maybe she can wave her wand and make me stop thinking about Luke."

"You don't need magic, Shelby. You need a new man to help you forget about Luke."

The image of Matt popped into her head, but she quickly dismissed it. How could she think about someone else when she wasn't over Luke?

Shelby stopped walking and turned to Harper. "Can I ask you a personal question?"

Harper chuckled. "You can ask, but I'm not sure I'll answer."

"And I won't blame you if you don't because I'm totally being nosy. But I'm dying to know the story behind your adoption. My mom told me that Pritchard and Savannah dated in high school and that she got pregnant with you. But I don't understand why she put you up for adoption and ran away for thirty years."

Harper lowered her gaze to the sand. "It's not a pretty story, Shelby. And I don't think I should be the one to tell you. Maybe you should ask your mom or Pritchard."

"Does it have something to do with Izzy? I sensed tension between you two yesterday."

"I really shouldn't say anything, Shelby. Pritchard loves his mother despite what she did. And he takes good care of her. I respect him for that."

Despite what she did? Harper basically admitted Izzy was somehow involved in her adoption. She wouldn't press for more details today, but she would find out in time. "I understand, and I respect *you* for not telling me. I've seen a different side of

Pritchard these past few days. Or maybe I've never noticed it before. But he's a kind man and a good person."

Harper beamed. "Pritchard's the best. I'm a lucky girl to have him as a father. And you're pretty awesome too, Shelby. I'm going to like having my first cousin around," she said, her genuine smile matching her father's.

Looping her arm through Harper's, Shelby smiled as they turned back toward Magnolia Shores. "Me too. I'll trade my mean old sister in for a cool cousin any day."

eleven

. . .

Isabelle searched high and low for a quiet spot to collect her thoughts. The tiny cottage was cluttered with the clothes she'd yet to put away, and the sweltering Lowcountry heat was too much for the antiquated air conditioner. The main house was an ant hill, with little people crawling in and out of every crevice. Every chaise lounge by the pool was occupied. There was even a guest in her hammock—*her* Pawleys Island Hammock, which Edward had given her one year for Christmas.

Isabelle grabbed a towel and made her way down to the beach. She sat with her knees tucked under her chin, drawing a family of stick figures in the sand: Isabelle, Edward, Pritchard, and Kate—her family during the good old days, back when she was still a happy person.

She was so lost in thoughts of the past that she didn't hear Pritchard approach. "There you are. I've been looking everywhere for you. What are you doing down here?"

"Hiding. In case you haven't noticed, our home is a beehive. And I'm allergic to bees."

Pritchard chuckled. "Since when?"

"Since Friday." Isabelle wiped the edge of her hand over her stick figures, erasing her sand family.

He helped her to her feet. "I have exciting news. Harper and Cody got engaged last night."

"How wonderful," Isabelle said in an unenthusiastic tone. They would expect her to get all gussied up and pretend she was happy about the wedding of a granddaughter who despised her.

"We need to talk about this," Pritchard said, handing her a yellow sheet of paper from a legal pad.

Isabelle read the list of guest complaints about her cooking and rude behavior. She thrust the paper back at him. "So? What do you expect me to do with this?"

"I expect you to be nice. You can't treat people this way, Mother. You told one woman she was gaunt."

"Because she insulted me for being too old to understand the concept of dairy-free milk."

Pritchard folded the paper into a square. "These people are guests in your home. You need to treat them as such."

"They are here against my will. Which makes me the hostage and them my captives."

Pritchard threw up his hands. "I give up. What is wrong with you? Why do you have such a chip on your shoulder?"

Isabelle's skin prickled. Kate had said something similar. "What's so wrong with having high expectations?"

"Because you crucify those who don't meet those expectations."

"That is not true, Pritchard."

"Yes, it is." He raked his fingers through his salt-and-pepper hair. "Becoming an Eagle Scout is the only thing I've ever done that you approved of. Why do you think Kate moved to Texas? To get away from your constant criticism."

"That's a boldfaced lie. You're the one who is constantly criticizing me. I'm done with this conversation." Isabelle scrambled to her feet and took off down the beach.

Pritchard caught up with her. "Can you please try to be more agreeable?" He flagged the folded paper at her. "A bad review on social media will ruin our reputation before we ever get started."

Isabelle's face fell. "Oh. I didn't think about that."

She considered telling Pritchard what she'd learned from his father's journal. She sensed her son was considering an early retirement from his job as a country music talent manager. Isabelle would be off the hook if he willingly took over running the bed and breakfast. And the sooner this new building was completed, the sooner Isabelle could return to her home.

Isabelle broached the subject as they headed back toward the house. "A guest discovered one of your father's journals hidden in a book safe. I read it from cover-to-cover last night. His vision for this place was more elaborate than he ever let on. He even named the property Magnolia Shores."

A thoughtful frown creased Pritchard's forehead. "I like the name. Tell me more."

Yes! He's taking the bait, Isabelle thought, and outlined Edward's vision for the new building, including the various amenities.

When they reached the pathway to the house, Pritchard stopped walking and stared over the dunes. "What you describe is way more than a bed and breakfast. We're talking about a full-on resort. I wonder why he never mentioned this expansion to you."

"Because he knew such a project would scare me off. You realize I'm incapable of designing and overseeing the construction of a building of this magnitude."

"Dad would never have expected that of you. At least not alone. But we have plenty of space to expand. I need to give this some more thought. Do you mind if I read the journal?"

"Not at all. It's in the cottage. If you can wait, I'll get it for you now."

"I have plenty of time. I'll walk with you," Pritchard said, motioning for her to go ahead of him up the pathway.

Isabelle trudged through the thick sand, stopping short at the sight of Blossom treading water in the center of the pool while her little dog paddled in circles around her. "What is that dag-blasted dog doing in my pool?" she hollered, not thinking about the other guests lounging around the pool.

Pritchard whispered to her, "Let it go, Mother. Don't you dare cause a scene in front of all these people."

Ignoring her son, Isabelle marched over to the edge of the pool. "No dogs are allowed in this pool. Get it out now!" she said, gesturing wildly at the steps.

"Geez, Izzy! Hold on to your granny panties. I'm getting out as fast as I can," Blossom said, tucking the dog under her arm as she waded toward the steps.

Pritchard rushed to Blossom's aid, holding on to her elbow while she climbed out of the pool. "I'm so sorry, ma'am."

"Don't worry, son. I live to irritate your mama," Blossom said, flashing Isabelle a mischievous grin.

"What a cute dog. What's her name?" Pritchard asked.

Blossom held the little dog up for him to see her face. "Jolene."

Pritchard scratched behind the dog's ears. "I love it. Believe it or not, I'm close friends with Dolly Parton."

Blossom winked at him. "So am I."

Isabelle grabbed Pritchard by the arm. "Let's go, son," she said, dragging him away from Blossom.

"Slow down, Mother." Pritchard wrenched his arm free of her grasp. "What is wrong with you? If any of our guests videoed your little scene back there, they could post it on social media."

Isabelle increased her pace as they crossed the courtyard. "I'm sorry. But that woman is driving me crazy. I told her to be mindful of her dog, and she let the nasty little creature swim in *my* pool."

Pritchard hurried along beside her. "Since when are you a dog hater?"

"Not all dogs. Just hers," Isabelle said with a thumb over her shoulder.

"Who is she anyway? How did she know I'm your son? And how does she know Dolly Parton?"

They stopped in front of the cottage. "Her name is Blossom. I have no clue how she knows Dolly Parton, but she somehow knows everything about our family."

Pritchard glanced back toward the pool. "So that's Blossom? Blossom with no last name who's booked a room for the entire summer?"

"Yep." Isabelle lowered her voice and leaned in close to her son. "I think she's a spy."

Pritchard peered at her over the top of his sunglasses. "A spy? Like for the CIA?"

"More like an angel spy your father sent down from heaven to keep tabs on me."

Pritchard's brow hit his hairline. "How long were you out on the beach, Mother? I think you may have suffered a heat stroke."

"I'm perfectly healthy, thank you very much." With Pritchard on her heels, Isabelle entered the cottage and retrieved Edward's journal from her bedroom. "Yesterday, I visited your father's grave, asking him to share his vision for the bed and breakfast. And voila, Blossom magically appeared with this journal full of his ideas. You have to admit it's quite the coincidence."

"That's exactly what it is, Mother. A coincidence."

Isabelle unlocked the journal and handed it to him. "Here. Your father wasn't concerned about protecting his private thoughts from prying eyes. He used our Magnolia Shores' address as the code."

Pritchard thumbed through the pages. "Whoa. This is a lot to absorb. He went into full detail about this building he envisioned. Can I take this home? I want to read through it more carefully."

"Sure." She flicked her wrist, gesturing for him to get the journal out of her sight. "Do with it what you will. I have no use for it since I obviously can't make that dream a reality."

Pritchard fanned himself with the journal. "Why is it so hot in here? No wonder you're having a heat stroke."

"Hush!" Isabelle smacked his belly with the back of her hand. "I'm not having a heat stroke. The air conditioner isn't working properly."

Tucking the journal under his arm, Pritchard crossed the room to the thermostat. "Geez. It's eighty-four degrees in here." He fiddled with the controls. "Your air-conditioning isn't working at all." He pulled out his phone, clicked on a contact number, and reported the outage to his HVAC company's after-hours service hotline. "I realize it's a holiday weekend, but this heat isn't good for my elderly mother," he told the woman on the phone.

Isabelle fixed her gaze on him while she waited for him to finish his call. "Who are you calling elderly?" she asked when he hung up.

"No offense, Mother. I was trying to get a technician out here today."

"And? Are they sending someone?"

"She said they'd try. We need to get some air in here." Pritchard checked all the windows, but they were painted shut. "You should hang out in the main house today. If they haven't fixed it by tonight, you can stay with Savannah and me."

Isabelle turned up her nose. "No thanks. I'd rather have a heatstroke."

Pritchard shrugged. "Suit yourself." He headed toward the door. "I'll check in with you later."

After he left, Isabelle propped the door open to let in fresh air. Grabbing a kitchen knife, she pried open a window in her bedroom and one in the living room. With the ceiling fan on in both rooms, the temperature inside the cottage soon dropped to seventy-six.

With nothing else to occupy her time, Isabelle set about organizing her clothes in the closet. She was folding her nightgowns into the chest of drawers when, through the open window, she heard the rumble of an outboard boat engine. Through the palmetto tree fronds, she could make out her granddaughter talking to a young man in a center-console boat. *So that's where Shelby was last night.* She hadn't been here a week, and her granddaughter had found a local boy to sleep with. Where Isabelle came from, they called such loose women hussies.

twelve

. . .

Shelby was sitting on the dock, leaning against a piling with her feet dangling over the side, when Matt's boat sped past. He slowed, turned around, and headed back her way. He called out to her as he grew closer. "Afternoon, Shelby. What're you up to?"

She held up her grandfather's camera. "Waiting for the golden hour to take more pics of the house."

As he nosed the boat up to the dock, he asked, "Wanna go for a ride in the ocean? I've just come from there, and the water is as calm as glass. You could get some great photographs of the sun setting over the house."

Shelby jumped to her feet. "That'd be awesome if you can spare the time."

"I'm free as a bird," he said with a laugh as he gave her a hand onto the boat and pushed off the dock.

Shelby stood at the leaning post beside him, his toned body pressed against hers. He smelled delicious, the outdoors clinging to him with the subtle hint of exertion that whispered of days spent under the sun. Was she crazy to go out in the ocean with a total stranger?

As though reading her mind, Matt said, "Will your boyfriend

get mad if he finds out you went for a boat ride with a strange guy? Or is he back home in Texas? Out of sight, out of mind."

Shelby bit down on her lower lip as she considered how much to tell him. Something in his kind smile and genuine demeanor told her she could trust him. "I lied earlier. Correction. I didn't actually lie. I mentioned my boyfriend out of habit. We broke up over a year ago, but we'd been together since middle school, and I'm learning to live without him. It hasn't been easy. My parents sent me here, hoping I'd get my life back on track. I just want . . ." Her voice thickened with emotion. "I want this all-consuming pain to end."

He nodded. "I get it."

Her head jerked up. "You too?"

"Yep," he replied, keeping his eyes fixed ahead as he navigated the boat through the swells at the mouth of the inlet where the sound met the ocean. He waited until they reached calmer water before explaining. "Kayla and I had also been together for a long time. Then, out of the blue, she accepted a job in London." He snapped his fingers. "And just like that, she was gone. It's probably for the best though. We'd grown apart."

Shelby could see the pain etched in his face. He was far from over Kayla. "How so?"

"Kayla is a wild child who loves to live on the edge. I'm sure she's digging big-city living. I, on the other hand, prefer to stay home on Friday night and cook steaks on the grill. I'm ready to settle down with a wife and kids. She will likely never get married."

Shelby had originally guessed Matt to be in his late twenties, but his comment made him sound at least thirty, which was way too old for her. She thought about her social life back home in Austin. She'd gone out every night, not because she enjoyed partying but because she'd been afraid of missing an opportunity to see Luke. Maybe her parents had done her a favor by sending her to the Lowcountry.

Matt slid onto the leaning post and crossed one foot over the opposite knee. "It's a beautiful evening. Even though the sun doesn't set for another hour, you should be able to get some nice photographs."

Shelby stared up at the cloudless sky. "I agree. The sunlight is already much softer and warmer, almost golden."

"I'll get you as close to the beach as possible. Are you comfortable going up to the bow alone?"

"I'm fine. I have sea legs. I used to go out on my grandfather's boat all the time when he was alive."

Matt chuckled. "Which boat? He had a few."

Shelby smiled. "Right? His fleet. My favorite was his old wooden-hull Chris Craft."

Matt let out a low whistle. "She was a beauty, all right. Whatever happened to his *fleet*?"

"Good question. Most are in storage, I think."

Matt took the boat out of gear. "Let's do it. Signal when you're ready, and I'll move inland."

Shelby made her way to the v-seats at the bow of the boat, giving him a thumbs-up over her shoulder. The sprawling white house, partially hidden by an expanse of dunes and sea grass, stood out against the gorgeous pink sky, creating a stunning backdrop. After taking dozens of photographs, she reviewed them on her camera's viewfinder to ensure she had captured enough good shots before making her way back to the leaning post.

"Thanks, Matt. The images are excellent."

"You're welcome. Would you like to go for a ride, or do you need to get back to work right away?"

Shelby checked the time on her phone. "Most of our guests have gone to town for dinner. I should be okay for another hour."

"Great." Matt eyed her camera. "We should do something about that though." Tugging his T-shirt over his head, he took the camera from her, wrapped it in his shirt, and tucked it behind the windshield. "That should keep it dry."

His bronzed chest and tight abs made her shiver. Luke had certainly never made her break out in goosebumps.

The roar of the wind and hum of the outboard motor made conversation difficult. They rode in comfortable silence up the coast, looping around the uber-contemporary home occupying the northern end of the island and continuing back through Catawba Sound. Matt slowed the boat as they passed under the Merriweather Bridge and rode past the shops and restaurants lining the town's waterfront commercial area.

When Matt returned Shelby to her grandmother's dock, he asked, "What are your plans for the holiday tomorrow?"

"I'll be working. What about you? Do you have big plans?"

"I'll be doing chores most of the day, and then I have a family cookout at my sister's tomorrow evening." Unwrapping her camera from his T-shirt, he held it while she climbed out of the boat.

She took the camera from him. "Thanks for the boat ride."

"Anytime. I'll see you around." He waved his T-shirt like the white flag of surrender as he drove away.

Shelby followed his progress until his boat was merely a dot on the horizon. She was disappointed he hadn't asked her for a date when he found out she didn't have a boyfriend. Was he no longer interested? Did she do something to turn him off? Was it the freckles?

She wondered where he kept his boat and what chores would occupy his day tomorrow. Did he live alone? What did he do for a living? Was he a lawyer or doctor or independently wealthy like so many of her friends back home? She imagined them getting married. He would buy them a waterfront home, and she would spend her days playing tennis at the Sandy Island club. Until she had children, and then she would be a stay-at-home mom. She chuckled to herself as she strolled up the dock. Her professionally driven sister would cringe at Shelby's lack of ambition. She was getting way ahead of herself anyway. She and Matt hadn't even been on a first date. But after so long, she was finally able to daydream again.

Pritchard took his father's journal home to the daybed swing on the porch and didn't move until he'd read the last word. Without turning on any lights, he went inside for a whiskey and returned to the swing. He found the setting romantic, with the moon's rays shimmering off the water and the twinkling lights of the Merriweather Bridge in the distance.

He was still sitting there, plotting and daydreaming, when Savannah arrived home from work. She curled up beside him. "What're you doing sitting alone in the dark?"

"Thinking." He stroked the smooth leather cover of the journal in his lap. "Mother found one of Dad's journals. It's filled with ideas for Magnolia Shores. His vision was grander than any of us realized. He dreamed about building a separate hotel offering a host of different amenities. He calls this boutique hotel The Sanctuary at Magnolia Shores."

"I love the name. It's elegant and suits the property. What did Izzy say? She can't handle a bed and breakfast, let alone what you describe."

"I don't know what to think about my mother," he said, lifting the journal. One of her guests, a woman named Blossom, found this journal in Dad's study. She thinks Blossom is an angel spy Dad sent down from heaven to keep tabs on her."

Savannah's olive eyes popped. "What?"

Pritchard gave her an incredulous nod. "Those were her exact words. I'm worried about her. The stress is getting to her."

"Then why would you pressure her into expanding?" she asked, gesturing at the journal.

"I wouldn't. I might take over running the resort."

Savannah's jaw went slack. "But you already have a career."

"I'm ready for a change, Savannah. I'm burned out, and I hate spending so much time in Nashville." He put an arm around her, drawing her in. "Now that I've got you back in my life, I can't stand being away from you for even one minute."

Savannah snuggled in close to him. "I don't like it when you're away either. But you've worked so hard to build your reputation, I'd hate for you to throw it away."

"In hindsight, I became a talent agent because I wanted to represent you. I've enjoyed my career, but I can easily walk away."

"But you know nothing about managing a resort?"

Pritchard shrugged. "Neither did Dad. But that didn't stop him. I'll figure it out as I go." He shifted toward her. "I haven't felt this passionate about anything since we were kids, Savannah. But I can't do this alone. I need you by my side. Together, we'll build a future for the next generations of the St. Clair family."

Savannah jumped back as though scalded. "No offense, Pritchard. But there is no way I can work with your mother."

He expected this initial reaction and decided not to pressure her. They were far from being ready to make this decision. However, given that Savannah thrived in the hospitality industry, he suspected she would eventually come around. "I thought you might say that. I'm getting ahead of myself anyway. First, I need to see what's involved in designing and constructing a building of this magnitude."

"Good thing we have an architect and a builder in the family," she said about her sister and brother.

He flashed her a devilish grin. "I've already texted Ashton. We're having coffee first thing on Tuesday morning."

thirteen

. . .

The ai-conditioning repairmen failed to show up, and Isabelle spent a sleepless night tossing and turning in the stuffy cottage. Dragging herself out of bed before dawn, she threw on yesterday's clothes and trudged over to the main house. She'd given no thought to her breakfast menu. Scrambled eggs and bacon would be the easiest to prepare and satisfy the majority. She wasn't sure if eggs were vegan. She knew they weren't dairy, but the real butter she used to cook them was. The dairy-free guest could either suck it up or starve.

When she opened the refrigerator, she realized she'd forgotten to go to the market yesterday for more eggs. Panic gripped her chest. The first guests would be down in thirty minutes, and she had nothing to feed them. She was pacing the floor, rubbing her chest with one hand and chewing on a thumbnail of the other, when Blossom burst through the back door. Her arms were laden with cartons of eggs as the little dog ran circles around her feet.

"Morning! I found these beside the back door," Blossom said, gingerly setting the egg cartons on the counter.

Isabelle looked from the cartons to Blossom. "How did they get there?"

Blossom shrugged. "I have no clue. Maybe your wholesale food distributor left them?"

"I haven't employed a wholesale food distributor yet. Even if I had, I'm certain they wouldn't deliver at dawn on a holiday." Isabelle opened a carton and inspected the gorgeous eggs. "These aren't your ordinary run-of-the-mill eggs. These are fresh from a henhouse. *You* are the egg fairy, Blossom. What is it you want from me?"

"Why don't you tell me?" Blossom asked with a look that made Isabelle squirm, as if she were searching deep within her soul.

"I don't have time for riddles. I have to prepare breakfast for my guests," Isabelle said, turning her back to Blossom and counting scoops of ground coffee in the percolator.

Out of the corner of her eye, Isabelle watched Blossom open a can of dog food and dump it in one of her crystal bowls. Isabelle was so grateful for the eggs, she decided to let it slide.

Once the coffee was perking, she opened a package of bacon and arranged slices in a skillet. Sensing Blossom behind her, she turned and found herself nose-to-nose with the woman. "Can I help you?'

Blossom jabbed a finger at the skillet. "You realize it's easier to cook bacon in the oven."

Isabelle gave her a skeptical look. "I've heard of that, but doesn't it make a mess of the oven?"

"Not at all. I'll show you. Do you have any parchment paper?"

"Sure." Isabelle located the roll of parchment paper while Blossom rummaged in the cabinets for two baking sheets.

Blossom was lining the baking sheets with the paper when something outside the window caught her attention. "Are you expecting someone? There are two men in blue uniforms wandering around in the courtyard. They seem lost."

Isabelle glanced out the window. "They're my air-conditioning repairmen. I can't deal with them right now. They'll have to come back at a more convenient time."

Blossom grunted. "If you tell them that, you'll never see them again. I'll cover for you while you give them instructions."

Isabelle hated relying on this annoying woman for anything. But she needed to get her air conditioner fixed. "Fine. I won't be but a minute," she said, washing her hands at the sink.

She was gone only long enough to point the repairmen toward the cottage. When she returned, Blossom was seated at the table drinking coffee and thumbing through a magazine, her little dog sleeping on the floor at her feet.

"What're you doing?" Isabelle asked, aghast. "You're supposed to be cooking the bacon."

"The bacon is cooked, and your breakfast is ready, awaiting your first guests."

Isabelle's chin dropped to her chest. "How is that even possible? I was only gone a few minutes."

Blossom nodded at the dining room. "See for yourself. By the way, I moved a few things around on your buffet. I hope you like my presentation."

"There was nothing wrong with *my* presentation." Marching into the dining room, Isabelle could hardly believe her eyes. An enormous bouquet of blue hydrangeas was in the center of the dining table, and the buffet boasted a spread fit for royalty with pastries, fresh fruit, and yogurt parfaits.

"Well? What do you think?" Blossom said near her ear.

"Did you leave any blooms on my hydrangea bushes?"

Blossom barked out a laugh. "These didn't come from your bushes."

"Then where did they come from?"

"You wouldn't believe me if I told you." Blossom's breath on Isabelle's neck sent a shiver down her spine.

Isabelle inspected the contents of the chafing dishes—scrambled eggs, bacon, sausage, and hash browns. "No normal person could whip something up like this in five minutes. You're obviously a miracle worker. Where did you come from, Blossom? Who sent you, and why are you here?"

Blossom was saved from having to respond by the appearance of their first guests. Isabelle greeted them and motioned them to the buffet. Watching the guests serve their plates, she whispered to Blossom, "You're hiding something, and I aim to find out what it is."

The guests raved about the delicious food and lovely presentation. Their flattery irritated Isabelle. She didn't deserve the credit. Blossom did.

Blossom sniffed. "What's that smell?" She sniffed again, her nose close to Isabelle. "It's you. When's the last time you bathed?"

Isabelle made certain no one was watching before smelling her armpit. And it wasn't a pleasant odor. "What do you expect? My air conditioner is broken, and my cottage is hot as blazes."

"Maybe your repairmen have the air conditioner up and running. I can hold down the fort if you want to shower."

The thought of a hot shower appealed to Isabelle. At the very least, she needed a fresh change of clothes. "I won't be long."

As she emerged from the kitchen, Isabelle spotted the uniformed repairmen getting into their service van. She flagged down the driver. "Yoo-hoo! Mr. Repairman! What did you find out about my system?"

He left his van door open and strolled toward her. "Your coils are leaking. We added some freon. You're good to go for now. Who knows how long it'll last though. Maybe a couple of months—the summer, if you're lucky. Eventually, you'll need to replace the unit."

"Can you give me a price to replace it?"

"I can't. But I can send someone over tomorrow who can?"

"Do that," Isabelle said, brushing past him on the way to the cottage.

The majority of the guests departing on Monday had requested late checkouts. With their staggard departure times, Silas spent the afternoon running up and down the stairs, helping with their luggage, while Shelby remained at the desk, preparing their bills and processing credit card charges.

Despite being busy, thoughts of Matt kept creeping into Shelby's mind. She fantasized about kissing him, about laying her head on his glorious bare chest and feeling his toned body against hers. She can't remember her desire for Luke ever being this intense, even after they lost their virginities to each other and started experimenting. There had never been anyone else for Shelby. She and Luke had remained faithful throughout their relationship. After being with the same person for so long, maybe the excitement over someone new intensified the attraction. Was it like this for Luke with Alexis?

The last of the departing guests were leaving around six o'clock when Matt arrived with two paper plates covered in aluminum foil. His face lit up when he saw her at the reception desk. "There you are! I felt sorry for you having to work on the holiday, so I brought you dinner from my sister's cookout."

Shelby flashed him her brightest smile. "And just in time because I'm starving." She stood and stretched and smoothed out the wrinkles in her sundress. "I've been sitting at this desk all afternoon. I'm ready for a break. Let's go out by the pool."

"Lead the way," he said, following her down the hall to the kitchen.

Shelby explored the refrigerator's contents. "What would you like to drink? We have beer, bottled water, or sweet tea."

"Water is fine."

Shelby grabbed two bottles and a handful of napkins, and they exited the back door. After people had been crowding the house all weekend, she was grateful to find the pool empty. They sat at a small round table near the dunes, palmetto fronds rustling over their heads.

Matt handed her a plate. "I wasn't sure whether you liked hamburgers or hot dogs, so I brought you one of each."

She noticed that the contents of his plate mirrored hers. "Is that why you brought one of each for yourself?"

He gave her a boyish grin. "I like both, and I'm not embarrassed to admit it."

They'd taken their first bites when Blossom appeared with Jolene at her feet. Shelby waved them over and provided introductions. She lifted the miniature basset hound onto her lap. "And this is Jolene."

"Jolene?" Matt asked in disbelief. "What a great name. I love it."

"It fits her." As Shelby cuddled the dog, Jolene licked at her face.

"She sure does love you," Blossom said.

Shelby giggled. "She loves the ketchup on my face."

Blossom took the dog from her. "We'll leave you two lovebirds alone. It was nice meeting you, Matt."

Shelby waited until Blossom was out of earshot before bursting into laughter.

Matt appeared wounded. "What's so funny? Is it that outrageous to think of us as lovebirds?"

Shelby couldn't tell if he was teasing or being serious, so she ignored his question. "Did you stay long at the cookout? I hope you're not in trouble with your parents."

"I made an appearance. I even helped my brother-in-law cook. I waited until everyone sat down to eat before sneaking out. My three older sisters all have young children. My sister's house was a Romper Room. I doubt they even missed me." He stuffed the rest of the hot dog in his mouth and waited until he finished chewing. "Actually, I had an ulterior motive in coming here."

"Really? What's that?" Shelby asked, biting into a deviled egg.

"I've been thinking about you all day. I wanted to talk to you, but I didn't have your number, so I used the excuse of bringing you food to get it."

"I'm flattered. And grateful. I didn't realize how hungry I

was." She pushed her empty plate away. "Are you always so honest?"

He wiped his mouth with his napkin. "Pretty much. In a world filled with lies, I challenge myself to be truthful, no matter the cost."

"That's refreshing." She planted her elbows on the table. "Are you ready?"

He furrowed his brow. "Ready for what?"

"For my number."

"Oh! Yes!" He tugged his phone out of his pocket and entered her number as she called it out. Seconds later, her phone pinged with a text from him. "And now you have mine. In case you're thinking of me later when lying in bed."

Imagining the lustful thoughts that would undoubtedly be running through her mind in bed made her face warm. "What am I supposed to do if I happen to think of you later?" she teased.

"Text me. To thank me for bringing you dinner of course." Matt pushed back from the table. "Do you have to get back to your command post, or can you go for a walk on the beach?"

Shelby jumped up. "A walk sounds good. Our remaining few guests have gone to town for dinner. They won't be back for a while."

Gathering their empty plates, she glanced around for a trash can but didn't see one. Another item added to the growing list. They would need at least two, one near the beach access and another at the opposite end of the pool. Who would empty them? Silas? Or the cleaning crew? Shelby gave herself a pat on the back. She was starting to think like a manager.

"I need to throw these away. Be right back," Shelby said, taking the trash to the kitchen and grabbing two fresh bottles of water from the refrigerator.

Leaving their shoes at the pool, they cut through the dunes to the beach and walked in the edge of the surf toward the Sandy Island Club.

"So . . . are you originally from here?" Shelby asked.

Matt hesitated, a guarded expression settling on his face.

She gave him a playful shove. "That's an easy question. Are you not sure where you're from?"

"I'm from here, born and raised." He hung his head. "Let's not talk about the past. I'd hate to scare you off with my baggage."

Shelby thought about her drinking and driving incident the day before she left home. "I get it. I have my share of baggage as well."

"I want to know important things about you, like your favorite color, what kind of books you like to read, and how you drink your coffee."

"Blue, urban fantasy, and cream with tons of sugar. This is fun. My turn. What kind of car do you drive? What kind of music do you like? What is the last thing you do before going to sleep at night?"

"A pickup truck. Country. Pray."

Shelby's teal eyes grew wide. "I just learned a lot about you in three simple questions."

"What? That I'm a Christian redneck."

She laughed. "Isn't every guy in South Carolina a redneck?"

"You'd be surprised. We have our share of preppy pricks."

Luke was a preppy prick. He hated country music, but she loved it, and they'd always fought over control of the music. "I like country music too," she said softly.

"Which makes us a perfect match. Since we're auditioning for Lovebirds, we should probably start on the right foot by going on an official date. What does your week look like?"

"I'm free until Friday. We have a large group coming in for the weekend."

"Then how about dinner in town on Thursday night?"

"Sounds perfect." *A date with Matt and a chance to explore the town.*

As they strolled on, they quizzed each other about their likes and dislikes. Shelby learned that Matt played the guitar and enjoyed tinkering with boat engines. He also liked to read, his favorite genre being mysteries. Seafood was a favorite food for them both, and they both stayed in shape by running. Although Shelby hadn't been on a run since she got to South Carolina. She made a mental note to start first thing in the morning.

When they turned around to head back, Shelby's breath hitched at the sight of her grandmother's house washed in the orange glow of the setting sun. "I wish I had my camera." She snapped several pics with her phone and studied the results. "The phone doesn't do it justice."

"No camera will do it justice. But the sun isn't going anywhere. You can try again another time."

"Does it look like this every day?" Shelby asked, spreading her arms wide. "It's magnificent."

Matt chuckled. "As long as you can see the sky, it is almost always this spectacular."

"I think I'm going to like living in the Lowcountry."

"I think you will too. It's an extraordinary place." He took her hand in his. "Holding hands is what lovebirds do."

Shelby's heart skipped a beat. Luke's is the only guy's hand she'd ever held. While his skin was calloused, Matt's grip was firm. She felt safe in his presence, as though she could count on him to protect her. Something she'd never experienced with Luke. Why did she keep comparing the two guys when they were nothing alike?

fourteen

. . .

Isabelle was eating a dinner salad at the kitchen table when, through the window, she noticed Shelby coming up from the beach with the same young man she'd seen her with on the dock late yesterday afternoon.

Eating the last bite of salad, Isabelle placed the plate in the dishwasher and hurried down the hall to the living room. She settled at the reception desk to wait. As soon as Shelby entered through the front door, Isabelle leapt to her feet. "There you are. I've been fielding guest inquiries about rates and availability for future dates. As our receptionist, this is your job."

Shelby glanced around the room. "Where? I don't see anyone."

"They're all gone now. Where have you been anyway?"

"Taking my dinner break. A friend brought over food from his family's cookout. We ate by the pool and went for a short walk on the beach. According to Pritchard, I don't have to sit at that desk 24/7."

"Is this *friend* the guy you've been sleeping with?" Isabelle asked in an accusatory tone.

Shelby's head jerked back. "I'm sorry, what?"

"You heard me. I think it's sinful how promiscuous young people are these days."

A flush crept up Shelby's neck. "I only just met Matt. I certainly haven't slept with him. Are you calling me a slut?"

Blossom appeared from down the hall. "What's all this racket about? I heard your loud voices in the kitchen."

Isabelle glared at her. "Butt out. This is none of your business."

Blossom's annoying little dog darted into the living room, growling and baring its teeth at Isabelle.

"Stop that!" Isabelle demanded of the dog, which made it growl more fiercely.

"Don't blame her," Blossom said. "She's merely protecting me from the likes of you."

When Shelby picked up the dog, it calmed down, nestling into her arms.

Blossom brushed a lock of Shelby's strawberry-blonde hair off her face. "What's the matter, sweet girl? Are you and your granny having another spat?"

Shelby gave Isabelle the stink eye. "Yes! Izzy accused me of sleeping with a guy I've only known for two days."

Isabelle folded her arms over her chest. "Then where have you been sleeping, if not with that young man? You certainly haven't been in the cottage."

"One of our guests had to cut their stay short due to a death in the family," Shelby explained. "I've been sleeping in their room upstairs."

Isabelle put on her poker face, not letting her relief show. She felt responsible for her granddaughter's safety and was concerned about Shelby's virtue. "Those rooms are off-limits."

Shelby planted her hands on her hips. "Says who? I don't see why they're off-limits. I'm not bothering anyone, and you snore like a freight train."

"And where will you sleep when every room is occupied next weekend?" Isabelle challenged.

"In a lounge chair by the pool if it means not having to share the cottage with you."

Blossom took the dog from Shelby. "All right, ladies, that's enough. Sounds like you two would benefit from having your own space. I have a pull-out sofa. Shelby, you can bunk with me if necessary."

Shelby gave Blossom a thin smile. "Thanks. I may take you up on that."

Isabelle looked down her nose at her granddaughter. "If I'd known you would be this much trouble, I never would have agreed to you coming here."

"You *didn't* agree. Mom insisted. I was already here when you found out I was coming." Shelby held out her hand. "Pay me what you owe me, and I'll get out of your hair right now. You'll never have to see me again." She gestured at the desk. "If you can manage the reservations better than me, have at it."

Panic struck Isabelle. She could barely get breakfast on the table, and she didn't need the added responsibility of reservations. "Calm down, Shelby. We can work this out. We're family."

"You have some nerve lecturing me about family after what you did to Savannah and Pritchard."

The color drained from Isabelle's face. "What're you talking about?"

"I don't know exactly. Harper wouldn't tell me. But you had something to do with her adoption. How could you do that to your own flesh and blood?" Shelby brushed past Blossom as she fled the room and dashed up the stairs.

"What an ungrateful child." Isabelle stumbled over to the sofa and collapsed onto the soft down cushions.

Blossom sat down beside her with the dog on her lap. "What did you do to Savannah and Pritchard?"

Isabelle rolled her eyes. "As if you don't already know."

Blossom appeared genuinely confused. "I have no clue what you're talking about. But it sounds like you have unfinished business with your family."

"Humph. That business is in the past. No one even thinks about it anymore."

Blossom arched an eyebrow. "Clearly, they do."

"I've had enough drama for one day." Isabelle pressed a hand to her chest. "Please leave me in peace before I have a heart attack."

"I can't do that," Blossom said with a stubborn shake of her head. "I'm here on assignment. You're stuck with me until I complete my mission."

"Who sent you? Was it Edward? Are you even real?" Isabelle massaged her temples. "Or am I imagining all this? If you're a miracle worker, give me back my life."

"Going back in time is impossible, Isabelle. My job is to help you cope with your new life. The sooner you accept me, the sooner we can work on sorting you out."

"I don't need sorting out, thank you very much."

Isabelle got up from the sofa and left the house for the safety of her cottage. She stretched out on her bed and stared up at the ceiling. "Why, Edward? Why are you tormenting me? You never thought I needed *sorting* out when you were alive."

Deep down inside, Isabelle knew that wasn't true. Her husband had hounded her to take ownership of her mistake. But apologizing was the one thing she could never do.

Shelby stood at the window in her room, staring at the ocean. With this view, her grandmother could and should charge more for the oceanfront rooms.

Her head throbbed from holding back her emotions, but she refused to let Izzy make her cry. There was so much Shelby didn't understand. She needed to talk to someone. For the first time since arriving in the Lowcountry, she felt homesick. She clicked on her mom's number, and the phone only rang once when there was a knock on her door.

Ending the call, she tossed the phone on the bed and went to the door. Worried it might be her grandmother, she said, "Who is it?"

"Blossom," came the muffled voice on the other side of the door.

The dam broke, and Shelby burst into tears. She flung open the door and threw herself into Blossom's arms, squishing the dog between their bodies.

Blossom stroked her back. "There, now. Everything's gonna be all right. Just give it some time."

Jolene let out a yelp, and Shelby pulled away. "I'm sorry, Jolene."

Setting the dog on the floor, Blossom entered the bathroom and ran cold water over a washcloth. "Here," she said, handing the washcloth to Shelby. "This will help with the puffiness."

They sat side by side on the end of the bed as Shelby dabbed at her eyes. "I don't care what Izzy thinks about me. I'm not a slut, and I haven't had sex with Matt. I don't know what's wrong with her. She used to be such a nice grandmother. But she's changed. She's a vindictive old bitch. Whatever she did to Savannah and Pritchard is so bad Harper wouldn't even tell me. I'm not sure I want to be part of the same family as Izzy."

Blossom chuckled. "The greatest gift of family is not in the happy moments but in the unwavering presence and acceptance during difficult times."

Shelby's eyes grew wide. "Whoa. Did you just make that up?"

"Yep." Blossom snapped her fingers. "Just like that. I've got dozens of similar sayings if you want to hear them."

"Maybe later." Jolene pawed at her leg, and Shelby lifted the dog onto her lap. "My mother thinks I'm like my grandmother, that we're both stubborn and headstrong and have chips on our shoulders. Do you think that too, Blossom?"

"It's not my place to judge, baby girl. What matters is in your heart." Blossom touched her finger to Shelby's chest.

Shelby buried her nose in the dog's fur. "Is that why you're here? To fix Izzy and me?"

Blossom let out a deep chuckle, causing her turkey neck to jiggle. "What makes you ask that?"

"You're either a fairy godmother or a guardian angel. Isn't that what they do?"

"I'm not here to fix anyone, Shelby. I can offer guidance. The rest is up to you." Blossom rose slowly from the bed. "I will say this though. If you believe in fairies and angels, you're off to an excellent start."

"I'm curious, Blossom. Who sent you here?"

Blossom took the dog from her. "That's top-secret information, baby girl," she said and vanished from her sight.

Shelby squeezed her eyes tight. When she opened them, the room was still empty. Did Blossom actually disappear before her eyes? Was Shelby losing her mind? Whoever she was, Blossom left Shelby with a sense of hopefulness she hadn't felt in a long time.

In the bathroom, Shelby splashed cold water on her face and pulled her unruly hair into a ponytail. She went downstairs to her desk and spent the next hour poring over their reservations for the next three months. Only one night—the Friday of July Fourth weekend—was completely booked. By rearranging the room assignments, she freed up a tiny room on the second floor of the pool house. With its slanted ceilings and dormer windows, the room offered no closet space and only a glimpse of the courtyard. Despite its shortcomings, Shelby would call this room home for the summer.

fifteen

. . .

With fewer guests to feed, breakfast preparation on Tuesday morning took less time. Isabelle even made one woman a special-order omelet. Pearl and Hilda were doing the dishes, and Isabelle was sipping coffee and reading the morning paper at the table, when Blossom bustled in. She dumped a can of dog food into a bowl for Jolene, helped herself to coffee, and plopped down at the table opposite Isabelle.

"Are you ready to be sorted out?" Blossom said with a smirk as she lifted her coffee cup to her lips.

"Go away," Isabelle said, returning her attention to the newspaper.

"I can't leave just yet. Jolene is still eating, and you may need me for your meeting."

Isabelle lowered the newspaper. "What meeting?"

"This meeting," Blossom said and snapped her fingers. The sound of the front door closing was followed by footfalls in the hallway and the appearance of Silas and a woman Isabelle had never seen before.

"Sorry to interrupt." Silas gestured at the guest. "Marilyn Daily with Waterside Wholesale Food Distributors is here for her nine o'clock appointment."

Feeling Blossom's eyes on her, Isabelle resisted the urge to stick out her tongue. "You must be mistaken. I didn't make an appointment for this morning."

"Your son made it for you." Helping herself to an empty chair, Marilyn took a handful of glossy brochures from her leather tote and fanned them out on the table. "We offer every food item imaginable, from Doritos to Philadelphia-style cheesecake."

"We don't need either. Thank you for your time," Isabelle said, bringing the newspaper up before her face.

Blossom snatched the paper away from her. "You're expecting a houseful of guests this weekend. Unless you plan to serve them burnt pancakes again, I suggest you listen to Marilyn's pitch."

"Fine," Isabelle said with a huff.

For the next few minutes, Marilyn talked about her service's wide variety of breakfast items. "Myrtle's guests love our mini quiches," she claimed.

The mention of Myrtle, the proprietor of Myrtle's Bed and Breakfast, made Isabelle sit up straighter. Myrtle was one of the Lowcountry's most renowned cooks. On slow weekends, she offered Sunday brunch to the locals, who raved about her food. "I can't believe Myrtle serves her guests anything that isn't made from scratch."

"You're right," Marilyn said with a nod. "She does most of the cooking and baking herself, and we supply the majority of her raw ingredients. She does, however, add variety to her buffet by serving some of our prepared items."

Blossom picked up the brochure for the mini quiches. "You don't even have to dethaw these. Just pop them in a preheated oven for a few minutes."

"Or an air fryer," Marilyn chimed in.

Isabelle turned up her nose. "I don't own an air fryer."

"You should get one. They're extremely useful." Marilyn set down the brochures and opened her iPad. "I suggest we start with samples of our most popular breakfast items. You can try them out next weekend and see what you think."

Isabelle threw her hands up. "Fine! I'll try your service. But only on a trial basis."

"Understood." Marilyn eyed her refrigerator. "Do you have a second freezer for storage?"

While there was a freezer in the cottage, Isabelle refused to haul heavy boxes of frozen foods across the courtyard. "Nope. You'll have to make smaller, more frequent deliveries."

"No problem." Marilyn handed Isabelle an order form, and together, they went down the list, choosing easy-to-serve foods she thought her guests would enjoy.

After seeing the woman off, Isabelle went to her cottage to shower. Dressed in navy linen slacks and a white silk blouse, she headed off to run errands in town. She needed a break from her guests, Blossom, and the stuffy cottage.

On a whim, after picking up her dry cleaning and alterations, she decided to stop in at Coastal Hardware. She was inspecting the selection of air fryers when someone tapped her on the shoulder. She looked up to find Blossom smiling down at her.

"Fancy meeting you here. I see you took Marilyn's suggestion about purchasing an air fryer. I have this model on my bus." Blossom removed a box from the shelf and deposited it in Isabelle's hands. "You won't be disappointed."

Isabelle dropped the box in her cart. "Are you following me, Blossom?"

"Heavens, no. I'm shopping." Blossom gestured at her cart, loaded with gardening tools and bags of potting soil. "I'm sprucing up your containers with fresh plants. They have a nice selection of annuals in the nursery out back."

Isabelle's jaw went slack. "But I just planted those containers in April."

"And I'm sure they looked lovely in April. But flowers die if you don't water them." Blossom reached into her cart for a coil of black plastic tubing. "Which is why I'm installing an irrigation system for the planters."

"Who gave you permission to do all this? I'm certainly not paying for it."

Blossom flicked her wrist, dismissing her concern. "I'm doing it as a favor to you. And don't worry. It's on the house."

"Well . . . um . . . thanks," Isabelle muttered as she wheeled her cart down the aisle.

Isabelle's next stop was Fancy Pantry. The food distributor would make a large delivery on Thursday, including everything from bottled water to the breakfast foods they'd selected. But they needed a few items to tide them over until then.

She was scrutinizing the selection of salad greens in the produce section when a familiar voice behind her said, "What a coincidence! And here you are again."

Blossom's playful shove caught Isabelle off guard, and she tumbled forward. Fortunately, the woman grabbed hold of Isabelle before she face-planted in the lettuce.

Blossom held onto her while she steadied herself. "Good gracious! Are you all right?"

"I'm fine." Isabelle wrenched her arm free of the woman's grip.

A goofy smile spread across Blossom's face, revealing a smudge of pink lipstick on her front tooth. "Where are you going next? I'll meet you there."

"Home! Where I plan to sequester myself in my cottage, away from the likes of you, until the next guests arrive on Thursday." Isabelle dug through her purse for a tissue. "By the way, you have lipstick on your tooth."

Blossom scrubbed the lipstick off her tooth. "Don't be a spoilsport. I was going to ask you to play bridge. You do play, don't you?"

"Of course. But we need four people to play."

"I can easily arrange for additional players," Blossom said, winking at her.

Isabelle imagined playing bridge with Blossom and two women wearing white robes, angel wings, and halos. She pressed her temples between two pointer fingers. This woman was starting to get to her.

She inhaled a deep breath, reminding herself to be polite. "I'm not in the mood for bridge today, Blossom. I'm not feeling well. I'm going home to rest," she said and hurried to the checkout counter with only half the items on her list.

Isabelle hadn't played bridge in years. She quit her bridge group around the time she dropped out of her other social circles. She grew tired of those silly women blabbering ad nauseam about their petty lives.

"Don't cut off your nose to spite your face," her mama used to say when she turned down invitations to birthday parties and school dances—not that there had been many invitations. Isabelle had never truly fit in with any social group. She found it easier to be alone than forced to converse with someone she cared nothing about.

sixteen

. . .

Shelby waited until her grandmother's car left the driveway before beelining it to the cottage, packing her belongings, and moving them to her new room in the pool house. She loved her new home. She felt safe and secure, a bit like Eloise tucked away in the small back corner room of the hotel.

After the last guests left on Tuesday morning, the house grew quiet, and Shelby's days fell into a routine. After running for miles on the beach in the early mornings, she took hundreds of photographs with her grandfather's camera and set up the new reservation system the web designer had approved.

Thoughts of Matt were never far from Shelby's mind. They sent flirty texts back and forth. On Wednesday afternoon, he gave her the choice of two restaurants for their date on Thursday night —The Nest, the town's iconic tavern, or the more upscale Clam and Claw. Shelby didn't hesitate in picking The Nest. She'd been there many times with her family, and she thought the tavern's relaxed vibe would help break the ice on their first date. When the reservations were sold out online, she texted Savannah, who managed The Nest, asking for help in securing a table.

After eating a salad for dinner, Shelby retreated to her room, where she tried on every outfit she'd brought from Texas. She finally decided on a dressy black shorts set with a cropped top that showed off a sliver of her tanned tummy.

She was beyond herself with excitement as she showered and dressed on Thursday evening. She was eager to see Matt and could hardly wait to venture into town after being confined to her grandmother's property for a week. Had it only been a week? It felt like a year.

Matt picked her up at seven o'clock sharp, and they said little on the way to town. She sensed he was as nervous as she. His fresh scent filled the inside of his truck—an exhilarating combination of sunshine, wind, and rain.

"They've renovated since I was here last summer," Shelby remarked to Matt while waiting for the hostess to seat them. The wooden floors had been refinished in a lighter stain, and the booths recovered in cheerful orange leather.

"They had no choice," Matt said. "They rented the tavern to a private party. The guests got out of hand and demolished the place."

Striking photographs of sea turtles in various nesting stages hung from exposed brick walls. "I miss the other turtles though. I used to love them as a kid," Shelby said, thinking about the mounted turtles that had hung on the walls since she was a child.

"Didn't we all? They didn't survive the party." He shook his head in dismay. "I don't understand the senseless vandalism."

When the hostess showed them to a booth, Shelby asked about the stage set with musical instruments. "We're having live entertainment tonight," the hostess explained, handing them menus.

"Cool!" Matt said. "The Nest has really upped its game since Savannah took over as manager."

Shelby spotted Savannah conversing with a couple at a nearby table. "Savannah is my aunt."

"I knew that! I've done some work for Pritchard and Savannah in the past."

Shelby wondered what kind of work. Legal? Was Matt an attorney? But since the past was off-limits, she didn't ask.

Savannah made her way to the table. "Welcome. I'm glad to see you out on the town, Shelby."

"Me too. I needed a break from Magnolia Shores." Shelby's hand shot out. "Don't get me wrong. I'm enjoying the job. And Pritchard's been great."

Savannah smiled. "He's extremely impressed with what you've accomplished so far."

Matt gestured at the stage. "Who is the live entertainment tonight?"

"Retro Rewind, a cover band that has been popular with our customers. I think you'll like them. They'll be starting their first set around eight." Savannah flagged down a waitress. "Sheila will be serving you tonight. Sheila, this is my niece, Shelby, and her friend, Matt. Take good care of them."

Sheila nodded, her auburn ponytail bouncing. "You know I will. Good evening, folks."

Savannah squeezed Shelby's shoulder. "Let me know if you need anything."

Sheila flipped to a clean page on her order pad. "Can I start you out with some drinks?"

"I'll have a glass of rosé," Shelby said. After a week of living in her grandmother's prison, she was in the mood to party, and she was disappointed when Matt ordered sweet tea.

"I don't drink," Matt said. "But don't let that stop you."

Where was the fun in drinking alone? Shelby thought and changed her order to a Diet Coke.

Shelby was curious why he didn't drink. Did he not like the taste? Was he a recovering alcoholic? Was drinking against his religion? If they didn't discuss the past soon, they would run out of things to talk about. But neither was at a loss for topics to discuss. Matt spoke about the offshore fishing trip he had planned for Saturday, and Shelby speculated about the large party booked at the bed and breakfast for the weekend.

"When Izzy took the reservation, she didn't think to ask them what occasion they were celebrating," Shelby said.

Matt considered this. "Hmm. It could be a family reunion. Or a bachelor party. Prepare yourself to have a bunch of drunk guys hitting on you all weekend."

With a mischievous glint, Shelby said, "I'll need something to occupy my time since you'll be fishing."

Matt's face darkened. "Maybe I'll cancel my trip."

Shelby placed her hand on his. "I'm just joking, Matt. Why would a group of guys book a quiet bed and breakfast for a bachelor party? They usually go to hot spots like Las Vegas and Miami Beach."

Relief washed over his face. "You're probably right."

Sheila appeared with their beverages. Instead of ordering entrees, they decided to share several appetizers. They had just finished eating when the band began tuning their instruments. After the lead singer welcomed the crowd, the band launched into Van Morrison's "Brown Eyed Girl."

"Let's dance." Matt slid out of the booth and pulled Shelby to her feet.

Shelby couldn't remember the last time she'd danced sober—if ever. But Matt was an excellent dancer, expertly twirling her around and making her giddy with laughter. They danced to two more classic rock songs before the band slowed its tempo.

Matt hooked an arm around Shelby's waist and pulled her close. "I've been waiting for this moment all week."

"What moment is that?" Shelby teased as she gazed up at him.

He tightened his grip on her. "Holding you in my arms."

"And? What do you think?"

He leaned in, his voice near her ear. "We're a perfect fit."

They danced until they were both covered in sweat. Shelby couldn't take her eyes off him. His damp shirt clinging to his tight body made her eager to do more than dance. When they finally returned to their table, Matt summoned the waitress for their check and two glasses of water, which they gulped down.

Shelby tied her hair back with an elastic band. "I'm dying, I'm so hot," she said, fanning herself.

"I agree. This place is an inferno." He signed the check and tossed the pen on the table. "Are you ready to go?"

"Sure!" While Shelby didn't want the night to end, she longed to be alone with Matt, to feel his arms around her, for him to kiss her.

But during the ride back to Sandy Island, she panicked about what to do with him when she got him home. Taking him to her room would be an invitation to have sex, which she wasn't ready for. Despite what her grandmother thought, she wasn't that kind of girl. She could feign a headache or make an excuse about needing to check on something for work. However, Shelby was saved from doing either when Matt saw the pool lit up.

"It's like a blue spaceship. Let's go check it out," he said, taking her by the hand and leading her across the courtyard.

They strolled around the pool, slipping off their shoes and dipping their toes in the water. When they reached the hammock, Matt fell into it, pulling her along with him. She burst into a fit of giggles, and he silenced her by pressing his lips to hers. He tasted sweet, like honey, and the way his mouth explored hers ignited sparks of electricity throughout her body. Luke had never kissed her with such passion. Why was she even thinking about Luke at a moment like this?

When the kiss ended, Matt fell back in the hammock, his eyes squeezed shut. "Wow! I see stars!" he said, opening his eyes. "Oh, wait. I actually do see stars."

She smacked his chest. "Stop! Although I admit the kiss was pretty amazing." She snuggled her body against his. "There's something I should tell you."

"Uh-oh. I don't like the sound of that. Please don't tell me you're really a man."

Shelby sat bolt upright. "What? No! Are you crazy?"

"Just checking." He pulled her back down beside him. "You never know these days. I have nightmares about misunderstandings in romantic situations where things aren't what they seem."

She jabbed her elbow into his ribs. "I'm being serious, Matt."

He turned on his side so he could see her. "Okay. I'm being serious now. What's wrong?"

"Nothing's wrong." Her face warmed. "This is embarrassing . . . Luke is the only guy I've ever been with. I've never even kissed anyone else before tonight."

He traced his finger around her lips. "Thank you for telling me, Shelby. I promise to be a perfect gentleman. We won't do anything until you're ready."

She cupped his cheek. "You're a good guy, Matt."

"I'm glad you think so," he said, kissing her again.

Her body yearned for more. She could so easily get carried away, but she would hate herself in the morning if she let things go too far. "We'd better stop. I'm sorry, but I'm just not ready."

"No worries. You're calling the shots."

They tumbled out of the hammock in a tangle of arms and legs, and he walked her to the front door of the pool house. "Sweet dreams," he said, pecking her cheek. "Don't be surprised if I stop by tomorrow afternoon to stake my claim. I want the bachelors to know you belong to me and to keep their hands off."

Shelby laughed. "You're ridiculous. You don't need excuses to stop by. I look forward to seeing you."

Locking the door behind her, Shelby floated up the stairs to her room, watching from her window as Matt's silver pickup disappeared down the driveway in a cloud of dust. Her feelings for him were more than physical. She could easily fall in love with him. After Luke, she vowed never to be hurt by another man again. She would proceed with caution, protecting her heart. She needed to find out more about him and his mysterious past before things went any further.

seventeen

. . .

The loud tooting of a car horn brought Shelby outside to the courtyard around five o'clock on Friday afternoon. She watched with wide eyes as a group of young women piled out of the party bus. They were all dressed from head to toe in varying shades of pink—stiletto heels with short skirts and low-cut tops that revealed an obscene amount of their fake boobs. Their eyes were caked with heavy eyeliner, their pouty lips painted hot pink, and their blonde hair extensions curled and teased. Shelby recognized the type—girls from questionable backgrounds with lousy taste, no manners, and wealthy daddies.

The last young woman off the bus wore a slim-fitting white sundress. Shelby covered her mouth to hide her smile. This wasn't a *bachelor* party. It was a *bachelorette* party.

A striking brunette wearing gray slacks and a white silk top emerged from the passenger-side front seat. She approached Shelby with an outstretched hand. "Hey! We're here for the Tucker bachelorette party."

"We have your reservation for twelve people booked in seven rooms in the main house, although we were unaware of the occasion." Shelby feared this seemingly rowdy crew might be disappointed with the remote setting. "Are you a bridesmaid?"

She cut her eyes at the women tripping over one another as they removed their luggage from under the bus.

Jenna peered at Shelby over the top of her sunglasses. "Do I look like one of them?"

Shelby laughed. "Just checking."

"I'm an assistant to the wedding planner. Brandi, the bride, hired me to organize the weekend. I booked my room separately, under my name, Jenna Blevens."

Shelby gave a curt nod. "I remember the name. If I'm not mistaken, you're booked in the garden house. Will that be okay?"

Relief crossed her face. "That'd be great. Also . . ." Jenna pulled Shelby to the side, out of earshot of the others. "I realize it's last minute, but do you have any extra availability? Brandi made the room reservations, and I neglected to check behind her. She hired the bus driver for the entire weekend but forgot to get him a room."

As best she could remember, Shelby's was the only available room, and she wasn't ready to give it up. "I'm pretty sure we're booked solid, but I can check our reservations system just in case."

Brandi teetered toward them on black Christian Louboutin pumps. "I'm ready to go to my room now." Following closely behind her, wheeling two suitcases with tote bags strung around her neck, was a woman who looked enough like Brandi to be her sister.

Jenna whispered to Shelby, "That's her twin, Candi."

Shelby's brow hit her hairline. *Brandi? Candi?* "I'm not touching that with a ten-foot pole," she whispered back to Jenna.

Silas rushed to Candi's aid, relieving her of her luggage.

"You can take the group upstairs," Shelby instructed Silas. "They can decide who sleeps in which room. I'll bring them their keys in a bit."

Shelby and Jenna followed Brandi's entourage inside.

Brandi stopped midway up the stairs and called out to Shelby, "Have a bottle of Champagne sent to my room right away."

"I'm sorry, but we don't offer room service," Shelby said.

Brandi gasped. "Surely, you're joking. No room service?"

Shelby shook her head. "Sorry. We only offer breakfast, which is why we call ourselves a bed and breakfast."

Brandi's head swiveled to her wedding planner. "Jenna! Get Alvin to drive you to the store. Load up on Champagne, bottled water, and snacks. And buy me some cigs while you're there."

"Sorry again," Shelby said. "Our property is nonsmoking."

"Then I'll smoke on the beach."

"Suit yourself. But be sure to pick up your butts." Shelby turned away from the staircase and went to her desk in the living room.

She was searching her reservations system for a vacancy when a notification regarding a cancellation for the weekend popped up on her screen. "You're in luck!" she said to Jenna. "I have an extra room in the garden house for the bus driver."

A loud crashing noise followed by laughter reverberated throughout the house. Shelby had a bad feeling about this bachelorette party. She worried her grandmother's beloved house would never be the same. She held a hand out to Jenna. "I'll need a credit card to cover the cost of the rooms plus a five-hundred-dollar deposit for any damages."

Jenna slapped a credit card with Brandi's name in Shelby's hand. "If I were you, I'd charge that deposit on each room."

"If you say so. The deposit will be credited to her account when they check out, provided there are no damages." Shelby slid two keys across the desk to Jenna. "Here are the keys to the two rooms in the garden house. Both are the same size, but number four has a better view."

"Then I'll take number four," Jenna said, sliding the key into her pants pocket. "I'll earn every bonus I get this weekend."

"For sure. Have you made dinner plans yet? Reservations are recommended for a party this large."

Jenna nodded. "I've booked a large table at The Nest for tonight. And tomorrow, we're making a day trip to Charleston."

"Sounds like fun." Shelby spotted Silas coming down from upstairs and called out to him. "Silas! Can I borrow you for a second?"

"Sure. What's up?" Silas asked, joining them at the desk.

Shelby introduced him to Jenna. "She's in charge of the bachelorette party."

A slow smile spread across his face. "Nice to meet you, ma'am."

"Please take Jenna to the garden house," Shelby said. "And be sure to show her how to use the keypad entry systems to enter the buildings. They're going to dinner in town and might be late returning."

"Sure thing," Silas said, and the twosome headed outside together.

No sooner had they left than Matt entered the house. Squeals of laughter from above greeted him in the foyer. He strolled into the living room, his neck craned as he looked up the stairs. "I gather that's not a bachelor party."

"Nope. Wrong gender. Your bachelor party is a bachelorette party." Coming from behind the desk, Shelby took him by the arm and hurried him to the front door. "You need to go."

Matt placed a hand on his chest, wounded. "I don't understand. Why are you making me leave?"

"I'm saving your life. When they see you, those women will be all over you like bees on honey."

Shelby was reaching for the knob when the door swung open, and there stood Izzy, her face flushed with anger and hair on end.

"Whose god-awful vehicle is that parked in my driveway?" she said, tossing a thumb over her shoulder.

"That's the party bus for the bachelorette party."

Izzy flinched at the sound of laughter from above. "Did you say *bachelorette* party?"

"You heard me. And you booked it," Shelby said, unable to resist the urge to rub it in. "From now on, ask more questions when taking group reservations."

"I won't be taking future reservations. That's now your job." Izzy turned her attention to Matt. "You're the young man Shelby's been sneaking around with."

"Izzy! Geez! I told you, we haven't been sneaking around. This is Matt Hitchcock. Matt, this is my rude grandmother, Isabelle St. Clair."

Izzy narrowed her eyes at him. "Hitchcock? And who are your people, son?"

Shelby stared down, wishing the ground would open up and swallow her whole. "Izzy, please. You're embarrassing me."

Matt chuckled. "No worries. You probably know my grandmother, Adele?"

"I know her." Izzy's reaction gave nothing away regarding her feelings for Adele.

Shelby's gaze shifted to Silas who was speaking to a couple in a Cadillac with handicap tags. Silas left the car and rushed over to Shelby. "Pardon the interruption, but our new arrivals need a wheelchair-accessible room."

Izzy zeroed in on his tattoos. "Cover up those vulgar inkings. Can't you wear a long-sleeve shirt?"

Silas's lips twitched as though suppressing a smile. "With all due respect, ma'am, I refuse to wear long sleeves in this heat."

"Then put makeup on them. I find them offensive." Izzy spun on her heels and strode across the courtyard to the cottage.

Silas watched her go and then turned back to Shelby. "About a room that is wheelchair accessible—do we have one?"

"Not one that is officially designated as such. We may have something suitable on the first floor of the pool house. I'll check the room chart."

"They're a real nice couple. The man was paralyzed from the waist down in a boating accident years ago. I'll take them some bottled water while they wait," Silas said, heading down the hall to the kitchen.

Matt followed Shelby to her desk. "You were kinda hard on

your grandma, Shelby. She's an old lady. You should show her some respect."

"Respect works both ways, Matt. Izzy has been mean to me since I got here." She swiveled her chair toward her computer. "Now, if you'll excuse me, I need to find suitable accommodations for the man who just arrived."

"I didn't mean to make you mad. I'll let you get back to work," Matt said, slipping out of the house.

Tears blurred Shelby's vision as she attempted to study the room chart. Who did Matt think he was reprimanding her like that? She felt like a child being called out by her parents for dissing her elders.

Shelby was dabbing at her eyes with a tissue when Blossom entered the room. "I ran into Matt outside. He looks like he lost his best friend."

"He'll live." A thought occurred to Shelby as she turned away from her computer. "Say, Blossom. I could use your help. I have a guest in a wheelchair, but we don't have an official accessible room. Another one of our many oversights."

Coming behind the desk, Blossom peered over Shelby's shoulder at the rooming chart. "Are you sure? Look at pool house number three. The print is small, but isn't that the handicap icon I see?"

Shelby squinted at the computer. Once again, Blossom had waved her magic wand. "I do believe it is." She shot out of her chair and threw her arms around Blossom. "You're the best. Thank you so much."

"You're most welcome." Holding her at arm's length, Blossom said, "Make things right with Matt, baby girl. He's one of the good guys. You'd be a fool to let him get away."

eighteen

. . .

The sound of car doors slamming and loud voices in the courtyard woke Isabelle during the night. She glanced at the clock on her nightstand. It was nearly three in the morning. The guests grew quiet again, presumably having gone to bed. But a few minutes later, the sound of music pierced the silence.

Throwing on her robe, Isabelle stuffed her feet into her slippers, grabbed her cell phone, and strode across the courtyard to the main house. When she discovered the front door locked, she returned to the cottage and spent ten minutes searching for her house key. In all the years she'd lived here, she'd only locked their doors when they traveled.

Locating her key in the bottom of her purse, she returned to the house and let herself in. A pungent skunk odor greeted her in the foyer. Someone was smoking something in her home. And it didn't smell like cigarettes. Starting up the stairs, she gasped and stumbled when she saw naked men and women chasing each other in the second-floor hallway. Steadying herself, she bolted down the stairs and out into the night.

She should call someone. Where was the bellman with the tattoos when she needed him? Shelby was of no use. She needed a man. She clicked on Pritchard's number.

Her son answered in a groggy voice on the third ring. "What's wrong, Mother?"

"Those people are having an orgy in my house!"

"Wait a minute. Slow down. What people are you talking about?"

"The bachelorette party staying here this weekend. I admit I'm to blame for booking the reservation without asking questions. But I never wanted to turn my home into a brothel. This is all on you, Pritchard. You and your father."

"Why is this *my* fault? Never mind. Forget I asked that. I'm not having this argument with you at three in the morning. What makes you think the guests are having an orgy?"

"Because I went over to ask them to turn down the music and saw them with my own eyes. Those women brought men home with them from town. And they are currently running around naked in the upstairs of my house."

"Why didn't you call Silas?" Pritchard asked.

"Because I don't have his number," Isabelle snapped.

"All right," Pritchard said with a reluctant sigh. "I'll call him. Sit tight. One of us will be there in a few minutes."

Less than five minutes passed before a beat-up white pickup truck came speeding up the driveway with Silas behind the wheel. Isabelle was so intent on watching Silas get out of his truck that she didn't hear Shelby approach from behind.

"What's going on, Izzy?"

Isabelle's hand flew to her chest, grasping at her robe. "Jiminy Cricket, child! You nearly gave me a heart attack!"

"Sorry. Why are you awake?"

Isabelle gestured at the house. "Who can sleep with all that racket going on?"

"I know, right? It's obnoxious. I called Silas to come deal with them."

Isabelle eyed her granddaughter's nightclothes—flannel pajama bottoms and a flimsy tank top that revealed her nipples. "You should put on a robe."

Crossing her arms over her chest, Shelby glared at her. "I don't own a robe."

"You're welcome to borrow one of mine." Isabelle turned to Silas. "I went inside to ask them to turn off the music. They're having an orgy in there, and they're smoking something too. Probably heroin or meth."

Shelby rolled her eyes. "I doubt they're smoking heroin or meth, Izzy. It's probably just weed."

"*Just* weed! They shouldn't be smoking anything in *my* house." Isabelle took Silas by the elbow and marched him up to the front door. "Tell those hussies to put on some clothes and get rid of those vile men."

"Yes, ma'am," Silas said and disappeared inside the house. A minute later, the music died, and a stream of disheveled men filed out.

Silas brought up the rear. "I threatened to call the police. You shouldn't have any more trouble out of them tonight." He gestured at the men, who were now packed like sardines in his truck. "I know a couple of the local boys. I'm going to drive them home."

Shelby smacked Silas on the back. "You're a good man, Silas. I don't know what we'd do without you."

"Yes, thank you, Silas," Isabelle added, suddenly grateful for the man with the tattoos. "Plan on spending the night tomorrow. I'll pay you overtime, of course."

Isabelle returned to the cottage, but she couldn't fall back asleep. Every time she closed her eyes, she saw the naked men and women playing chase in her upstairs hallway. She'd never seen such toned bodies. People worked out to the extreme these days, and she wondered if having such tight muscles prevented them from relaxing.

At dawn, she dressed and dragged herself over to the kitchen. Preparing for breakfast was considerably easier with the foods provided by the wholesale distributor. She heated the items, arranged them on a pretty tray, and displayed them on her buffet.

Around eight o'clock, sleepy guests from the pool and garden houses started making their way over. They grumbled about the overnight commotion and threatened not to pay their bill if it happened again tonight. Isabelle was at a loss for what to say. She didn't blame them. If she'd been in their shoes, she would have already checked out.

Isabelle was sipping coffee at the table while Pearl and Hilda cleaned up when an attractive young woman entered the kitchen through the back door.

"Good morning!" the young woman said in a cheerful voice. "I'm Jenna Blevens, the organizer for the bachelorette weekend. The girls would like their breakfast served out by the pool."

"Breakfast ends at ten." Isabelle gestured at the wall clock. "It's now quarter past."

Jenna appeared taken aback. "That's unfortunate since there's nowhere nearby to get food. I'm not asking you to go to any trouble, but would you mind if I prepared something light for them? Maybe some muffins and juice."

"We have leftovers." Pearl presented Jenna with an assortment of breakfast pastries covered in plastic wrap. "I'll get you some orange juice."

Jenna took the tray. "Thank you. These are perfect."

As she removed two pitchers of orange juice from the refrigerator, Pearl asked Jenna, "Are the girls out of their rooms yet? We want to start cleaning as soon as possible."

"Everyone is out by the pool." Jenna glanced skeptically at the ceiling. "I'm sure it's fine."

Isabelle worried the condition of those rooms would be anything but fine.

Pearl headed upstairs to start cleaning while Hilda helped Jenna carry the juice and pastries to the pool.

Alone in the kitchen, Isabelle got up from the table and walked over to the percolator. As she filled her cup, she looked out the window at the *girls* stretched out in the lounge chairs. They all wore dark glasses and sun hats. Most were in blue bathing suits, except the bride, whose white bikini was so tiny that she might as well have been naked. She watched in horror as Jenna popped the cork on two bottles of Champagne, adding the golden liquid to the pitchers of orange juice.

Shameful, Isabelle thought. *Those girls partied all night, and here they are, drinking again before noon.*

Pearl had just returned to the kitchen when Hilda came flying back down the stairs. She spoke to Hilda in such rapid Portuguese Isabelle couldn't make out a word.

Hilda pulled Pearl in for a hug, stroking her back and whispering for her to calm down.

Isabelle planted her hands on her hip. "For the love of Pete, what's she saying? Did she find a dead body upstairs?"

Pearl looked at Isabelle from over Hilda's shoulder. "No, Mrs. St. Clair. No need for you to worry. It's nothing we can't handle."

Isabelle didn't want to know anymore. She'd had enough for one day. "I'll be in the cottage if you need me."

nineteen

. . .

The staff breathed a collective sigh of relief when the bachelorette party left for their outing. According to Jenna, the girls would return late from Charleston. With checkout at eleven tomorrow morning, Shelby hoped they'd seen the worst from the group. The house couldn't withstand another night like last night. Fortunately, Hilda reported only minor damage to the upstairs, including a broken lamp, bloody sheets, and a trail of vomit from the bed to the toilet in one room.

Shelby went outside to see them off, a parade of green-clad bridesmaids led by the bride in a flowing white pantsuit. As she watched them drive away, she thumbed off a text to Matt but erased it before pressing send. Blossom's words came back to her. *Make things right with Matt, baby girl. He's one of the good guys. You don't want to let him get away.* Matt had overstepped a boundary when he'd called her out for being rude to her grandmother, and he owed Shelby an apology.

Around dinnertime, Shelby took a bag of trail mix and her Colleen Hoover novel out to the dock. Leaning against the piling with one calf dangling off the end of the dock, she had just settled in when she noticed Matt speed by in his boat. When she waved at him, he slowed down and turned back toward her.

"How was fishing?" she asked as he pulled up beside her.

Matt hooked a rope around a cleat. "Phenomenal. We released two blue marlin and three sailfish. We also caught several large mahi. Dad was beside himself with excitement."

Shelby set the paperback down and shifted on the dock to face him. "I guess so."

His face grew serious. "I owe you an apology for yesterday. What I said about your grandmother was out of line."

"Apology accepted. My relationship with my grandmother is complicated. To explain, I'd have to revisit the past," Shelby said in a teasing tone.

His lips parted in a sad smile. "I sense a bond developing between us, Shelby. I'm ready to venture into the past if you are."

She wasn't sure she was ready for this next step, but she thought they would better understand each other if they shared their histories. "If you're sure."

"I'm positive. I would suggest we talk right now, but I'm sweaty and fishy, and I prefer to be clean when I confess my past sins. What does your day look like tomorrow?"

Shelby ran down her mental list of their guests' arrivals and departures. "I should have a window of opportunity between one and three."

Matt thought for a minute. "Why don't I pick you up here on the dock at one? We'll zoom over to town and grab some lunch at Comet Dogs."

Shelby curled her upper lip. "Dogs, as in hot dogs?"

Matt laughed. "These aren't your normal hot dogs. Everyone raves about them," he said, pushing off from the dock.

As he drove away, a sense of dread overcame Shelby. She hoped the revelations of his *sins* would not alter her opinion of him.

Shelby was reading in bed around ten o'clock that night when she heard the party bus return—slamming doors, squeals of laughter, men's riotous voices. She sat up straight in bed. *Men? Not again.*

Shelby jumped out of bed and flew to the window. A crowd of approximately thirty men and women migrated from the van into the house. Accompanying the bachelorettes was a clown, a male stripper in a gold metallic thong, and a large muscular guy cradling the passed-out bride. Her dark hair was draped over his arm, and one foot was missing a gold sandal. Noticeably absent was Jenna. The last person to enter the house, a beast of a man with Rastafarian hair, slammed the door behind him.

Seconds later, Silas's truck appeared in the driveway, screeching to a halt in front of the house. He strode up to the door and punched in the code to unlock it. But the door wouldn't open, as though something on the other side was blocking it. He hammered on the door with his fist, yelling, "Security! Open up!"

Music blared from inside the house in response.

Shelby slipped a T-shirt over her sleep camisole and hurried outside. She approached the bus driver, who was leaning against his vehicle, scratching his head in bewilderment. "You have a right to be upset. I couldn't stop them." He gave his head a grave shake. Those women are a disgrace to society."

"I won't argue with that," Shelby said. "Where's Jenna?"

He shrugged. "She didn't make roll call for the ride home."

Shelby's jaw went slack. "What do you mean? Where is she?"

"I don't know. She was with the group at the bar in Charleston. I tried to send someone back inside to fetch her, but they refused. I was afraid to leave my bus unattended with that unruly mob. I'm sorry, ma'am. I don't know what else to say." With shoulders round and head bowed, he shuffled off toward the garden house.

Turning away from him, Shelby marched over to Silas on the front stoop. He was staring at the door, looking completely miffed. "What's going on?" she asked.

"They've barricaded the door from the inside. They either don't hear me, or they're ignoring me. I'm sorry to say I'm in over my head in this situation. Because of my prison record, I'm not allowed to carry a weapon. There's only so much I can do."

Loud noises came from within—hollering and banging and shattering glass.

"They're out of control," Shelby said, pulling out her phone. "I'm calling the police."

When the emergency operator answered, Shelby identified herself as the manager of the Magnolia Shores B&B and briefly explained the situation. "Please! Send the police before they tear the place up!"

"I have a patrol car in the area, ma'am. They'll be there momentarily," said the operator.

As she ended the call, Shelby noticed her grandmother standing in the open doorway of the cottage. She called out to her, "Stay where you are, Izzy. The police are on the way."

Izzy nodded, pulling her robe tight around her.

Within minutes, a patrol car bumped down the driveway, and two young officers climbed out, one baby-faced and the other awkwardly thin. "You're Shelby," said the baby-faced officer. "I'm Cody Porter, Harper's fiancé. She told me a lot about you."

Shelby accepted his outstretched hand. "I've heard a lot about you as well, Cody. Thanks for getting here so fast. We have a situation." She briefly told him about the bachelorettes, the offensive crew they brought home from Charleston, and the barricaded door.

"We'll take care of it." Cody glanced around, his eyes zeroing in on Silas's truck. "You two take cover behind that truck."

Shelby and Silas followed his instructions. The truck was parked close enough to the house for them to see and hear what was happening on the front stoop.

Cody rapped on the door with his billy club. "Police! Open up!"

"Go away, pig. We don't want any," came a deep voice from inside, followed by female laughter.

Cody turned to his partner. "Call for backup. Tell them to bring the paddy wagon."

While the partner stepped away to make the call, Cody surveyed the exterior of the house. When he returned, he reported to Silas and Shelby that the party was a banger. "We could break in through the French doors, but with that many out-of-control drunks, I'd rather wait for backup. They should be here soon."

Shelby nodded. "Whatever you think is best."

The sounds of the raucous party inside the house made Shelby sick to her stomach. She was sure all her grandmother's priceless antiques, fine china, and expensive trinkets were being destroyed. Twenty minutes later, as the first of a long line of headlights was coming down the driveway, a second-floor window opened, and one of Izzy's large heirloom Chinese vases flew out, smashing to pieces on the cobblestones. Shelby screamed, and Silas shielded her with his body as a straight-back chair sailed past.

Everything happened so fast. Patrol cars parked haphazardly in the courtyard, and officers swarmed the house, breaking in through the kitchen window. The music died, the front door flew open, and police officers wrestled handcuffed men and women into the awaiting paddy wagon. The dazed bride was the last to be escorted out.

In the commotion, Shelby failed to notice Pritchard arrive until he was standing beside them. "This is a disaster."

Shelby glanced sideways at her uncle. "Tell me about it. Did Izzy call you?"

"Not Izzy. Cody called Harper, and she called me."

A tearful Izzy joined them. "Pritchard! Thank goodness you're here. They've destroyed my house, our beautiful home."

Pritchard pulled her close. "I know you're upset, Mother. Maybe the damage won't be so bad."

Izzy brought her fist to her mouth. "Maybe. But I doubt it."

The paddy wagon, followed by the convoy of patrol cars,

departed the driveway. Luggage-toting guests filed out of the pool and garden houses, got in their cars, and drove away.

After helping his wife into the car, one furious man stormed over to Shelby and Izzy. "What kind of place are you running? We were terrified during that hostage crisis."

When Izzy looked to Shelby to respond, she chose her words carefully. "I understand you were afraid, sir. But you were never in any danger. No one was being held hostage. Our guests hosted a party that got out of hand. You won't be charged for your stay."

Incensed, the man said, "Charged? I certainly hope not. You'll be lucky if we don't sue you."

Silas stepped forward as if to intervene, but Shelby grabbed his arm, holding him back.

"Sir, I'm sure you're aware this is only our second weekend in operation. We're still working through some issues. If you allow us, we'd like to comp you a stay at a weekend of your choosing in the future."

"Well, okay. That might be all right. Let me think about it," the man said and stomped off.

"Nice job, Shelby," Pritchard said, patting her back. "You handled him beautifully."

Noticing Cody in the doorway, the foursome walked toward him. "Can we go inside?" Pritchard asked.

"Not tonight," Cody said. "Our crime scene investigation team is on the way."

"What about the bachelorettes?" Shelby asked. "Will they be coming back tonight?"

Cody shook his head. "They'll spend the night in jail. Because we arrested such a large group, the judge may hold a special session of the magistrate court in the morning. Otherwise, we'll hold them until Monday. Once released, they'll have to come back for their belongings."

Shelby grimaced. "Ugh. Can't we just ship them their stuff?"

Cody appeared to consider this. "You could. But it would cost you a fortune in shipping. If something gets lost, they'll blame you."

"I agree," Pritchard said. "We should proceed with caution in case we have to sue them for damages."

"I guess you're right," Shelby said in a reluctant tone, dreading the thought of facing the bachelorettes again.

As though reading her mind, Cody said, "Don't worry, Shelby. You won't have to interact with them. Our officers will take them to their rooms and supervise them while they're inside the house." The sound of an approaching vehicle grabbed his attention. "There's the CSI team now."

Pritchard stepped down off the front porch. "I guess there's nothing left for us to do. We might as well get some sleep. We have a long day ahead of us tomorrow."

"Do you want me to hang around for a while?" Silas asked. "I can stay the night if you need me to."

"I don't think that's necessary. The house is crawling with police. I imagine they'll be here for a while." Pritchard placed an arm around Izzy, pulling her in close. "If it makes you feel more comfortable, you and Shelby are welcome to stay with Savannah and me tonight."

Shelby and Izzy shook their heads in unison. "We'll be fine here," Shelby said. "I'll keep an eye out for Izzy."

"I'm only a phone call away if you need me," Pritchard said, kissing Shelby's cheek before walking Izzy to the cottage.

Shelby felt an overwhelming sense of foreboding at the thought of what they might find inside the house tomorrow. Her grandmother's house held her fondest memories of childhood. She and Grace rarely argued during the weeks they spent here over the summers. Their grandparents doted on them, and their days were filled with exciting activities. Maybe she belonged at Magnolia Shores after all.

Pritchard tiptoed around the room, undressing and slipping into bed, trying not to disturb his sleeping wife, but Savannah was already awake.

"Is everything okay?" she asked in a groggy voice as she threw her leg over his body.

He put his arms around her, holding her close. "There was an incident at Magnolia Shores. Fortunately, no one was hurt. Go back to sleep. I'll tell you about it in the morning."

"I've been awake since you left. You might as well tell me what happened now."

Pritchard gave her the abbreviated version of the night's events.

"That's awful, Pritch. How's your mother? She must have been terrified."

Pritchard kissed the top of Savannah's head. "She's pretty upset, mostly about the condition of her house. Shelby handled this situation like a pro though. She's turning out to be a valuable asset."

"Good! She's a nice girl. This is the second night in a row you've been called out for an emergency. If you decide to move forward with the expansion, we'll have to live on-site."

"And sell our love nest? No way! I've learned a valuable lesson this weekend. If we expand, we'll be able to hire an entire security team. I won't be called during the night for emergencies. If we remain a simple bed and breakfast, a mom-and-pop operation, we can only afford Silas, which means I'll have to be more hands-on."

"I haven't thought about it like that." Savannah rolled onto her back. "I've been thinking a lot about your father's idea for Magnolia Shores. And I admit the project excites me. I'm not agreeing to anything yet. Izzy and I would need to iron out our differences. But I might be willing to help you manage the resort."

While Pritchard couldn't see his wife's face in the dark, he could hear the smile in her tone. "It means a lot that you're even considering it. We would make an amazing team. Through reading Dad's journal, I feel as though I absorbed his passion for this project. But one step at a time. I'm terrified of what we'll find inside the house tomorrow. We have an enormous challenge ahead of us getting the bed and breakfast back up and running."

Savannah hooked an arm around his neck, pulling his head to her chest. "I know, sweetheart. Close your eyes and try to get some sleep."

twenty

. . .

When Isabelle woke on Sunday morning, the events of the previous night rushed back to her. Squeezing her eyes shut, she pulled the covers over her head and prayed for sleep to return. But her efforts were a lost cause. She'd never been one for sleeping in, and since she couldn't hide, she might as well get out of bed and face the day.

After being awake half the night, Isabelle needed caffeine, and because there was none in the cottage, she dressed and walked over to the main house. She could hardly believe her eyes when she found the kitchen spotless.

Blossom looked up from opening a can of dog food. "Morning! You must be starving after last night's commotion. Coffee is perking and mini muffins are warming in the oven."

Isabelle gave her head a bewildered shake. "I don't understand. Was the kitchen spared vandalism? Or did you do all this?"

"I've been cleaning for hours," Blossom said, even though she appeared as fresh as a daisy in jean overalls and a pink cotton shirt. "I've never seen such a mess in my life. They smeared condiments from the refrigerator all over the counters and emptied the trash on the floor."

Isabelle experienced an unfamiliar emotion. *Was this what gratitude felt like?* "That magic wand of yours comes in handy."

Blossom chuckled. "I'll take that as a thank you. And you're welcome."

"What about in here?" Isabelle asked, walking toward the closed door leading to the butler's pantry.

Blossom warned, "I wouldn't go in there if I were you. You should wait for Pritchard and Shelby before inspecting the rest of the house. Here. Your coffee's ready." She handed Isabelle a mug, the coffee prepared the way she liked it with a dollop of cream and a spoonful of sugar.

The back door opened, and Silas, Pritchard, Savannah, Harper, and Shelby filed in, with Shelby bringing up the rear. She stopped short at the sight of the gleaming kitchen. "Whoa," she exclaimed, turning to Blossom. "You did this, didn't you?"

Blossom shrugged. "Maybe. I figured y'all could use the kitchen as home base these next few days."

Shelby threw her arms around Blossom. "You're a godsend."

Blossom let out a belly laugh. "Don't I know it?"

"Can't you fix the rest of the house too?" "Shelby asked.

Blossom kissed the top of Shelby's head and drew her away. "I'm sorry, baby girl. I've already used up all my energy for today."

"All right then," Pritchard said, inhaling a deep breath. "Are we ready to assess the damage?"

Isabelle slowly rose from the table. "No time like the present."

Blossom shooed the small crowd out of the kitchen. "Go! Make your rounds. I'll have breakfast ready when you come back."

Isabelle had expected the damage to be bad, but she was unprepared for what awaited them in the other rooms. The walls, furniture, and hardwood floors were covered in a sticky substance, which Shelby identified as Champagne. The shattered remains of her china and crystal collections covered the floor in the butler's pantry. Her crystal chandelier dangled from a single wire over her dining room table. Multiple windows and picture frames and the desktop computer screen had been smashed. Feathers from slashed pillows and down cushions covered every surface in the living room, a few still floating in the air. In the study, her husband's books had been pulled from the shelves, the spines of some broken and pages torn from others. Edward's Oriental rug was saturated with whiskey, and the bottles from his rare collection stood empty on the bar behind his desk. When they ventured upstairs, broken lamps, ruined carpets, stained walls, and shredded linens greeted them in the bedrooms.

Harper attempted to repair the bent neck of a lamp. "My storage unit is full of odds and ends, including a wide assortment of lamps. You might want to take a look," she said, tossing the unfixable lamp on the bed.

"I already have a decorator," Isabelle snapped.

Harper leveled her gaze on Isabelle. "Oh, really? Who?"

Isabelle squared her shoulders. "Rose Cain at Lowcountry Living Interiors. She has impeccable taste."

Harper nodded in agreement. "She certainly does. I bought Rose's business last summer."

Pritchard nudged Izzy with his elbow. "I told you that, Mother. Don't you remember?"

"Apparently not, Pritchard," Isabelle said with a huff.

"If you're interested, I can give you the accessories at cost," Harper volunteered.

"I'm not looking for a handout, Harper." Isabelle pointed at her son. "But all this is coming out of your father's estate."

"I'm counting on insurance to pay for everything," Pritchard said.

Isabelle's eyes fell on the stained carpet. "It'll cost me a fortune to replace this wool carpet."

Harper produced a screwdriver from her backpack and pried the carpet from one corner of the room. "You have hardwood floors under here. Why not refinish them and leave them bare? Most hotels are going that route now. It's cleaner, and you don't have to worry about carpet stains."

"I like that idea," Shelby chimed in. "We'll save a fortune in carpet cleaning."

Isabelle's shoulders deflated. She suddenly felt ancient. She said little as she followed the others downstairs to the kitchen, where a smorgasbord awaited them. In addition to the warmed muffins, Blossom had made waffles, scrambled eggs, and sausage. They loaded their plates and gathered around the pine farm table.

Pritchard slurped his coffee. "I've contacted RestoreEase, a commercial cleaning and restoration service. They'll be starting first thing in the morning. Today, our goal is to restore order as best we can, pick up trash, and salvage valuables. Most of you know Savannah's brother, Will, is a building contractor. His crew will come in after the cleaners to paint, repair windows, refinish the floors if we decide to go that route, and take care of whatever else needs fixing."

Shelby crunched on a slice of bacon. "I can access the reservation system through my laptop. We don't have anyone booked for tonight. I'll cancel the reservations for this week. How long do you think it'll be before we can reopen? Is next weekend out of the question?"

Pritchard thought about it as he peppered his eggs. "Next weekend might be pushing it. But I can't say for sure until I talk to Will. Why don't you hold off canceling next weekend for now?"

"Okay," Shelby said and popped a mini muffin into her mouth.

While they ate, they divvied up cleanup chores. Isabelle was relieved to be excluded from the list. After breakfast, she remained in the kitchen to help Blossom with the dishes.

"You were awfully quiet during breakfast," Blossom noted.

Isabelle set down her dish towel and fell back against the counter. "I no longer belong in my own home. I can't stay here, but I don't have the money to leave either."

Blossom placed the last dish in the dishwasher. "Why can't you stay here?"

"Because I know nothing about running a bed and breakfast."

Isabelle pressed her hands to the sides of her head. "All this is my fault. I failed to check out the group when I took the reservation."

Blossom picked up Jolene and held the dog close to Isabelle's face. "Jolene says for you to stop being so hard on yourself."

Isabelle smiled despite her dislike of the dog.

Blossom nuzzled the dog to her neck. "So, you made a mistake. You learned from it, didn't you?"

Isabelle hunched a shoulder. "All I ever do anymore is make mistakes."

Blossom frowned. "You don't strike me as someone prone to having pity parties. So you have some damage to repair, but it could be worse. Those awful people could've burned the house down."

Isabelle chipped the red polish off her fingernails. "I'm allowed to have a pity party, Blossom. I'm seventy-five years old, and my life has drastically changed, thanks to my dead husband."

Blossom cocked her head to the side. "Would your husband intentionally put you in a position he didn't think you could handle?"

Isabelle jerked her head up. "You have all the answers. Why don't you tell me?"

Blossom stood so close to Isabelle she could feel the heat emanating from the large woman's body. Isabelle would normally resent the invasion of her personal space, but after the trauma of the past twenty-four hours, she found Blossom's presence oddly comforting. "I think maybe your husband is testing you."

Isabelle's throat thickened, and she fought back tears. She was certain Edward was testing her. And she was sure to fail, just as she'd failed all the previous times.

twenty-one

. . .

The cleanup was grueling, but Shelby enjoyed the camaraderie of their small crew. Silas entertained them with funny stories from life in prison. Savannah made up humorous songs about the bachelorettes. Both Harper and Savannah had lovely voices, and Shelby wasn't surprised to learn they'd once considered careers as country music singers. Harper talked excitedly about the wedding plans they'd begun to make for next May—a ceremony and reception on the lawn at Marsh Point, Savannah's family's waterfront home on Catawba Sound.

When Jenna appeared around ten o'clock, she was appalled at the state of the living room. "Oh my god. What happened in here?"

Shelby wiped her sweaty forehead with the back of her hand. "Your girls brought *company* home with them from Charleston. They had a raging party and vandalized the place. Where have you been?"

"They left me in Charleston. I was having a drink with a friend on a different floor of the bar. When I went to find them, they were gone. Nobody would answer their phone, not even the bus driver. I assume they're still sleeping. I'll go wake them up. We need to get on the road," Jenna said, approaching the stairs.

"They're not here," Pritchard said. "They're in jail."

Jenna stopped in her tracks and turned back around. "Seriously? Was the party that bad?"

Pritchard spread his arms wide. "Look around you. They ruined my family's home."

Jenna made a quick tour of the house. "You're right. This is bad. I hope you're planning to sue for damages."

"We have no choice," Pritchard said. "They destroyed some very valuable antiques."

"Let me see what I can find out," she said, her phone pressed to her ear as she exited the house.

Jenna returned two hours later with three female police officers and the hungover bachelorettes. As they trekked up the stairs for their belongings, not a single one made eye contact with Shelby, let alone apologized for the damage and disruption they'd caused.

Shelby was furious. She wanted to give that bride a piece of her mind. But Pritchard warned her to keep quiet. "Don't say anything they could potentially hold against you if this thing goes to court."

When the bridal party came back downstairs, Shelby followed them into the courtyard and watched to make certain the party bus left the property.

Blossom grilled hamburgers for their lunch and served them homemade pizza late afternoon.

At six o'clock, Pritchard declared their job complete. He said to their group, "The professional cleaning service can handle the rest. You have all worked hard today, and I don't know how to thank you."

An empty feeling overcame Shelby as she watched Pritchard leave with his wife and daughter. She longed to go home with them, to be part of their lovely little family.

Shelby had left her phone charging beside her bed that morning, and she'd been too preoccupied during the day to retrieve it. When she returned to her room, a long string of Matt's missed calls and texts greeted her. How could she have been so careless and insensitive to have forgotten their date?

She clicked on his number, and when he answered, she exclaimed, "Matt! Oh my gosh! I'm so sorry." She babbled on about the vandalism last night, and the day she'd spent cleaning up. "Why didn't you come to the main house to get me?"

"I figured something had happened with work, and I didn't want to bother you."

Shelby laughed. "It's probably a good thing you didn't. Pritchard might have put you to work. What're you doing right now?"

"Meal prep for the week."

Meal prep? Shelby thought. *Do people actually do that?* "I was thinking about going for a swim in the pool. All the guests have left. There's no one here except Izzy, Blossom, and me. Wanna come over?"

He paused a beat before letting out a sigh of resignation. "Sure. Why not? I'll be there in a few minutes."

"Are you coming by boat or truck?" Shelby asked, rummaging through her bathing suit drawer.

"Boat. It's a nice night, and I could use the fresh air."

"Then I'll meet you on the dock. I promise I'll be there this time."

Ending the call, Shelby peeled off her sweaty clothes and slipped on her black, ruffly bikini. She was waiting on the dock twenty minutes later when his boat pulled up.

Matt greeted her with a tight smile and said little as they walked to the pool. He was clearly irritated at having been stood up earlier.

Shelby dove into the pool and swam to the other end without coming up for air. Treading water, she yelled down the pool to him, "Is there an oily streak around me? I'm polluting the water with all the sweat and grime from my body."

This made him smile, and he dove in after her. When he came up beside her, he asked, "How old are you, Shelby?"

"Twenty-four. I'll be twenty-five in August."

Matt's smile faded. "That's what I thought."

Shelby splashed him and said in a teasing tone, "Why? How old are you? Thirty?"

His face grew serious. "Thirty-one, actually."

Shelby's lips formed an O. "That's a big age difference."

"Yes, it is. If only you were a few years older, but you're so young." Matt grabbed two Styrofoam noodles from the side of the pool, handing one to her. "When you didn't show up for our date earlier, I worried I'd scared you off by talking so much about the past. You're not old enough to even have a past."

"That's not fair, Matt. I have no control over my age. I'm sorry if I'm not as mature as your old girlfriend."

He shook his head. "And that statement shows just how juvenile you are."

"*Juvenile*? Ouch."

"If the shoe fits. Kayla and I were never going to get married. But she was my best friend, and she helped me through a difficult time," he said, his expression pained.

Shelby swam closer to him, touching her fingertips to his arm. "You don't have to tell me this if you don't want to."

"I need to clear the air. I made my past sound worse than it is. I don't want you to think I'm an ex-con or something." He raked his fingers through his damp hair. "Like many other guys, I chose a career path that was all wrong for me. I was miserably unhappy, and I lost my way for a while. But I'm much better now."

"I'm glad." Shelby didn't know what else to say. She sensed he was only touching the tip of the iceberg of his past, but she didn't encourage him to continue. Something had shifted in their relationship, and a void the size of a universe now separated them. Their spark had been extinguished, and their aura was now awkward. He no longer trusted her, whether because she'd stood him up or because of her age.

Matt pulled away from her and kicked toward the shallow end. Drying himself off with a towel, he said, "I should go. We're both tired. Let's forget about today and see what tomorrow brings."

He walked Shelby to the pool house but didn't kiss her goodnight, not even a peck on the cheek.

Shelby showered, put on her pajamas, and climbed into bed. She stared up at the ceiling, wondering about the career Matt had given up. Was he a med school dropout? Did he finish two years of law school before deciding a law profession wasn't for him? How had he lost his way? Did he have a substance abuse problem? Alcohol? Drugs? Their bond had seemed so strong in the beginning. How had it gone south so quickly? Was their age difference so important?

Pritchard startled, his heart skipping a beat, when he noticed Harper in the kitchen doorway. He and Savannah had been too engrossed in his father's journal to hear the front door open. After eating a light dinner, they'd remained at the table, sipping tea while he shared his father's dreams for Magnolia Shores.

"Harper! I didn't hear you come in," Pritchard said to his daughter.

"Obviously. You two were lost in your own world." Harper entered the kitchen. "What're you working on?"

"We were just discussing the work required to reopen the B&B."

Harper eyed the journal. "What's that?"

"Nothing." Pritchard closed the journal. "I was just making some notes for tomorrow's meeting with Will. It's getting late. Why aren't you at home?"

"I left my iPad in your car earlier. I'm sorry to bother you, but your car is locked."

"The keys are on the tray beside the front door." Pritchard stood to face her. "Since you're here, I'd like to officially hire you to refurbish the house. I'm not sure I made that clear earlier."

Harper shook her head. "I wasn't sure. Thanks for clarifying. I appreciate the business."

"You have excellent ideas and flawless style," Savannah chimed in.

Harper smiled. "Thank you. I still have a lot to learn. But I'm fortunate to have a talented team."

"When you get a chance, I'd like you to create a simple drawing of what you had in mind to turn Dad's study into a cocktail lounge. I'm going to ask Will to give us an estimate."

"That's exciting. I'll get right on it." Harper backed out of the kitchen. "I'll just grab my iPad and be out of your hair."

"I'll go with you." Pritchard followed her, grabbing his keys on the way out the front door. He unlocked the car and waited while she retrieved her iPad. "Good night, sweetheart. Have I told you lately how grateful I am that you're back in my life?"

"Hmm. I'm not sure. Does yesterday count as lately?" she asked, a smirk tugging at her lips.

He laughed. "I apologize in advance. I may never get tired of saying it."

"Good. Because I'll never get tired of hearing it." Harper stood on her tiptoes to kiss his cheek. "Good night, Daddy."

Tears filled his eyes. "That's the first time you've called me that."

Harper blushed. "I hope it's okay. I wasn't sure you wanted me to. I feel like we're more friends than father and daughter."

"We can be both. Our relationship is evolving," he said, opening her car door. "Drive safely. I'll see you soon."

Pritchard returned to the kitchen, his fingers still touching his cheek where she kissed him. He lowered himself to his chair. "She called me Daddy. But she also said she thinks of me more as a friend than her father."

"That's understandable," Savannah said. Our situation is unusual. She'll think of you as her Daddy when you walk her down the aisle next spring. Why didn't you tell her about Magnolia Shores?"

Pritchard withdrew his hand from his face. "I started to, but telling her would make it official. Are we ready to commit to this project?"

"Hmm. I'm not sure," Savannah said, biting down on her lower lip. "Maybe we should give it a few more days. This will drastically change our lives, and I need a little more time to get comfortable with the commitment."

"If we decide to move forward, I very much want Harper to be involved. Do you think she's ready to handle all the design work?"

Savannah placed her hand on his. "Not alone. But she has Bridget to help her. And she's a real dynamo."

Pritchard frowned. "What if Harper wants nothing to do with this project? I'm building a future for her, as much as for you and me."

"And Shelby and all future St. Clair offspring."

Pritchard relished the idea. "Wouldn't it be amazing if generations from now, our great-great-grandchildren were running Magnolia Shores?"

twenty-two

. . .

On Monday morning, Savannah's brother, Will, brought a small crew of workers to assess the restoration project. One of those workers was Matt.

A construction worker? Shelby thought, dumbfounded. Unfortunately, she didn't get a chance to speak with him before the meeting started.

As they toured the house, Will told Pritchard, "You're fortunate. Most of the damage appears to be superficial. It'll only take RestoreEase a couple of days to clean. If we start Wednesday morning, we'll be done by midweek next week."

Shelby's heart sank. "So that means we'll have to cancel all reservations for this weekend."

Will gave her a grim nod. "I'm afraid so. At least in the main building."

Shelby's mind raced. "We could keep the reservations for the pool and garden houses, but we would need somewhere to serve them breakfast. The kitchen is in working order. Could you prioritize the dining room so we could have possession of it by Friday?"

Pritchard beamed at her. "Good thinking, Shelby."

Will consulted his legal pad. "That shouldn't be a problem. The painters can start in the dining room first, and I'll schedule the electrician to rehang the chandelier."

Shelby pulled Matt aside after the meeting. "Are you the project manager or something?"

"Nope. I hope to be a project manager one day. Right now, I'm a lowly construction worker. Your disapproval is written all over your face."

She brought her hand to her cheek. "I don't disapprove, Matt. I'm just . . . I don't know what I think."

"I know exactly what you think. You hate the idea of being with a blue-collar worker. I was wrong about you, Shelby. It turns out you *are* a spoiled rich girl after all," he said, turning his back on her and rejoining his crew.

Is what he said about her true? So what if she couldn't see herself with a blue-collar worker? What was wrong with wanting to be with a man who could care for her in the manner she was accustomed to?

Shelby spent Monday afternoon by the pool, working on her tan while canceling and confirming reservations for the upcoming weekend. The guests booked for the pool and garden houses seemed unfazed when she alerted them to the construction that would be taking place in the main house. The reservations she canceled were rebooked for a different weekend later in the summer.

Hearing the sound of a car engine, Shelby looked up from her computer to see Harper parking her 4Runner in the courtyard. She put on her cover-up and flip-flops and hurried over to greet her cousin. "Hey there! What're you doing here?"

Harper removed her tote bag from the back seat. "Pritchard officially hired my firm to handle the restoration."

Shelby's face lit up. "Cool! Welcome aboard!"

Harper checked her watch. "I'm meeting a man about cleaning the downstairs rugs in thirty minutes."

"RestoreEase doesn't do that?" Shelby asked.

"I'm sure they do, but I don't trust them with Izzy's Oriental rug. In the meantime, I need to take measurements and make lists."

Shelby relished the idea of spending more time with her cousin. Do you want some help?"

"Sure! That would be great." Harper retrieved a tape measure and legal pad from her tote. Hanging the pad to Shelby, she said, "We'll start in Edward's study."

Shelby followed Harper inside and jotted down the measurements as Harper called them out to her. "So, Pritchard is seriously considering turning this room into a cocktail lounge?"

"Yes! He asked me to create a drawing for Will to use for the estimate."

Following Harper's instructions, Shelby took one end of the tape measure and walked it to the French doors. "I hope he's planning to hire someone to manage it."

"I'm sure he will. Unless Savannah manages it." Harper retracted the metal tape measure and called out the measurement for Shelby to note on her pad. "I have a hunch Savannah and Pritchard are up to something."

Shelby frowned. "What makes you say that?"

"I can't put my finger on it. They've been secretive lately." Harper shrugged. "I guess they'll tell us when they're ready."

Shelby wondered if Pritchard was considering selling the property. After last weekend, she wouldn't blame him. What would that mean for her future?

After finishing with the measurements, Harper and Shelby went upstairs to the second floor. They moved from room to room, making a list of accessories that needed replacing—lamps, decorative pillows, and knickknacks. Completing their task, they returned to the courtyard to wait for the rug cleaner.

Shelby leaned against the porch railing, crossing her ankles.

"Cody seems like a nice guy. How long did you date before you got engaged?"

A dreamy expression overcame Harper's face. "Almost a year."

Shelby tried not to show her surprise. She and Luke had dated for over ten years, but they were young, in high school and college. If she met someone now, would she marry them after only knowing them for such a short time? "Aren't you worried about his career?"

Harper's smile faded. "Of course. I worry about his safety every day. Fortunately, Water's Edge has very little crime."

Shelby furrowed her brow. "I'm talking about his salary, not his safety. He can't be making much money."

Harper chuckled. "Money isn't everything, Shelby. Cody loves being a police officer. He takes great pride in protecting this community. That's more important to him than money. I've dated plenty of wealthy guys. Most were shallow and pretentious. But Cody has heart."

Shelby mulled over the expression *has heart.* That phrase seemed spot-on in describing Matt.

She felt Harper's eyes on her. "What's going on, Shelby? Is there anything you want to talk about?"

"I was sort of dating this guy, Matt Hitchcock. Do you know him?"

"Of course. Everyone knows Matt. He's a great guy. What happened?"

"It's complicated. Remember I told you about Luke?"

"Sure. He's your old boyfriend," Harper said, leaning against the railing beside her.

"Luke is brilliant and ambitious, determined to make his first million by the time he turns thirty. He promised me the lifestyle I've always wanted, to be a stay-at-home mom and raise a house full of children." Shelby picked at a loose thread on her cover-up. "I majored in hospitality with a concentration in event management. I figured a party planning degree would serve me well as being the wife of a successful businessman. But the guy is now engaged to someone else, and I'm stuck with a hospitality degree."

Harper shoulder-bumped Shelby. "It sounds to me like you're having a career crisis, not a man crisis."

Shelby's throat thickened. "I'm having a life crisis. Nothing is turning out the way I hoped."

"Let's sit down." Harper lowered herself to the top step, pulling Shelby down beside her. "I majored in English, thinking I would follow in my adoptive mother's footsteps and become a lawyer. I worked as a paralegal, but I could never bring myself to apply to law school. When I moved to Water's Edge and met Cody, he encouraged me to reconnect with my creative side. And now I own a design firm." She shifted to face Shelby. "Your hospitality degree makes you an excellent fit for your job here. Do you like working at the B&B?"

Shelby pondered the question before answering, "That's hard to say, considering our rocky start."

"True. But don't rush to judgment. Wait and see what Pritchard has up his sleeve. The property has serious potential. With the right person in charge, it could become a luxury hot spot. You're a St. Clair, Shelby. You're more than an employee. You're a principal. You could have a solid future here."

"That's true. I haven't thought of it like that."

"But only if working here makes you happy, Shelby. Being in charge of your own destiny and earning your own money is both rewarding and liberating. As for the man, sort yourself out first. The rest will fall into place."

A white van appeared in the driveway. "There's your rug cleaner," Shelby said, getting to her feet and pulling Harper in for a hug. "Thanks for the pep talk."

"Any time." She pushed Shelby away. "Thank *you* for helping me. What are you doing on Wednesday morning? Do you want to come with me to my storage unit? We can pick out accessories together and then have lunch afterward."

"That sounds great. See you tomorrow," Shelby said, waving as she headed back to the pool.

She reapplied sunscreen and settled back into her lounge chair. No sooner had she started a new chapter in her romance novel than she received a text from Emily.

It's working! Luke's heart is growing fonder in your absence.

Shelby's heart raced as she called Emily. "What makes you think that?" she blurted when her best friend answered on the first ring.

"I saw him at Caitlyn Morrison's wedding on Saturday night. He was asking about you. He wanted to know where you'd been."

Shelby's spirits deflated. "He was probably just drunk."

"Maybe. But I saw him again yesterday at the golf shop. We were both finishing up a round of eighteen with our dads. Luke pulled me aside, and he had definitely not been drinking. He seemed so sincere, so genuinely concerned about you. I couldn't lie to him, Shelby. I told him about your grandmother's bed and breakfast. He asked how long you would be in South Carolina, and I told him I didn't know. Maybe permanently. You should've seen his face. He was wrecked."

Hope blossomed inside of Shelby. "Really?"

"Cross my heart. I wouldn't be surprised if he shows up on your doorstep. He's familiar with your grandmother's place. He's been there with you plenty of times."

"Him coming here is a stretch, Emily. What about Alexis? Have you seen her?"

"She wasn't with him at the wedding. Maybe she's out of town."

"Probably. I assume they're still together. You would've heard if they'd broken up."

They talked for a few more minutes before ending the call.

Shelby rested her head against the back of the chair and closed her eyes. She considered the possibility that Luke and Alexis had broken up. Despite what Harper had said about being in charge of her own destiny and earning her own money, Shelby would much rather have the life Luke promised her than a career in hotel management.

twenty-three

. . .

Isabelle waited until Harper left before sneaking over to the main house. She slipped into Edward's study and retrieved her most valuable possessions from the locked cabinet behind his desk. She carried the leather-bound family photo albums and old wooden cigar box outside to the hammock, hugging them close. Closing her eyes, she recalled last night's dream about Edward.

She smiled at the memory of her dignified husband dressed in white robes with angel wings extending from his shoulders and a golden halo hovering over his head. He'd been guarding the pearly gates of heaven, refusing to let her through until she . . .

Isabelle had woken up before he'd told her the admission price, but she already knew what she had to do to get into heaven. Was this the only way? If she refused, would she go to hell?

During their married life, Edward had often been reduced to begging, pleading, and bribing Isabelle to get his way. He gave her a five-carat sapphire ring when she refused to travel to Egypt with him. When he wanted to build a swimming pool, she'd argued it would spoil the natural beauty of the surroundings. He'd gotten his pool, and Isabelle had gotten a new kitchen. And now he'd backed her into a corner.

Isabelle opened her eyes to find Blossom looming over her,

two glasses of sweet tea in her hands and her little dog running circles at her feet. "Why are you always sneaking up on me, Blossom?"

"You looked so peaceful, I didn't want to disturb you. But then I got to thinking you might be dead, and I thought I should make sure you were still breathing."

Isabelle struggled to sit up. "Well, it's a good thing I'm not dead. Otherwise, I'd be on an express elevator to hell."

The lines on Blossom's forehead deepened. "What makes you say that?"

"Don't play dumb with me, Blossom. Isn't that why you're here? To help me get into heaven?"

Iced tea sloshed out of the glasses as Blossom roared with laughter. "I wish I had that kind of power." She dipped her head at the photo albums in Isabelle's lap. "What's all that?"

"Memories," Isabelle said, clutching the albums and box to her chest.

Blossom's emerald eyes twinkled. "Ooh. I love family photos. Can I see?"

"I guess. Although you'll probably find them boring." Isabelle rolled out of the hammock, landing on her knees and clambering to her feet. "Gracious, I'm getting old."

They sat down across from each other at a table near the pool. Jolene curled up at their feet and soon fell fast asleep. Isabelle sipped sweet tea while Blossom hemmed and hawed at photographs of Pritchard's and Kate's childhood—birthdays, Christmases, and Easters, memories of simpler times. Isabelle had been a loving mother when her children were little. But Isabelle failed them during their teenage years when their problems became complicated.

Blossom closed the photo album and eyed the cigar box. "What's in there?"

"Stuff," Isabelle snapped.

Blossom chuckled. "I figured that. Can I see?"

Isabelle hunched over the box. "No way! I've never shown

anyone what's in here. Not even Edward." She slid the box off the table into her lap. "Keep your X-ray vision off my box. The contents are personal."

"I don't have X-ray vision, Isabelle. And I'm not here to work magic on you. I'm here to support you."

Isabelle gasped. "Support me? What're you talking about? You're here to do Edward's bidding."

"That's what you think, but that's not true." Blossom pointed at her. "You summoned me here, Izzy."

Isabelle's eyes blinked wide. "What on earth for?"

"You tell me. I sense you're at a crossroads. You're awfully concerned with getting into heaven. You seem to have something you need to get off your chest."

Isabelle was not perfect, but she was no stranger to the Lord. She rarely missed church and prayed often. She'd been distraught since Edward so drastically changed her life with his cockamamy will. She might have inadvertently asked for divine intervention.

"I understand if you're not ready to talk about it. I have all the time in the world." Blossom produced a deck of cards from her pocket. "Let's play gin rummy."

Isabelle wasn't in the mood for cards but hoped the distraction would lessen her tension. "Okay."

After dealing each of them ten cards, Blossom placed the remainder of the deck face down on the table and turned over the top card—a seven of spades.

Isabelle arranged her cards into matching sets and runs before drawing a new one from the deck. She discarded the six of diamonds from her hand and nodded for Blossom to take her turn.

As she drew a card from the deck, Blossom said, "I died in a tragic car accident at age fifty."

Isabelle's breath hitched. "You were so young. Your gray-streaked hair confused me."

"I was prematurely gray. But yes, I was too young when I died. I was completely unprepared for death. I had so many things left to do, but only one thing that really mattered." Blossom discarded the card. "My only daughter, my only *child,* and I had been estranged for years when I passed away."

"Why? What happened to cause the rift?"

Blossom rolled her eyes. "A man, of course."

Isabelle gave a knowing nod. "Of course," she said, drawing and discarding the same card.

"I suspected Melody's boyfriend was abusing her, but when I confronted her, she denied it. We had a nasty argument, and we both said things we regretted. Instead of forgiving her, I let my anger fester. I was the adult. I should've worked harder to mend our relationship. She eventually married a different man and had children. I never met my grandchildren."

"That's so sad," Isabelle said past the lump in her throat.

"After my death, I visited Melody in a dream and apologized. While it wasn't the same as doing it in person, it was my only choice. The next day, she attended my burial and stayed after the other attendees left. She sensed my presence at the graveside, and she also apologized. The moral of this story is—"

"Don't put off until tomorrow what you can do today," Isabelle said, and then abandoned her hand of cards face-down on the table. "I owe someone an apology too. The problem is, I can't bring myself to say the words."

Blossom furrowed her brow. "What words? *I'm sorry*?"

"Yes. I haven't said them in over seventy years." Isabelle peeked inside her cigar box and closed it again. "It's a long story. Are you sure you want to hear it?"

Blossom glanced down at her sleeping dog. "Jolene and I have nothing but time."

A thought occurred to Isabelle. "Is the dog an angel too?"

"All dogs are angels, Isabelle. I didn't bring her with me, if that's what you're asking. I discovered her along the way."

Isabelle was sorry she asked. She settled back in her chair. "I was an only child of a single mother. I never met my father. I'm not even sure my mother knew who he was," she said and watched for her reaction. If this shocked Blossom, she did an excellent job of hiding it.

Despite the warm day, Isabelle shivered as the memories flooded back to her.

Isabelle's mama worked as a maid for the Sterns, the wealthiest couple in their tiny Georgia town. Isabelle often helped out on Saturdays and during the summer months. She was eleven years old, helping prepare for the Stern's annual Christmas party, when Lilith Stern accused her of stealing a pearl bracelet.

"I didn't take it, Mrs. Stern. Cross my heart with my hand on the Bible. I saw the bracelet on your dressing table when I was vacuuming your bedroom. Are you sure you didn't put it somewhere?"

Mrs. Stern's face flushed blood red. "Why, you little cretin. Are you calling me a liar?" She grabbed Isabelle's wrist with one hand and snatched the butcher knife Mama had been using to carve a ham with the other. "Give me back my bracelet, or I'll cut off your fingers with this knife."

Isabelle tried to wrench her arm free, but Mrs. Stern was surprisingly strong for a small woman. She pressed Isabelle's hand on the counter with the knife poised to strike. "Say you're sorry."

"But I didn't take it," Isabelle sobbed.

Mrs. Stern lifted the knife higher. "Say you're sorry, or I'll chop off your fingers."

Pee trickled down Isabelle's leg. "I didn't take it."

Mrs. Stern tightened her grip on Isabelle's wrist. "Say you're sorry, you little ingrate."

Anger surged when she noticed Mama watching in horror but not saying a word. "I said. I didn't take. The bracelet."

"I'm counting to ten. Say you're sorry, or off go your fingers."

Isabelle started screaming bloody murder, her cries

reverberating throughout the house until the woman finally let go of her hand. Mrs. Stern spun around and brandished the knife at Mama. "I'm docking your pay for a month."

Mama bowed her head. "Yes, ma'am."

Neither Isabelle nor Mama spoke on the drive home. Something seemed off to Isabelle. Why didn't Mama come to her rescue? Did Mama believe Isabelle stole the bracelet? Or did Mama want Mrs. Stern to *think* Isabelle stole the bracelet?

Isabelle waited until Mama got in the tub for her nightly soak to search her purse. Inside the zippered pocket, she found Mrs. Stern's pearl bracelet.

Isabelle opened the cigar box and slid it across the table to Blossom. She stared down at the bracelet but didn't remove it from the box. "Did you confront your mama when she got out of the tub?"

"Nope." A smile tugged at the corner of Isabelle's lips. "I wore the bracelet to dinner instead."

Blossom's emerald eyes doubled in size. "I love your style, Isabelle St. Clair. Did you really think Mrs. Stern would cut off your fingers?"

"At the time, I did. I was only eleven years old, and despite her size, she was an imposing figure. I have no doubt that Mama would've let her. Like your daughter, Mama blamed me for everything wrong in her life."

She slid the box back to Isabelle. "Now I understand why saying you're sorry doesn't come easy."

"It doesn't come at all. I simply can't bring myself to say it." Isabelle's expression grew serious as she lifted the bracelet from the box and fastened it onto her wrist. "This little trinket became a bone of contention between Mama and me. I held the theft over her head. We both knew she would lose her job if I ratted her out to Mrs. Stern."

"So you bribed her to get what you wanted instead."

"We were dirt poor, Blossom. There wasn't much to want for. I never caused my mama any trouble. I was a good girl and an excellent student. I worked hard and earned a full-ride scholarship to a small girls' college in Georgia. I left home and never spoke to my mother again." Isabelle expelled the air from her lungs as decades of pent-up tension left her body.

Blossom offered her a soft smile. "Feel better?"

Isabelle fell back in her chair. "Indeed. I can't believe I told a total stranger my deepest secret."

"Because you've never had a close friend to confide in other than your husband." Reaching across the table, Blossom placed her hand over Isabelle's. "I want to be your friend if you'll let me."

Isabelle realized she desperately wanted and needed this heavenly creature in her life. "I'd like that," she said.

"Why didn't you ever tell Edward about the bracelet?"

Isabelle looked away, staring at the sun's rays glistening off the ocean. "That's a story for another day. For now, I want to relish this profound sense of peace. I've never felt anything quite like it. Am I experiencing your celestial aura? Is this what heaven feels like?"

Blossom held her hands out, palms skyward. "Maybe."

twenty-four

. . .

Around six o'clock that evening, Isabelle was inspecting the meager contents of her refrigerator when the cottage door flew open, and Blossom sashayed in on a cloud of floral perfume. She was dressed in a green flowing jumpsuit that matched her emerald eyes, and her silver coils were tied in a loose knot at her nape.

"Get dressed!" Blossom demanded. "We're going to town for dinner."

"No thank you. I'm exhausted. I'll eat a quick bite here and go to bed."

"You've been resting all afternoon," Blossom said, peering over her shoulder into the refrigerator. "It doesn't look like you have much in the way of food here anyway. Besides, when's the last time you had any fun?"

Isabelle couldn't remember when she last went to town for dinner, and she knew Blossom wouldn't take *no* for an answer. She closed the refrigerator door. "Okay. I'll go with you." She glanced down at her seersucker slacks and white blouse. "I should change though."

Blossom gave her a once-over. "Why? What you have on is fine."

Isabelle lowered her gaze to Blossom's feet. "Where's Jolene?"

"Shelby is dog sitting for me."

"Then what are we waiting for? I'm starving." Isabelle grabbed her purse and followed Blossom out of the cottage. When she saw the blue school bus idling in the courtyard, she stopped in her tracks. "Surely you don't expect me to ride in that contraption. We'll take my car."

Blossom kept on walking. "Sorry, Charlie. The Blossom Bus is way more fun."

"If you say so," Isabelle said, lacking the energy for an argument.

Gospel music sung by rich, soulful voices greeted Isabelle inside the customized school bus. The interior boasted an all-white decor featuring leather seats, velvet pillows, and faux sheepskin rugs. There was a small galley kitchen outfitted with white and chrome appliances, and at the rear was a bed made with fluffy white linens.

"It's like heaven in here," Isabelle said in awe.

Blossom laughed out loud. "Exactly. This is my home away from home." She put the bus in gear, and they glided out of the driveway.

"The ride is so smooth."

Blossom winked at Isabelle. "Because the tires aren't actually touching the road."

On the way to town, she tooted her trumpet-sounding horn at every car they passed. Most of the other drivers responded in kind. Isabelle pressed her lips tight to hide her smile. She didn't know when she'd had such fun.

They never discussed where they would eat. But Isabelle wasn't surprised when Blossom parked in front of her favorite restaurant, Clam and Claw, or when the hostess showed them to the table in the front window where she and Edward always sat.

When the waitress arrived, Blossom took the liberty of ordering a glass of Champagne for Isabelle and a sparkling cider for herself.

"What're we celebrating?" Isabelle asked.

"Your resurrection," Blossom said with a straight face as she studied the menu.

The color drained from Isabelle's face. "My *resurrection*? Did I die? Was the ride in the Blossom Bus my trip to heaven?" she asked, taking in her surroundings. "Is Clam and Claw my eternity?"

Lowering her menu, Blossom set her gaze on Isabelle. "You're not dead, Izzy. I'm referring to your emergence from the past that's been holding you hostage for too long."

"Oh. That again." Isabelle lifted the menu to hide the tears welling in her eyes. She'd been an emotional wreck since she'd told Blossom about her mama and the pearl bracelet. With blurred vision, she ran down the menu items. As much as she loved peel-and-eat shrimp, she found them too messy to eat in public.

When the waitress returned with their drinks, Blossom once again ordered for them. "We'll have house salads, hush puppies, and peel-and-eat shrimp."

Isabelle waited until the waitress left. Leaning across the table, she whispered to Blossom, "You're either a mind reader, or Edward told you everything about me in great detail."

"I told you Edward did not send me here. You summoned me."

"That's the most preposterous thing I've ever heard."

"Believe what you will. As for the shrimp, I'm blessed with a keen perception, and I sensed you were longing for them."

Isabelle gave her a curious look. "What about the hush puppies? Since you know so much about me, you know I never splurge on carbs."

"I'm aware. But you *should* splurge on carbs. Life is short. Enjoy every minute."

Isabelle braced herself against the table. "Are you trying to tell me something, Blossom? Am I going to die soon?"

Blossom laughed. "I'm not privy to such information. My job

is to help you live whatever time you have left to the fullest." She held up her glass of sparkling cider. "To new beginnings."

Isabelle clinked her glass and took a sip, the bubbles tickling her nose. The Champagne was dry and crisp. She couldn't remember the last time she drank Champagne, the last time she had reason to celebrate. Her hopes soared as she realized she very much wanted a new beginning. But her hopes came crashing back down when she realized a new beginning was beyond her reach.

Blossom settled back in her chair. "Tell me about your relationship with Edward. How did you two meet?"

Isabelle inhaled an unsteady breath. "We met our senior year in college when his fraternity at the University of Georgia came to Lindenwood College for a mixer. We hit it off right away." She drained the rest of her Champagne and summoned the waitress for another.

"How much did you tell him about your background?"

Isabelle waited until the second glass of Champagne was in hand before answering. "I never told Edward the truth about my upbringing. I lied. I told him that my parents had died in a car accident when I was a young child and that my mean aunt, from whom I was estranged, had raised me. While he was suspicious of my story, I don't think he wanted to know the truth. When he suggested we elope, I packed my suitcase, and we ran off to the nearest justice of the peace. Our elopement didn't sit well with Edward's socialite mother, who had in mind for him to marry her best friend's daughter, the season's most sought-after debutante."

The waitress delivered their food, and Isabelle dug into the peel-and-eat shrimp, not caring how messy her fingers and lips got. They ate in silence until a pile of discarded shells was the only evidence left of the shrimp. When the waitress suggested Key lime pie for dessert, Isabelle shook her head and asked for decaf coffee.

Blossom held up two fingers. "Make that two, please." She folded her hands on the table. "Did you and Edward move back to Water's Edge after college?"

"Not immediately. At the time of our elopement, Edward had been accepted to law school at the University of South Carolina." Isabelle's features softened as she reflected on the early years of their marriage. "I supported us by working at the makeup counter at Tapp's Department Store. Those were the happiest times of my life." She stiffened. "Then he graduated, and we moved in with his parents at Magnolia Shores."

"How was that?" Blossom asked as she dumped spoonfuls of sugar into her coffee.

"Terrible. Edward's mother hated me. She made my life a living hell." Isabelle lifted a finger. "I'll say this much about Bethany. I learned a great deal from her about social etiquette and taking care of a fine home. I also learned how to be a snob."

"Being Edward's wife and Bethany's daughter-in-law secured my admission into the right social groups. But their friends merely tolerated me. I never truly belonged—even to this day."

Blossom planted her elbows on the table as she sipped her coffee from the mug. "Is that your perception or reality?"

"What do you mean?"

"You have a chip on your shoulder, Isabelle. Maybe you psyched yourself out. Is it possible your feelings of inferiority skewed your perception of reality?"

Here we go again with the chip-on-the-shoulder nonsense. "I'm not sure, honestly. I never let anyone get too close for fear they would discover the truth about my past."

twenty-five

. . .

Shelby sensed the kind of sisterly bond growing with Harper that she'd never experienced with Grace. After spending two hours selecting accessories for Izzy's house, Harper treated Shelby to lunch at The Nest. They talked about guys and careers and family. When Harper dropped her off around two o'clock, they made a date to install the chosen accessories after the bedroom floors had been refinished early next week.

Amazon had delivered their new computer while she was out with Harper. She wrestled the big box through the front door and across the foyer. When she came up for air in the living room, she was startled by the sight of Luke seated behind her desk.

"Geez, Luke!" She placed a hand on her pounding heart. "You scared me. What're you doing here?"

Ignoring her question, Luke came from behind the desk and took her in his arms. The feel of his body against hers made her ache with longing for the relationship they'd once shared.

He held her at arm's length. "You look amazing, Shelby. The Lowcountry agrees with you."

Shelby's face warmed. "Thank you. I love it here." As the words left her lips, she realized that not only did she love South Carolina, she felt at home here.

He dropped his hands from her arms. "What's going on around here? The place is crawling with workers. Are you renovating the house?"

"An unplanned renovation. A group of guests got out of hand last weekend and caused a lot of damage to the house. You didn't answer my question. What are you doing here?"

He raked his fingers through his dark hair. "I'm not sure, honestly. I missed you. I've been thinking a lot about you lately, and I needed to see you."

"What about Alexis?"

Again, he ignored her question. "Do you have any available rooms? Or are they all under construction?"

"Only the ones in the main house. You have your choice between the pool and garden houses."

"The pool house will be fine. If possible, I'll stay in the room I usually stay in." Luke was partial to the front corner room on the first floor nearest the pool.

Shelby should not have given him a choice. Now they would be the only two occupants of the pool house, an arrangement a little too close for her comfort. When he handed her his credit card, she told him to wait until he checked out to pay. "By then, I'll have the new computer working."

"Or maybe you'll comp me since I'm a family friend."

He stopped being a friend of her family when he broke up with her. "Sorry. No freebies allowed." Going behind the desk, she retrieved his room key from the board and handed it to him. "Here, you go. Room 101. I trust you can find your way."

He looked down at the key and back up at her. "Don't you have a bellman to help me with my luggage?"

"Silas is off today. We don't have any other guests at the moment. Can you handle your bags? Or would you like me to carry them for you?" she asked in a sarcastic tone with a sweet smile.

"Ha ha. I've got it. I have only one bag." He moved toward the front door. "Do you have to work? Or can we hang out by the pool?"

Installing the new computer could wait. Shelby was dying to spend time with him to discover why he was here. "I can spare a couple of hours."

"Cool. Do you have beer for sale?"

"Sorry. Breakfast is the only thing we provide. You're on your own for everything else."

"Ugh. All right, then. I'm going to my room to change. I'll see you in a few."

Shelby gave him ample time to get his bag out of the car before crossing the courtyard to her room. After trying on every bathing suit she owned, she decided on the modest one-piece that revealed just enough cleavage to get his attention. If he were here to win her back, he would have to work for it.

When she arrived, Luke was relaxing in a floating lounger, drinking a beer. "Where'd you get the beer?" she asked.

"From the kitchen refrigerator. Izzy won't mind. She loves me."

Shelby glared at him. "She *loved* you when we were dating. Not anymore."

"I'm not worried about Izzy. I'll have her eating out of my hand in no time. Get in! I'm saving you a seat," he said about the empty floating lounger beside him.

"Give me a minute. I need to put on some sunscreen." Shelby felt his eyes on her as she slowly covered her body in sunscreen. She plugged her phone into a portable speaker and selected their favorite playlist from Spotify. She was dipping her toe into the pool when she spotted Blossom walking Jolene in the garden. When she called out to the dog, Jolene sniffed her way over.

Shelby scooped up the dog and introduced Blossom to Luke.

Blossom smiled at him. "Nice to meet you, Luke."

Luke barely acknowledged her with a curt nod.

"Does Matt know about your visitor from home?" Blossom asked Shelby in a voice loud enough for Luke to hear.

"Troublemaker," she whispered to Blossom as she dropped the dog into her arms.

Blossom chuckled as she sauntered back to the garden.

"You didn't have to be so rude," Shelby said as she waded into the pool.

"Who is she anyway? And who is Matt?"

"Blossom is our summer guest. And Matt is a guy I've been seeing. We're not exclusive," Shelby said, unsure why she added the last part. Her relationship with Matt was none of Luke's business.

"Here." He removed a bottle of beer from the chair's cup holder. "I brought you a beer."

"No, thanks. I have to work later." Alcohol was a bad idea. She needed a clear head while she figured out what Luke wanted.

He popped the cap. "Good! All the more for me," he said, taking a long chug.

The music took them back in time, and they talked about their younger days in high school and college. Luke returned to the kitchen twice for more beer. Shelby wasn't worried. Izzy wouldn't miss the beer.

They'd been in the pool for over an hour when Luke asked, "Will you have dinner with me tonight at The Nest?"

Shelby smiled, remembering how much he loved the place. Having dinner with Luke was a bad idea, but Harper had mentioned that Savannah was performing tonight. And since she had no other way to get to town . . . "Sure, but only because Savannah is singing."

Luke appeared confused. "Who's Savannah?"

Shelby frowned but then remembered Luke hadn't been part of her life for over a year. "Uncle Pritchard got married last spring. Savannah is his new wife."

"Good for Pritchard."

Shelby noticed dark clouds building in from the west. "Looks like a storm is coming. We should go inside. I need to set up the computer anyway."

They slipped off the loungers and swam to the shallow end. Shelby was climbing the stairs ahead of Luke when he hooked an arm around her waist and pulled her back down. Spinning her around to face him, he covered her mouth with his. He tasted like beer and bad breath. She pushed him away. "Stop, Luke! What're you doing?"

Before he could answer, Shelby heard someone calling her name and turned to see Matt waving wildly at her from over by the kitchen. "There's lightning all around us. Get out of the water and come inside," he hollered over the sudden wind.

Shelby jumped out of the pool, stuffed her belongings in her beach bag, and darted to the kitchen, the first raindrops pelting her face.

Luke called out to her on his way to the pool house. "I'll see you at seven for dinner."

Matt opened the back door for her, and they went inside. "Who's that guy?"

"My ex, Luke. And before you ask, I don't know why he's here. He appeared out of the blue."

Matt cocked an eyebrow. "Come on, Shelby. You know why he's here. He just kissed you."

"And I pushed him away," she said, drying her face with a paper towel.

"But you're having dinner with him later."

"Because he loves The Nest." She held up a hand. "This is all very confusing for me, and I don't want to discuss it."

Matt appeared wounded. "I understand. I wanted to touch base with you before I leave for the day. The painters will be done with the upstairs tomorrow. If the floors get refinished on Friday as planned, we'll be out of your hair no later than Tuesday of next week."

"That's great news. Thanks for the update."

They walked together down the hall to the living room. "Will it be in your way if I set up the new computer?" she asked, gesturing at the computer box on the floor.

"Not at all. We'll drape plastic over it when we work in here. Would you like some help unpacking it?"

"Sure. That would be great."

Matt was electronically inclined, and they had the computer online in thirty minutes. He no longer seemed angry at her. He'd reverted to the genuine guy she'd first met.

When she walked him to the front door, he kissed her cheek. "Maybe I'll see you at The Nest later."

Shelby inwardly groaned. She finally had a chance to get Luke back. She didn't need Matt causing trouble. If she were honest with herself, the idea of seeing Matt tonight excited her more than going on a date with Luke.

twenty-six

. . .

Isabelle spent the rainy afternoon in the cottage, reflecting on the past. After all these years, the fog had finally cleared, and she was able to put her life into perspective. She'd been wrong about so much, and her mistakes had caused great heartache. But she had no idea how to go about making things right. Feeling the urge to confide in someone, she went out into the stormy evening in search of Blossom. She found the woman at the garden house, curled up on the daybed swing on the screened porch, reading a novel.

Isabelle plopped down in a rocking chair. "I'm ready to redeem my sins."

"I'm in the middle of something. Can't it wait?" Blossom held up an Ernest Hemingway novel.

The Old Man and the Sea cover brought back pleasant memories for Isabelle. "Hemingway was my husband's favorite."

"I know. He's mine as well. I've read all of his novels dozens of times. Hemingway was from my era. We met once in Key West through mutual friends. It was in the late twenties, just after he moved back from Paris."

Isabelle's jaw hit the floor. "You're lying."

Blossom stiffened. "I resent that. I was not a liar in life, and I'm certainly not one in death." She threw her legs over the side of the swing and smoothed out her mussed hair. "Now what is so urgent you need to talk to me about?"

"I'm ready to tell you what happened with Pritchard and Savannah."

Blossom cast a glance heavenward. "Praise, Lord. At long last." She stood and stretched. "I'll order us a pizza. We'll need nourishment for such a confession."

Isabelle rolled her eyes. "How can you think about food at a time like this? And who's going to deliver pizza way out here?"

"Sal's will." They heard a car with a loud exhaust pipe in the courtyard, followed by the ringing of the garden house doorbell. "That would be them now," Blossom said and disappeared inside.

Isabelle didn't ask about the immediate delivery. She was growing accustomed to Blossom's magic tricks.

A minute later, Blossom returned with a large veggie pizza, paper plates, and napkins, and they sat down at the small table. She said the blessing and helped herself to a slice of pizza. "You may begin whenever you're ready."

Isabelle inhaled an unsteady breath. "I need to say this fast in order to get it out. Pritchard and Savannah dated in high school. She was a year younger than he was. She got pregnant the summer before he left for his freshman year at Alabama. They were determined to keep the baby, but I was adamantly opposed to them getting married."

Poised to bite, Blossom looked at Isabelle over the top of her pizza slice. "Why would you be opposed? Savannah seems like a perfectly lovely person."

"She's okay, I guess. Her ancestor was one of the town's founding fathers. The was named after him." Isabelle's eyes traveled to the Merriweather Bridge connecting downtown to Sandy Island. Only a few of the bridge's lights were visible through the fog and mist. "But Savannah's mother had a terrible reputation as the town drunk, and I didn't want my son associated with that family. When I heard Pritchard and

Savannah were planning to elope, I took matters into my own hands."

Blossom groaned. "I'm almost afraid to ask what you did."

Isabelle squirmed in her chair. Despite the ceiling fan twirling overhead, she was sweating profusely. Once she confessed, there was no turning back. She snatched up a napkin and blotted the beads of sweat from her forehead. "I paid Eileen a visit. I told her I'd make Savannah's life miserable if she married my son. We conspired to make Savannah give the baby up for adoption. Only Eileen took things too far."

"How so?"

Isabelle shredded the napkin on the table in front of her. "The weather played in Eileen's favor. Savannah went into labor during an ice storm, and she delivered the baby at home. After the storm cleared, Eileen told everyone Savannah had willingly given the baby up for adoption and ran away in disgrace. Savannah took the truth with her to Washington State, where she lived for the next thirty years."

Blossom dropped her gnawed pizza crust on the plate. "When did she return to Water's Edge?"

"Last summer. Her mother had passed away, and she came home to visit her siblings. She brought the truth of what happened to her baby with her. Eileen tricked Savannah into signing adoption papers while she was in labor. And she hid the baby in their guesthouse until the adoptive parents came for her."

Blossom's mouth fell open. "Are you saying she *kidnapped* the baby?"

Isabelle nodded solemnly.

Blossom shook her head as though struggling to comprehend. "So, Eileen had previously arranged for the adoption? She'd planned all along to steal her own daughter's baby."

Unable to meet Blossom's gaze, Isabelle stared down at her empty plate. "Seems that way."

"Poor Savannah. I can't imagine the agony she must have suffered."

"What about Pritchard? He was devastated. He tried to find happiness. He even married a girl I wholeheartedly approved of. But it didn't last. His heart has always belonged to Savannah."

"How do you feel knowing you caused such heartache? Not only did you prevent Savannah and Pritchard from being together, but you also kept them from parenting their only child."

Blossom's disapproving tone brought tears to her eyes. "I may have initiated the plan, but the rest was on Eileen."

"But you got what you wanted nonetheless."

"What I *thought* I wanted at the time." Grabbing another napkin, Isabelle dried her eyes and blew her nose.

"How did Pritchard and Savannah find Harper?"

Isabelle left the table and stood at the screen door, watching lightning crack the night sky. "Harper's adoptive parents never told her she was adopted. When the mother passed away, Harper found documents that made her suspicious. Those documents led her to Water's Edge. She joined a genetic website where she was matched with Pritchard, who had been searching for his daughter for years."

Blossom joined her at the door. "Only it's not history. It's the present and the future if you don't do something about it. The animosity you feel toward Savannah and Harper, your own grandchild, is evident to everyone around you. This is about more than you saying you're sorry, isn't it?"

Isabelle hesitated.

Blossom pointed at the ceiling. "We're not alone, Isabelle. If you truly want redemption, you must tell the truth."

"Yes! Darn it. I want my son back. We had a special bond. He has always been my rock, especially during Edward's illness. Now I have to share him with Savannah and Harper." The confession took her breath away. "What a selfish, vindictive person I am."

Blossom let out a humph. "You won't get an argument from me about that. But there's enough room in Pritchard's heart for you, Savannah, and Harper."

Isabelle wrung her hands together. "Pritchard is an honorable man like his father. He takes his obligation to his mother seriously. But his feelings for me changed when he learned I had a role in the mess with Savannah and the baby. He hates me. I can see it in his eyes."

"He doesn't hate you, Isabelle. An apology is a start toward mending that rift."

"You make it sound so easy."

"It's not hard when you mean it." She placed a hand on Isabelle's shoulder. "You haven't lost your son, Izzy. You've gained a wonderful daughter-in-law and grandchild. And soon, you'll have a grandson-in-law. The only person you're hurting by holding on to your animosity is yourself."

twenty-seven

. . .

Shelby finished caking makeup on over her freckles and stood back to admire her reflection in the mirror. She'd spent an hour straightening her wild hair and chosen a blue-and-white strapless dress with a ruffled skirt that danced around her thighs. Because her black raincoat ruined her look, she located her yellow umbrella and dashed in the driving rain to the main house to meet Luke, who was waiting for her in the foyer.

"You look amazing," he said, kissing her cheek.

"Thanks. You don't look so bad yourself." Shelby thought he looked hot in stone-colored trousers that hugged his butt and a lavender T-shirt that made his chocolate-brown eyes pop. His cologne, a mixture of patchouli and sandalwood, was a new scent for him. Had Alexis chosen it for him?

"Say cheese!" Holding up her phone, she snapped a selfie of them and admired the photograph. They made for a handsome couple.

Luke pointed at her phone. "You can't post that to social media."

Irritation crawled across her skin. "Why not? Because you don't want Alexis to see?"

"Let's just go," he said, opening the door to reveal his rental car parked in front of the house, its engine idling.

They didn't talk much on the way to town. The rain was coming down in torrents, and Luke was focused on the road. Despite the nasty weather, the tavern's parking lot was full, but they arrived just as a car was vacating a spot near the front of the building.

The mood inside The Nest was lively. Nearly every table and seat at the bar was occupied, and a line was waiting at the hostess stand. Fortunately, Savannah had confirmed a reservation for them, and when Shelby provided her name, the hostess showed them to a prime booth near the dance floor.

They'd only been seated a minute when Savannah stopped by their table. Shelby introduced Luke as her friend from home, and Savannah extended her hand. "Welcome, Luke. How long are you in town for?"

"I'm not sure." He winked at Shelby. "As long as Shelby will tolerate me."

A flush crept up Shelby's neck as she looked at her aunt. "Thanks for getting us the reservation."

"Any time. And you're right. This place is hopping tonight."

Shelby gestured at the stage set for the upcoming performance. "I hear you're the star attraction."

"I am. I hope you'll stick around for the performance. I have a little surprise in store for the audience."

Shelby's face lit up. "Ooh. I can't wait."

Savannah excused herself, and their waitress arrived. Luke glanced at the menu before placing their order—a beer for him, a margarita for Shelby, and a plate of nachos to start. Shelby had outgrown her fondness for margaritas since they had broken up, but she didn't want to hurt his feelings.

When their drinks arrived, Luke monopolized the conversation by discussing his work. Money management was over Shelby's head, and she soon grew bored. He was still babbling on about his newest wealthy client when their favorite song, "Dancing in the Moonlight," came on the jukebox.

Shelby jumped to her feet. "Come on, let's dance."

Luke groaned. "Do we have to?"

"Yes! We have to. This is our song," she said, pulling him to his feet and leading him onto the dance floor.

Shelby and Luke had learned to dance at cotillion in middle school, one of the many firsts they'd experienced together. Luke was an excellent dancer, but tonight, he seemed bored as he swung her around with one arm. She was disappointed he didn't twirl her into a pretzel or dip her to the floor.

"Dancing in the Moonlight" ended, and a slow song came on the jukebox. Luke started to pull her into his arms when someone tapped her on her shoulder. Craning her neck, she was surprised to see Matt standing behind her.

He flashed that dazzling, dimpled smile at her. "May I have this dance?"

Luke's dark eyes shot daggers at him. "She's with me, bro."

Shelby smiled at Luke to placate him. "It's okay. One dance won't hurt." She saw no harm in making Luke jealous when he'd been flaunting his relationship with Alexis in Shelby's face for over a year.

Turning her back on Luke, Shelby stepped into Matt's arms. When he held her close, she felt a strong connection, a powerful sense of belonging.

He smiled softly at her as they moved slowly around the dance floor. "Why'd you cover up your freckles?"

"Why do you think? They're hideous."

Matt frowned. "Says who? Luke?"

She shook her head. Admitting that Luke hated her freckles felt like a betrayal.

Matt thumbed her cheek. "Your freckles lend a unique charm to your beautiful face." He twirled a strand of her silky hair around his finger. "And I like your hair better when it's wild and free. It brings out the vixen in you."

She sensed Luke watching them but didn't dare look his way. She brushed Matt's hand away from her hair. "A vixen?"

"You underestimate your beauty, Shelby. Your natural allure lights up a room. Why are you covering that girl up tonight?"

"Because I'm trying to win Luke back," Shelby admitted.

Matt's body tensed. "Why? Because he earns a big fat salary?"

"Among other reasons. Luke has always been my person. I don't know how to be me without him."

Matt dropped his arms from around her. "You're wrong, Shelby. You don't know how to be you when you're *with* him," he said, leaving her alone on the dance floor.

Pritchard watched his daughter watching Shelby and Matt on the dance floor. Even after nearly a year, he could hardly believe he had found his daughter and that she was such a phenomenal young woman.

"They make a nice couple, don't you think?" Harper said with a dreamy expression.

Savannah followed her gaze. "They do. But her friend from Texas doesn't appear too happy about sharing her with Matt."

Harper tensed. "What friend from Texas? Where?"

"Luke, he's the angry-looking guy seated alone in a booth on the other side of the dance floor," Savannah explained. "She introduced me when I stopped by their table."

Harper searched the crowd, her eyes landing on Luke. "He's attractive. You realize he's her old boyfriend, the guy who broke her heart. He's engaged to someone else." Lines appeared on her forehead. "I'm confused. What's he doing here? Is Shelby on a date with Luke? And why is she dancing with Matt? I know they've been seeing each other."

Pritchard chuckled. "Who knows? But Shelby's a beautiful girl. If she's not careful, she's liable to start a riot in here."

As the song came to an end, Matt suddenly pushed Shelby

away and walked off the dance floor. Harper brought her fingers to her lips. "Uh-oh. Looks like trouble in Paradise."

Savannah pressed her lips thin. "Mm-mm. I wonder what that's about."

"When is Cody getting here?" Pritchard asked, drawing Harper's attention away from her cousin.

"He gets off work at nine. He should be here soon."

Savannah glanced at the clock above the bar. "I didn't realize it was so late. It's almost time for me to go on." She locked eyes with Pritchard. "But before I go, Pritchard wants to discuss something with you."

Harper flashed Pritchard a smile. "Oh, yeah? What? Are you buying me a new car?"

Pritchard laughed. He was constantly buying her expensive trinkets to make up for all the gifts he missed giving her for birthdays, Christmases, and graduations. "Not quite. I'm building you a hotel."

Harper's expression turned serious. "What?"

Pritchard laced his fingers together on the table. "Izzy found one of your grandfather's diaries that outlines his plans for the future of Magnolia Shores. Turns out he had a lot more in mind than a bed and breakfast. He wanted to construct a new building that offered additional guest rooms, a cafe, a spa, a fitness center, and a cocktail lounge. We have the land, and he left us the money. The resort will be called Magnolia Shores."

"Are we doing this?" Harper asked, her blue eyes wide.

"I think so. Ashton is working on the plans. If we break ground in early September, she's confident we'll finish in time for next summer."

"So fast? Is that even possible?" Harper looked from Pritchard to Savannah.

"Will seems to think so," Savannah said. "He's committed to hiring the resources to make it happen."

Pritchard grinned. "And we want you to design the interior."

Harper's butt came out of the chair. "Yippee. I accept."

Pritchard's smile faded. "There's one hurdle we must tackle before we can proceed. Izzy."

Harper settled back in her chair. "Why is Izzy a hurdle?"

"Because she can't handle a bed and breakfast. There's no way she'll be able to manage a resort."

"Are you firing Izzy?" Harper asked.

"Not at all. I'm planning to negotiate with her. I'm going to see her tomorrow morning," he said, holding up his hands to show his crossed fingers.

Harper sipped her wine. "Who will run this resort if not Izzy? Shelby certainly doesn't have the experience."

"No, but she's doing an excellent job. I will find an important role for her." He rested an arm on the back of his wife's chair. "Savannah and I will run the resort together. We're both making midlife career changes."

Harper punched the air. "This is so awesome. Congratulations! This means you'll no longer have to spend so much time in Nashville."

Pritchard winked at her. "That's the idea."

Savannah smiled lovingly at Pritchard. "Your father has in mind to make Magnolia Shores the most exclusive five-star boutique resort on the East Coast."

Pritchard reached for Harper's hand. "I'm doing this for the family, Harper. I'm hoping it will finally bring us back together. Out of fairness, I'll offer Kate a chance to be part of the expansion. If she declines, I'll buy her out."

"Do you think she'll be interested?" Harper asked.

Pritchard shook his head. "Unfortunately, no. I'd love for my sister to move back to Water's Edge. But her life is in Texas. We'll see how things shake out. You have your own business now. But one day, if you're interested, I hope you'll join us in running it."

Harper shrugged, her shoulders nearly touching her ears. "Who knows? Maybe one day, I will."

Savannah pushed back from the table. "Showtime! The crowd is getting restless. Wish me luck."

Prichard leaned over and kissed her lips. "Break a leg, sweetheart."

Making her way to the stage, Savannah spent a moment tuning her guitar before welcoming the audience to The Nest. When the cheers died, she opened her act with one of her older songs, a heartbreaking ballad about a young runaway. Although he'd heard the song dozens of times, the lyrics moved Pritchard, and he reached for a napkin to dry his eyes.

When the song ended, Savannah said into the microphone, "I have a surprise for y'all tonight. My lovely daughter, Harper, will join me in singing a duet. "A Journey to Joy" is a new song I wrote about my recent good fortune in reuniting with my past love and finding my long-lost child. Let's hear a round of applause for Harper Boone."

The crowd erupted.

Harper looked at Pritchard with a panic-stricken face. "Did you know she was going to do this?"

Pritchard chuckled. "Nope. But nothing Savannah does surprises me."

"I can't believe she shanghaied me."

"You know this song well. I've heard you and Savannah practicing it in her studio. You've got this, sweetheart." Pritchard noticed Cody standing by the door. "Cody is here. Just in time for your performance."

Harper and Cody locked eyes, and he gave her a thumbs-up for encouragement. "Okay. Here goes nothing," she said and joined her mother on stage.

Pritchard's heart burst with pride as he listened to the loves of his life sing. As a talent agent, he'd represented some of the most successful professional singers in the country music industry. But none could compare with either Harper or Savannah.

Shelby hummed Savannah's song during the drive home. "Savannah and Harper have crazy vocals, don't you think?" she said to Luke. "Their performance blew me away."

Luke hunched a shoulder. "They were all right, I guess," he grumbled, apparently still sulking about her dancing with Matt.

The rain had finally let up, and when they arrived back at Magnolia Shores, Luke suggested a nightcap. "I drank all the beer earlier," he admitted. "Is there any booze around here?"

"There's probably some brandy in my grandfather's study." She punched in the code to unlock the front door and turned on the lights in the foyer. They navigated through a maze of paint cans, ladders, and construction debris in the living room to reach Edward's study. She was examining the few remaining liquor bottles that hadn't been destroyed when Luke spun her around and into his arms. Shelby had dreamed of this moment since they broke up, but the kiss wasn't what she remembered. She was as turned off by him now as she had been when he tried to kiss her at the pool earlier. Had they lost their chemistry? Would their passion return once they were officially back together?

When the kiss ended, Shelby touched her finger to his lips. "What about Alexis? Did you break off your engagement?"

"Let's not talk about Alexis." Luke pressed his body to hers, groping at her bottom.

Shelby pushed him away. She would not sleep with him until she got a straight answer about Alexis. She crossed the room to the French doors. The sky had cleared, and the moon shone bright, its rays sparkling off the inky ocean. "Wow! Look at the moon. Let's go outside."

"Not without the booze," Luke said, grabbing a bottle of Maker's Mark from her grandfather's stash.

He followed her across the terrace, and she sensed him behind her when she stopped at the edge of the dunes. She heard him unscrew the lid and chug the bourbon. He ran a finger down her neck and whispered, his breath hot near her ear, "When are you coming home, Shelby? Does your summer job end after Labor Day, or are you staying through September?"

"This isn't a summer job, Luke. I'm staying in the Lowcountry indefinitely." Drawing in a deep breath, she turned to face him. Whether she was ready or not, she needed to hear the truth. "Why are you here, Luke?"

"Isn't it obvious? I missed you, Shelby. I wanted to see you."

"Tell me you've broken up with Alexis, and you want me back in your life, and I'll fly home with you tomorrow."

"Come on, Shelby. Don't be like this. We used to be so good together."

When he tried to grab her boob, she smacked his hand away. "Don't you dare touch me."

Dropping the liquor bottle in the sand, he came after her, holding her tight and covering her mouth with his. She squirmed, but when she was unable to free herself of his grip, she kneed his crotch. He let out a yelp and dropped to the ground on his knees.

"Why'd you do that?" he croaked, writhing on the ground.

"Because you forced yourself on me. Are you broken up with Alexis or not?" Even though she suspected the truth, she needed to hear it from him.

He rolled onto his knees, his hands covering his crotch. "Alexis has a lot to offer. Her father is a billionaire several times over. I'd be a fool to give that up. But I still want you in my life, Shelby."

His words stung, and the implications rocked her to the core. Shelby wasn't good enough for him. Her family didn't have enough money or the right social connections. "You want me in your life as what, your side piece? Lurking in the shadows while you're parading Alexis around, buying her big houses and expensive jewelry?"

"It won't be like that. We'll be together as much as possible."

"What about the family we always dreamed of having? My children will be illegitimate, but Alexis's will bear your name."

"I'll be fair to you, Shelby. I promise I'll take care of you. I'll set you up in a swanky apartment, and later, I'll buy you a house."

Shelby's mouth fell open. "Are you out of your mind? I refuse to be your dirty little secret." She shoved him hard, and he fell over into the sand. "Get out of my life and off my grandmother's property."

"But it's late, and I've been drinking," he said, scrambling to his feet.

"Fine. Stay the night." She stormed off, calling over her shoulder, "But I want you out of here first thing in the morning."

twenty-eight

. . .

Isabelle fell asleep while looking at her family's photo albums and dreamed of happier days before she sabotaged her son's elopement with his pregnant girlfriend. Even though she never cared much for Savannah, she was willing to try to make their relationship work for the sake of her family. Truth be told, she thought her granddaughter, Harper, was an intriguing young woman—poised and striking, the apple of her father's eye. But Harper would be a difficult sell. Although she was never rude to Isabelle's face—she possessed better manners than that— Harper wore her heart on her sleeve, and her contempt for Isabelle was obvious.

Isabelle threw back the covers. She had her work cut out for her, and she might as well get started. She dressed in navy slacks and a crisp white blouse and left the cottage for the main house. She was crossing the courtyard when a small black sedan nearly ran her over. She stepped out of the way, her hand pressed against her pounding heart. Was it her imagination? Or was that Luke behind the wheel?

She found Shelby in the kitchen, her back to the room as she counted coffee grounds into the coffee maker. "My eyesight isn't what it used to be, but I'm pretty sure I just saw Luke speeding away in a black sedan."

Shelby, her eyes swollen and bloodshot from crying, was filling the coffee maker. Turning to face Isabelle, she said, "Your vision is fine, Izzy. Luke came for a visit, and I thought he was here to win me back. It turns out he hadn't broken up with his fiancée like I had hoped. He merely wanted some action on the side."

Isabelle stiffened. "I never liked that boy."

Shelby's lips parted in a sad smile. "You're lying. You loved him when we were dating. But he's changed. He's not the same person I fell in love with."

Sensing her granddaughter needed to talk, Isabelle gestured at the table. "Sit down and tell me about it."

Fresh tears filled Shelby's eyes. "I can't. It hurts too much," she sobbed and burst out the back door.

Izzy's chest tightened. Was she having a heart attack? Or was she experiencing her granddaughter's pain? She stared at the door, wondering if she should go after Shelby, then decided to let her calm down before trying again later.

She was filling a mug with coffee when Blossom bustled in with Jolene on her heels. "Good morning! You're looking awfully perky this morning."

"I feel much better after my confession last night. I'm ready to start making amends." She lifted her mug. "As soon as I finish my coffee, I'm going to see my son."

"Pritchard may have saved you a trip," Blossom said with a playful smirk.

"What do you mean?"

"I heard his car pull up out front."

Footfalls in the hallway preceded Pritchard's appearance in the kitchen. He gave Isabelle a perfunctory peck on the cheek. "Morning, ladies. Things are looking good around here. Will says we'll be ready to open midweek as planned."

Isabelle uttered an unenthusiastic "Woo-hoo."

Pritchard helped himself to some coffee. "Mother, if you have a minute, I need to talk to you about something important."

Isabelle glanced uncertainly at Blossom, who mouthed, "You can do this."

She got up from the table. "Your timing is excellent, son. There's an urgent matter I'd like to discuss with you as well."

Pritchard motioned Isabelle to the back door. "Shall we? I want to show you something outside."

The air was fresh and clear after yesterday's rain, and Isabelle filled her lungs with deep breaths as they headed toward the main road. "Where are we going?" she asked.

"You'll see." About a hundred yards from the house, Pritchard stopped walking and faced the ocean. Reaching behind him, he tugged Edward's journal from his back waistband. "I've given Dad's expansion plan considerable thought, and I believe we should move forward."

Isabelle's spirits deflated. She had hoped he'd forgotten about the journal. "That's the most ridiculous thing that's ever come out of your mouth, Pritchard."

He handed Isabelle the journal. "Dad didn't think it was so ridiculous. Did you even read this? He describes in great detail his vision for Magnolia Shores."

"Yes, I read it, and I'm adamantly opposed. I can't manage a simple B&B, let alone a full-size resort. How can you even consider such a thing after those crazed women destroyed our home?"

"And that would never have happened if we'd had proper security. We'll always be treading water as a bed and breakfast. Expanding will enable us to hire a full staff and better cater to our guests' needs."

"You don't have the authority to make this decision, Pritchard."

"Which is why I'm talking to you, Mother."

Isabelle recognized her son's determination in his set jaw. He'd already made his decision and would find a way to make it happen, with or without her approval. She stared down at the leather journal in her hands. She made a mistake in giving him the journal. "Where would I live?"

"You would continue living in the cottage until after the new building is complete. Then you can move back into the house. We'll use some of the bedrooms for overflow, but you'll have your suite all to yourself."

Isabelle tossed up her hands. "Great! So I can encounter strangers in the hallway when I go to the kitchen for milk in my pajamas."

"It won't be all the time, Mother, only when the other buildings are filled. I like the name Dad chose, The Sanctuary at Magnolia Shores, don't you?"

She glared at him. "Not particularly. I don't have a problem with just plain Magnolia Shores. Who's going to oversee this venture? I'm seventy-five years old, too old for a construction project of that magnitude."

Pritchard hesitated as though preparing himself to deliver news she wouldn't like. "Savannah and I will take over managing the business."

"Savannah?" Isabelle's anger surged at the mention of her daughter-in-law. "But you both have full-time jobs, and you love your music career."

"I've decided to take an early retirement. Now that I have a wife and daughter, I resent the time I'm away from them when I'm in Nashville." His unspoken words hung in the air between them—the years he missed being with Savannah and Harper because of Isabelle.

"I'm tired of everyone controlling my life. First your father and now you." Isabelle realized her mistake too late. She had controlled Pritchard's life by interfering with his elopement.

"I'm not trying to control your life, Mother. I'm trying to make it better. You have pushed back on this since the beginning. You even contested Dad's will, for crying out loud. I thought you'd be happy to turn the business over to someone else to run.

You're off the hook. You can go back to living your life as normal."

Off the hook means he no longer needs me, Isabelle thought. *I'm now worthless to my family.* She thrust the journal at him. "Do whatever you want with the place. Just leave me in peace to live out my last days." Spinning on her heels, she stormed off across the courtyard to her cottage.

He called after her. "Wait, Mother! Did you have something you wanted to talk to me about?"

"It can wait," she said with a dismissive wave of her hand.

Pritchard considered going after his mother but decided they both needed to cool off. Speeding home, he found Savannah returning from her morning run on the beach.

She followed him into the home office they shared. "How'd it go with Isabelle?"

"As I expected. She's being completely unreasonable," Pritchard said as he searched his desk drawer for his copy of his father's will. Thumbing through the pages, he continued, "Dad's will says I can take over if Mother opts out of running the bed and breakfast. There are no stipulations if she fails at her job or refuses to expand."

"What're you saying?" Savannah asked, mopping sweat from her face with a hand towel.

Pritchard dropped the sheaf of papers on his desk and leaned back in his chair. "Dad was extremely thorough. I'd be willing to bet he left out these provisions on purpose. I either convince my mother to go along with the expansion or take her to court, which Dad knows I would never do."

"Are you sure about that, Pritch? You're being presumptuous where your father is concerned."

"Because I knew my dad. He thought of everything, and he was a brilliant negotiator. He predicted this might happen. He put us in this situation so we have to work together. This is his way of getting our family to settle our differences."

Savannah's olive eyes grew wide. "That's a tall order."

Pritchard tugged his phone out of his pocket. "I need to call my sister."

"I'll give you some privacy." Savannah kissed the top of his head. "Good luck. Let me know what Kate says. I'm going to shower and head off to work."

Pritchard got up from the desk and walked with her out of the office. "Have a good day, sweetheart."

He grabbed coffee from the kitchen and went outside to the screen porch. Before making his call, he paused to breathe in the salty air and look out over the ocean, sparkling blue under a periwinkle sky and bright sunshine.

His sister answered on the first ring in an alarmed tone, "Pritchard! What's wrong? Is Shelby okay?"

"Yes, of course, Kate. Calm down."

She let out an audible sigh. "I'm sorry. You never call, and I haven't heard from Shelby since she arrived. Even Mom has been avoiding me. I've been terrified something bad had happened."

"You have nothing to worry about. Shelby is a hard worker, and she's doing an excellent job."

Kate let out an audible gasp. "Are we talking about the same Shelby? My daughter, strawberry-blonde with a face full of freckles?"

"Ha ha. Yes. She's doing great. Although we had a bit of a mishap last weekend."

Pritchard settled back on the bench swing as he filled his sister in on the weekend with the bachelorettes, the discovery of his father's journal with his expansion plans, and Pritchard's argument with Isabelle that morning.

Kate let out a low whistle. "Whoa, Pritch. That's a lot to take in. Sounds like Mom may be in over her head."

"I don't blame Izzy for being upset. Dad upended her life. But the more I think about it, the more I'm certain he did this on purpose, to bring our family back together. I realize you have a busy life in Texas, and you're planning Grace's wedding, but I would love for you to help manage the resort. Is there any chance Randall would consider an early retirement?"

Silence filled the line.

"Kate? Hello. Are you still there?"

"I'm here. Things haven't been great between Randall and me for a long time. With Shelby out of the house, we no longer have a reason to pretend. I've been homesick for the Lowcountry for years. Admittedly, I was jealous when I sent Shelby down there to work. Maybe a midlife change is just what I need."

"I'm sorry about your marital problems, kiddo, but I'm thrilled about the possibility of you moving back. We could rock this venture, Kate."

"Slow down, bro. You're getting way ahead of yourself. I have a lot to consider. Grace's wedding is at the top of the list. Let me look at my schedule. Maybe I can get away for a short visit sometime soon. I want to set my eyes on my daughter anyway, to see for myself that she's okay."

"That would be great. We can talk more about the expansion."

Kate chuckled. "And maybe I can talk some sense into Mom for you."

"You were always better at that than me." Pritchard put the call on speaker while he looked at his calendar. "I'm back and forth to Nashville during the next month. Text me some dates. I want to make certain I'm here when you come."

"Will do," Kate said. "Give my daughter a hug for me."

Pritchard remained on the porch long after he'd ended the call with his sister. He hadn't realized until now how much he relished the idea of running a resort with his family.

twenty-nine

. . .

Shelby collapsed in the hammock after a long run on the beach. Exhausted from a restless night spent crying over Luke, she quickly fell into a deep sleep. The sun was high in the sky when she woke to Jolene's barking and Blossom staring down at her. Blossom picked up the dog, dropped her in Shelby's lap, and sank into the hammock beside her. Her added weight made the hammock bounce, sending Shelby and the dog tumbling onto Blossom.

Blossom laughed out loud as she pushed them off of her. "I'm sorry to disturb you, but you looked so comfortable, I couldn't resist joining you."

Shelby's chin quivered as fresh tears threatened. "No worries. I'm happy for the company."

"Uh-oh. Why the long face?"

"Things didn't go well with Luke," Shelby said, swiping at her tears. "He just wanted to have sex with me. He never planned to break up with Alexis."

Blossom pulled a tissue from her pocket and handed it to her. "I say good riddance to him."

Shelby buried her face in Blossom's bosom. "I'm tired of crying. I've been crying all night. But I can't seem to stop."

"Why *are* you crying? Is it because you lost Luke? Or because he wounded your pride?"

"Good question." Shelby rolled onto her back with the dog on her chest, licking at the salty tears on her face. "We kissed a few times, but the chemistry wasn't there. Maybe I am finally over him."

"Then why the tears?"

Shelby shifted the dog to Blossom's arms as she struggled to sit up. "Because the jerk wanted me to be his side piece. He even offered to set me up in an apartment. I'm the runner-up because my father isn't a billionaire like Alexis's. To make matters worse, I treated Matt the same way when I discovered he's a carpenter."

Hoisting herself out of the hammock, Shelby went to the pool and sat on the edge with her feet in the water. She stared at the dark blob of her reflection, unable to make out her head and torso. For once in her life, she couldn't see her freckles.

Blossom came to stand beside her, hiking up her maxi dress and easing her body down beside Shelby. "Penny for your thoughts."

"Can you wave your magic wand and make my freckles disappear?" Shelby asked.

"Aww, baby girl." Blossom ran a finger down her cheek. "Were you teased about your freckles as a child?"

Shelby bobbed her head. "Mercilessly. To this day, my friends still call me Polka Dotty. You have to admit, I have an abnormal amount of them."

"I rather like your freckles. They add a certain wholesome beauty to your face." Blossom pulled a handheld mirror out of her pocket. "Is this the look you're going for?" she asked, holding the mirror out to Shelby.

Shelby looked suspiciously at the mirror. "Do you always walk around with mirrors in your pockets?"

"They come in handy sometimes. Go ahead. The mirror won't bite," Blossom said, placing the mirror in Shelby's hand.

Shelby held the mirror in front of her face. Her skin was

flawless, the cameo complexion she'd dreamed of her entire life. Her image freaked her out, and a chill traveled down her spine. Without the freckles, she was a stranger, even to herself.

"I guess I'll keep the freckles," she said, returning the mirror to Blossom.

"Altering your appearance won't change who you are on the inside, Shelby."

"That's the problem. I don't know who I am on the inside." She lay back on the pool deck and looked at the clear blue sky. "Luke and I had been together for so long that losing him was like cutting off my right arm. But I'm done mourning the loss of that relationship, and I'm ready to move on. But I don't know how or where. I'm definitely not going back to Texas, but I'm not sure I want to stay at Magnolia Shores either. I'm considering asking my mom to help me financially until I can find a job in Charleston." When the dog tried to lick her face again, Shelby gently pushed her away.

Blossom picked up Jolene and cradled her like a baby. "I got the impression you loved it here."

"I do! But this so-called bed and breakfast is a sinking ship. Izzy doesn't have a clue what she's doing, and the tension between us isn't healthy for either of us."

"Is this friction between you something new?"

Shelby rolled onto her belly and rested her cheek on her folded arms. "She was always just my grandmother, never overly affectionate but fun to hang out with sometimes. I learned so much from her about Magnolia Shores' natural habitat. She's the reason I love it here so much. Who knows? Maybe I'm seeing the real Izzy through my adult eyes."

"I don't think what you've seen of her recently is the real Izzy. She's going through a lot right now. As are you. If you tried, you two could work past your differences."

"Don't hold your breath. I don't like being an adult. Can you make me time travel back to my childhood?"

"I'm sorry, baby girl. I don't have that kind of power. Is that really what you want anyway? To relive your breakup with Luke all over again?"

"No! Please! I can never go through that again."

Isabelle was in the kitchen polishing silver when Blossom came through the back door.

"What're you doing?" she asked, filling a bowl of water for Jolene.

"What does it look like I'm doing?" Isabelle snapped.

"Doesn't your housekeeping staff polish your silver?"

"Hilda and Pearl are preparing the garden and pool houses for the upcoming weekend. Besides, I rather like the mindlessness of the task," Isabelle said, using elbow grease to remove the last of the dried polish.

Blossom chuckled. "If you're not careful, you'll polish the silver plate right off that candlestick."

"For your information, this *candelabra* is sterling silver. It is one of Edward's family's many heirloom pieces."

"I stand corrected." Blossom removed a pitcher from the refrigerator and poured herself a glass of sweet tea. "Based on your foul mood, I assume your apology didn't go well."

"I didn't get a chance to apologize. Pritchard was too busy discussing his expansion plans for The Sanctuary at Magnolia Shores. It's a ridiculous name. This place is anything but a sanctuary."

"I rather like the name," Blossom said.

Isabelle set down the candelabra. "Did you really find Edward's journal in his study? Or did you somehow fabricate it?"

Blossom held her head high, appearing genuinely incensed. "I beg your pardon. I would lose my wings if I did something so dishonest and underhanded. Like I told you, it was front and center on his desk."

"I must have overlooked it. I haven't been thinking clearly

since his death. Maybe my grief affected my eyesight." Isabelle went back to polishing silver. "Pritchard and I had a terrible argument. The bed and breakfast was a stretch for me, but this so-called Sanctuary is over the top. I'm a misfit in my own life. I don't even know where to lay my head at night." When Blossom didn't respond, Isabelle glanced over at her. She was tugging at her chin and staring into her tea. "What're you thinking, Blossom?"

"I'm wondering if you like soft-shelled crabs."

Isabelle frowned. "They're one of my favorites. But why are you thinking about soft-shelled crabs when my life is falling apart?"

"Because I'm going to cook us up a mess of them tonight." Blossom dumped her tea down the drain and placed her glass in the dishwasher. "I'll see you at seven o'clock sharp. And don't be late." She scooped up her dog and scurried out of the kitchen. Five minutes later, Isabelle heard Blossom's heaven mobile leave the courtyard.

thirty

. . .

When Blossom invited her to dinner, Shelby wasn't expecting her grandmother to join them. The mysteriously magical woman had been of great comfort to her lately, and she didn't want to have to share her with Izzy.

Based on the way she jerked the chair out from under the table, Izzy wasn't thrilled about eating with Shelby either.

"Where's Blossom?" Isabelle asked, glaring at Shelby over the table set with candles, blue-checked linens, white basketweave china, and an arrangement of blue hydrangeas.

Before Shelby could answer, Blossom emerged from the kitchen, calling out, "Here I am." She was dressed in chef's attire and carrying an ice bucket. She positioned the ice bucket near the table and popped the cork on a bottle of expensive Champagne.

"What're we celebrating?" Izzy asked.

"I'm glad you asked. Listen carefully as I outline your challenge for the evening," Blossom said as she poured a small splash of the golden liquid into each of their glasses. "To drink the Champagne, you must first agree on something to celebrate. You two have been sulking all day. I want you to focus on the positive and remember all the many blessings in your lives. One blessing earns you one sip of Champagne."

Izzy rolled her eyes. "Good grief. I should've known you were up to something."

"You'll thank me later." Blossom returned the bottle to the bucket and strolled off, calling over her shoulder, "I'll be out in a minute with your salads."

Izzy folded her hands on the table. "What have you been moping about? Luke?"

Shelby nodded. "He really hurt me. Turns out I'm not good enough for him. I can't compete with his fiancé's father's billions." Shelby sat up straight in her chair and reached for her glass. "But I refuse to shed another tear over him. I'm officially declaring him out of my life." She held out her glass to Izzy. "And that *is* a reason to celebrate."

"I'll drink to that," Isabelle said, clinking her glass to Shelby's.

The kitchen door opened, and Blossom hollered, "Remember! Only one sip per blessing."

Shelby set down her glass. "Ugh. She's so bossy."

Izzy gave her a rare smile. "That she is."

Shelby stared down at the table. "I wish I knew how to get back at Luke for what he did."

"I'm sure we can think of something," Izzy said with a devious smile. "Does his fiancée know he was here?"

"I doubt it." Shelby's face lit up as an idea came to her. She pulled out her phone and clicked on her photos. "I took this selfie before we went out last night." She flashed the picture at her grandmother. I could post it to social media."

"Do it!" Izzy demanded.

Shelby zoomed in on their faces. This would be the last picture taken of them together. "Do you really think I should? It could ruin his relationship with Alexis."

"Absolutely! You're doing Alexis a favor. She should know what her fiancé has been up to."

"That's true." Accessing her Instagram account, Shelby uploaded the image and thumbed off the caption. *Look who visited me in the Lowcountry this week.* She dropped her phone on the table. "Done. I feel better already."

Izzy lifted her glass. "Another reason to celebrate."

Shelby's face grew long as she sipped Champagne.

"What's wrong now?" Izzy asked.

Shelby lowered her gaze. "I'm not proud of the way I treated Matt. I blew him off when I found out he works construction. Luke gave me a dose of my own medicine. This whole experience has helped me realize how obsessed I've been with money."

"I hate to tell you, Shelby, but despite his occupation, Matt comes from a very old, well-established, and wealthy family."

Shelby jerked her head up. "What? Then why were you so rude about his grandmother the other day?"

Izzy appeared genuinely perplexed. "Was I rude? I didn't mean to be. Adele and I aren't close friends, but we've been in the same bridge club for years. Adele's son, Richard, grew up with Pritchard."

Shelby burst out laughing. "Cute! Richard and Pritchard."

Izzy smiled. "It's a mouthful. Richard is a nice man. He handles all our insurance needs."

"I'm glad Matt's family meets your approval. That's another reason to celebrate," Shelby said, draining the last of her Champagne.

Blossom arrived with their salads—arugula with perfectly ripened honeydew, tiny balls of mozzarella cheese, and prosciutto. She refilled their glasses and said, "I see you ladies are successfully identifying your blessings."

Shelby dug her thumb into her chest. "I have. Now it's Izzy's turn."

"I would be hard-pressed to find something to celebrate about my sad life."

Blossom lay a hand on Izzy's shoulder. "I have faith in you."

Isabelle toyed with her salad while considering how much to tell her granddaughter. Finally, she set down her fork without taking a bite and stared across the table at Shelby. The young woman was strikingly beautiful despite not wearing any makeup. Physically, Shelby reminded Isabelle of Kate at this age, but her granddaughter's personality was more like her own. Kate had been right. They were both stubborn and headstrong with chips on their shoulders. Perhaps Shelby could learn something from Isabelle's mistakes.

"Years ago, I made an error in judgment that greatly affected several people's lives," Isabelle said, and she told Shelby the saga of Savannah, Pritchard, and Harper. She stared down at her untouched salad while she talked. Tears blurred her vision, but she forced herself not to cry. When she finished her sad tale, she slowly lifted her gaze to Shelby's face, where she found the disgust she expected.

"That's bad, Izzy. *Really* bad." Shelby pushed her empty plate away and fell back in her chair. "Now I understand why Savannah and Harper hate you so much."

A searing pain ripped across Isabelle's chest. "Let's not mince words."

"You're lucky Pritchard still loves you."

Fresh tears pricked her eyelids. "Prichard doesn't love me. He tolerates me."

Blossom bustled out of the kitchen, balancing a large tray in one hand over her head. Noticing Isabelle's teary eyes, she said, "Uh-oh! If we can't make nice, I'll have to take away the Champagne."

Setting the tray down on a nearby table, she removed their salads and set their dinner plates in front of them. On each plate were two soft-shell crabs on a mound of garlic cheese grits covered in corn salad.

"This looks delicious, Blossom," Shelby said.

"Thank you, child. Be sure to save room for dessert. I'm making Key lime pie, as light and fluffy as a Florida cloud." After whispering something in Shelby's ear, Blossom retrieved her tray and went back to the kitchen without pouring them more Champagne.

Isabelle pointed her fork at Blossom's retreating figure. "What did she say to you?"

"That I should be nice to you because you feel awful about what happened with Pritchard and Savannah," Shelby said, breaking off a crab leg and crunching it with her teeth.

"I do feel awful. My actions shaped their lives," Isabelle said, running her fork through her grits.

"Have you tried apologizing?"

Isabelle shook her head. "I haven't been able to find the words. An apology seems inadequate after what I did."

"Maybe, but it's a start," Shelby said, breaking her soft-shell crab in half.

"I hoped to talk to Pritchard this morning, but then he sprung his expansion plans on me, turning my life upside down."

Shelby's teal eyes widened. "What expansion plans?"

Isabelle told her granddaughter about the discovery of Edward's journal and Pritchard's determination to see her late husband's plan through.

"Now that's something to celebrate." Shelby grabbed the Champagne bottle and filled both their glasses. "The Sanctuary sounds amazing. Tell me more about this new building."

"Thirty new guest rooms will be housed on the second and third floors. The ground floor will have a reservations lobby, spa, restaurant, cocktail lounge, and upscale gift shop. The main house will revert to being my home."

"How can you not be thrilled about this, Izzy? You're getting what you want."

"I've never wanted any part of this mayhem. You're young, Shelby, with a bright future ahead of you. If you decide to stay at Magnolia Shores, you could one day be running the resort. But I'm an old lady. I have nothing to contribute to either the family or the business."

"Oh. I see. You're upset because you're getting old, not because Pritchard is making Granddaddy's dream come true."

Isabelle's skin crawled. Was she that transparent? "When did you get to be so ruthless?"

Shelby shrugged. "I'm a chip off my grandmother's block."

Isabelle lifted her glass. "Touché."

"Seriously, Izzy. You're looking at this all wrong. You could play a vital role in this new plan. As grand mistress of Magnolia Shores, you could host afternoon teas. Think of all the interesting people you'd meet. You could take guests on nature walks like you used to do with Grace and me when we were little."

Isabelle's face softened. "You remember those?"

"How could I forget?" Shelby swept an arm at the dunes and ocean beyond. "You know more about the Lowcountry's natural habitat than anyone in our family. You should share that knowledge with our guests. As well as the history of Magnolia Shores. The story of how our family came to be here is fascinating. You could have bakeoffs in the kitchen and whiskey tastings in the afternoons. I mean, the possibilities are endless."

"When did you get so creative?"

Shelby pressed her hands to her head. "I'm not sure. The ideas keep coming. It must be the Champagne. I think I'll have some more." She emptied the bottle into her glass. "We can build a second dock and have our own mini marina, offering kayak and paddleboard rentals, sightseeing trips, and water taxis to town."

As they finished supper, Shelby babbled on about her ideas for the resort. Isabelle couldn't help but smile. The girl's enthusiasm was contagious.

Isabelle dabbed at her lips and pushed her empty plate away. "You need to write these ideas down to share them with Pritchard."

Shelby grew still, her fork frozen in midair. "I will. Does this mean you approve of the expansion?"

"As much as I'm ever going to approve. You've helped me see that it's time for me to step aside and let you young folks handle the dirty work. I will be the grand mistress of Magnolia Shores. Thank you for your vote of confidence, Shelby. I will focus my efforts on providing activities for our guests. As it happens, I am well versed in the art of entertainment." Isabelle frowned. "But before we can move forward, I must figure out how to apologize to Pritchard, Savannah, and Harper."

"That's easy," Shelby said with a flick of her wrist.

Isabelle planted her elbows on the table. "Okay, smarty pants. If it's so easy, tell me how I go about it."

Shelby tapped her chin. "Hmm, let's see. You should invite them over. Not for dinner. And definitely not for drinks. You need everyone to keep a level head. Maybe tomorrow afternoon around five. You can meet with them in the cottage or Edward's study if you can find somewhere to sit."

Isabelle bit down on her lower lip to keep it from quivering. "What do I say to them?"

"Tell them you're sorry. Own up to your mistake and let them know how much you regret what happened. It's not what you say, Izzy. It's how you say it. The apology must come from your heart."

"How do you know so much about apologies?"

"Because I've spent the last year apologizing to Luke."

Isabelle tilted her head to the side. "I don't understand."

"Luke never gave me a legitimate reason for breaking up with me. He said our relationship had run its course, but I convinced myself I'd done something wrong. I apologized for every single thing I might have done to turn him away. I basically apologized for being me."

Isabelle patted her hand. "You should never apologize for being yourself, Shelby. You have much to offer the world."

"Thanks for *your* vote of confidence, Izzy." Shelby glanced down at her phone on the table. "My friends are blowing me up about the picture I posted."

"Are you going to respond?"

"Nope." Shelby turned her phone face down. "I'll let them

wonder. I don't care about those people anymore. My life is here now."

Blossom came out of the kitchen with three slices of Key lime pie and sat down at the table with them. "I'm sensing a more positive vibe between you two. I assume this means you identified reasons to celebrate."

Isabelle looked over at her granddaughter. "We did. More importantly, I believe we've buried the hatchet."

Shelby gave Isabelle a definitive nod. "We did." She flashed Blossom a mischievous grin. "Can we have more Champagne?"

Blossom held out empty hands. "I don't have any more to offer you, child. Besides, I think you've had enough."

Shelby giggled. "You're probably right. I'm definitely a little tipsy."

After they finished their dessert, Blossom refused their offer to help clean up and sent them off to bed.

Isabelle and Shelby walked together to the courtyard. "Where are you sleeping these days?" Isabelle asked.

Shelby pointed at the far corner window on the second floor of the pool house. "The room at the end of the hall on the second floor. It's so small, I wouldn't feel right renting it to our guests."

"You're welcome to move back into the cottage if you change your mind."

Shelby hesitated. "Thanks. But we're better off having our own space."

Isabelle sensed something still bothering Shelby. "You're disappointed in me. I can see it in your eyes. I'm . . ." The word was on her lips, but she couldn't bring herself to say it. "I'll try to do better in the future."

Shelby embraced her. "No worries, Izzy. I'm not the one you need to apologize to."

thirty-one

. . .

Shelby was concerned when she found Blossom preparing breakfast for their guests on Friday morning. She'd been hard on her grandmother last night. While Izzy deserved it after what she'd done to Savannah and Pritchard, Shelby hoped she hadn't given her grandmother a stroke. Can traumatic events cause old people to have strokes?

"Where's Izzy? Is she okay?" she asked Blossom as she poured herself a coffee.

"Oh, she's fine. She's in her cottage, rehearsing her speech. She's meeting with her family this afternoon," Blossom said, removing warmed mini quiches from the oven.

Shelby added cream to her coffee. "So, she left you to serve breakfast to our guests?"

"I volunteered," Blossom said, brushing a stray silver curl off her forehead.

"Here, I'll help. You shouldn't have to do it alone. You're a guest." Shelby took the tray from Blossom and began transferring the quiches to a serving platter. "I'm glad Izzy's going through with the apology."

"Me too. Whatever you said to her last night got through to

her. She's already spoken to Pritchard and asked them to come over at five o'clock."

"Good for her for not wasting any time."

Blossom stared down her nose at Shelby. "Are you joking? She's wasted thirty-plus years."

"That's true." Shelby placed the metal tray in the sink and leaned against the counter. "Is that why you're here, Blossom? To help Izzy make things right with Pritchard and Savannah."

"That's one of many reasons. Turning her home into a B&B has rocked her world. I'm here to help her sort it out."

Shelby dropped down to a nearby stool with her coffee. "How could she do something so awful to her own son?"

"She was trying to protect Pritchard. She worried he was too young to have a wife and child. She didn't mean for things to go so far. She made a mistake, and it spiraled out of control. If she'd owned up to it right away, she could've done something about it."

"Instead, Savannah and Pritchard missed out on thirty years of their child's life. I was curious why Savannah and Harper hate Izzy so much. Now I wish I hadn't found out. I can't stop thinking about it."

"Hate is a strong word, baby girl. Savannah and Harper don't strike me as people who hate anyone." Blossom removed a bowl of fresh fruit from the refrigerator. "We should never judge anyone until we've walked in their shoes. The important thing now is for Izzy to make things right so her family can heal. She desperately wants this. I hope she has the strength to make it happen."

Shelby gave her a funny look. "Make what happen? All she has to do is say she's sorry."

"For some people, that's easier said than done, Shelby."

Two guests came through the back door, hungry for breakfast. When Blossom went to greet them, Shelby refilled her mug and sneaked outside to the hammock where she turned her thoughts to the proposed expansion plans. This revelation was a game changer, the reason she'd been looking for to stay at Magnolia

Shores. She could hardly wait to talk to Pritchard, but she would wait until things with Izzy were sorted.

Around four thirty, Shelby was seated on the front stoop with her laptop, checking in weekend guests as they arrived, when Matt emerged from the house and dropped down beside her on the steps. "Hey, kiddo."

She jabbed her elbow into his side. "Stop calling me that. I'm not a kid."

He leaned into her. "Sorry, *Shelby*. Things are looking good in the house. The floor refinishing is complete. Stay off of them through the weekend. The painters should be done on Monday afternoon. After that, we'll turn the house back over to you."

"Great! That'll give us plenty of time to put everything back together before next weekend."

"I haven't seen you around these past few days. How did things go with Luke? Is he still here?"

"Nope. He left first thing yesterday. Turns out he wanted less than I was willing to give him. Our relationship is over for good."

Matt looked at her quizzically but didn't press for more information. "I'm glad for you. That guy was a jerk. You can do better."

"I can't believe I wasted so much time on him."

"Time is never wasted if you learn something from your experiences, Shelby."

"Oh, I definitely learned a lot. Everything is much clearer to me now. I didn't realize how toxic my life in Texas had become. I found out something exciting last night about Magnolia Shores. I probably shouldn't say too much about it yet. But for the first time since Luke and I broke up, I feel like I have a real future."

Matt gave her a half hug. "That's awesome, Shelby. I'm glad for you."

The feel of his body stirred something inside of her. There was no denying their chemistry. Maybe the age difference wasn't such a big deal after all. "What're you doing later? You owe me a visit to Comet Dogs. I'll be finished here soon if you want to swing by in your boat."

"I'm sorry, kiddo. But I have a date." Kissing her cheek, he got to his feet and drove off in his truck.

Shelby's eyes stung, but she laughed out loud instead of crying. She needed to take a break from men and focus on herself for a change. If she impressed Pritchard with her brilliant ideas for the new resort, he might offer her an important role at The Sanctuary. She hugged herself. She just loved the way that sounded.

Pritchard glanced at Harper in the back seat. She was staring out the window, her mind seemingly a million miles away. "What're you thinking about back there?"

Harper met his gaze in the mirror. "Izzy. Why do you think she's summoned us?"

"There's no telling. But we'll soon find out," Pritchard said, returning his eyes to the road.

Harper let out a frustrated sigh. "I don't know how to shake this anger I feel toward her. It's eating me up inside. Because of Izzy, we missed out on thirty years of being together. I'm grateful I landed in a good home, but I can't help but wonder what my life would've been like if you two had raised me."

"The what-ifs will consume you if you let them." Savannah shifted in her seat to look at Harper. "But I know what you mean about the anger. I regret not coming home while my mother was still alive. I missed out on the opportunity to give her a piece of my mind." She patted Pritchard's arm. "I know it's difficult to hear us talking about your mother like this. If only she weren't so openly hostile toward us. She clearly resents us being a part of your life. Her animosity makes it difficult to be around her."

Pritchard slowed his speed when he reached the entrance to Magnolia Shores. "I agree. It makes it awkward for everyone.

How do you feel about the three of us seeking counseling? If we're going to be working together to expand the resort, we need to manage our feelings and figure out how to handle Izzy."

"That's not a bad idea," Savannah said as Pritchard parked in front of the house.

"What will you do if she refuses to go along with the expansion?" Harper asked.

Pritchard turned off the engine. "Good question. The bed and breakfast will never be profitable on its own. If we're not careful, it could burn up every last cent in Dad's estate."

The threesome piled out of the car and stopped to speak to Shelby on the way inside.

"Matt says they'll be finished with the house on Monday afternoon," Shelby reported.

"Great news," Harper said. "I'll block off some time on Tuesday to bring the new accessories over from my storage unit."

Shelby's teal eyes brightened. "Cool! Let me know if you want some help."

Harper smiled at her cousin. "That'd be great. I'll text you about a time."

Shelby shifted her attention to Pritchard. "By the way, Izzy told me about the expansion plans. When you get a chance, I'd love to share some ideas I have."

Pritchard nodded. "Sure thing! I look forward to hearing them. How did Izzy seem when she told you about the project? When I spoke to her about it yesterday, she was adamantly opposed to the idea."

"She's coming around," Shelby said. "Honestly, I think she's feeling old and unappreciated. She's not sure how she fits in the picture."

Pritchard stroked his chin. "I haven't considered that, but you may very well be onto something. We'll talk more later," he said, giving Shelby's shoulder a squeeze.

When her family entered the study, Isabelle came from behind her husband's desk to greet them. "Thanks for coming on such short notice," she said, motioning them to the sitting area.

Savannah, Harper, and Pritchard sat together on the sofa opposite Isabelle in a wing chair. She clasped her hands in her lap and held her shoulders high. "This conversation is long overdue. I made a grave error in judgment years ago that cost each of you dearly. I won't make excuses for my actions except to say I truly believed I was doing what was best for you." She set her tearful eyes on Pritchard. "You were so young. I underestimated your love for Savannah. I thought your obsession with her was a passing fancy. Obviously, I was wrong."

Savannah moved to the edge of her seat. "You weren't alone in your conspiracy. Did you know my mother tricked me into signing the papers and secretly arranged for the adoption?"

"Not at the time. I never would have approved of such a criminal act. But I knew something wasn't right when you ran away, and I did nothing to try to find you or make it right. You were gone, and that's all I cared about." Isabelle paused to gather her wits before continuing. "What's worse is how I've treated you and Harper since your return. I've had my son to myself for thirty years, and I resented your intrusion into our lives." Her gaze shifted to Prichard. "I'm a selfish old woman. I hated having to share you. Seeing how happy Savannah and Harper make you leaves me positively green with envy. But you're a wonderful man, Pritchard. I could not have asked more of a son. And you deserve to be happy."

"Thank you, Mother."

Isabelle can't remember the last time Pritchard called her *Mom*. Definitely not since Savannah came back into his life, since he discovered what Isabelle had done to break them up all those years ago. "Your father threw me for a loop with his crazy plans for this bed and breakfast. At my age, change isn't easy. I realize I've been difficult and unpleasant to be around. If you're willing to give me a second chance, I promise to do better in the future."

Uncertainty clouded her daughter-in-law's face. Savannah was waiting for an apology. Isabelle wasn't sure she could give her one. A shooting pain traveled through her brain, causing her eyes to see flickers of light.

"Does this mean you'll go along with the expansion?" Pritchard asked.

"You don't need my blessing, son. However, thanks to Shelby, the idea is growing on me. I'm stepping aside. From now on, running this business is your responsibility."

"The idea is for us to run the business together. You will have a role here if you want one."

"We can talk about all that later. I've lived with this deep remorse long enough. There's no way to compensate for the time you three lost together because of me. I invited you here today to say . . . I'm . . ."

"Mother? What's wrong? Are you okay?"

The light dimmed, and Isabelle's vision blurred as the world around her slipped away.

thirty-two

. . .

Pritchard shot off the sofa like a cannon, rushing to his mother's aid as her crumpled body slid out of the chair to the floor. He yelled to Savannah, "Quick! Call an ambulance. Tell them to hurry."

"I'm on it," Savannah said, moving into the living room for better cell service.

Harper pulled out her phone. "I'll call Cody. He knows all the paramedics. He can make the ambulance get here quicker."

"Good thinking. And ask Shelby to find out if there's a doctor or nurse in the house."

Pritchard grabbed a throw blanket from the sofa and draped it over Izzy's still body. All color had drained from her face, and her skin was cold. He stroked her hair and spoke softly to her. "Don't die on me, Mom. We've been through so much this past year. It's now time to put our differences aside and be a family."

Harper returned with Blossom on her heels. "Shelby is checking with the guests to see if any trained medical professionals are on the property."

Pritchard's eyes darted around the room. "Where's Savannah?"

"She's in the courtyard, waiting for the ambulance," Harper said.

Blossom knelt beside Izzy and gently shook her. "Wake up, Izzy. This is no time for theatrics."

Izzy's body remained lifeless, her chest barely rising and falling.

"Is she dying?" Pritchard asked with fear in his eyes.

"I don't know, son." Blossom pressed her finger to Izzy's wrist. "Her pulse is weak. I'm not a doctor, but she's probably had a stroke."

A winded Shelby appeared in the doorway. "No medical professionals are on-site, but I heard the ambulance's sirens approaching."

Less than a minute later, a team of paramedics filled the room. They went to work on Izzy, attaching an oxygen mask to her face and transferring her body to the gurney.

"Where are you taking her?" Pritchard asked, hurrying alongside them as they wheeled his mother out of the house to the awaiting ambulance.

"Beaufort County Regional," one of the paramedics said.

"Don't let her die," Pritchard said with a pleading tone as they lifted her into the back of the ambulance.

The paramedic gave him a curt nod. "We'll do our best, sir."

After the ambulance took off, Blossom herded everyone toward her sky-blue school bus. "I'll drive us to the hospital," she said.

"What about our guests?" Pritchard asked Shelby.

"Everyone with a weekend reservation has checked in. Silas ran out on an errand. He should be back any minute. I'll text him to let him know what happened. He can cover for us while we're gone."

Shelby had stopped walking, her thumbs flying across her phone screen, when a patrol car screeched to a halt in the courtyard, and Cody hopped out from behind the wheel. "I passed the ambulance on my way in. How bad is it?"

"We're not sure," Harper said. "She's unconscious. They're taking her to Beaufort County General."

Cody motioned Harper to his passenger side. "Get in. You can ride with me. I'll escort the others to the hospital."

The rest of the small group hurried over to Blossom's bus. Shelby climbed into the front passenger seat beside Blossom, and Pritchard got in the back with Savannah. They fastened their seat belts, and Blossom sped off behind Cody.

Shelby swiped at her eyes. "Is this why you're here, Blossom? Did you come to escort Izzy into heaven?"

"I was wondering that too," Pritchard admitted.

Blossom shook her head. "Death is not my department. I'm a lowly servant. If that is what the good Lord has planned, I would not have been notified. I'm sorry. I wish I could tell you more."

"Actually, I'm glad you *don't* know," Shelby said. "We still have hope."

When Savannah sniffled, Pritchard looked over to see tears streaming down her face. He reached for her hand. "Are you okay?"

Savannah shook her head. "Izzy was trying to say something when she went pale and fell out of the chair."

"She was probably trying to say she was sorry," Shelby said.

Blossom bobbed her head, her silver coils dancing atop her crown. "Mm-hmm. Something traumatic happened to her as a child that makes saying she's sorry difficult. She should be the one to tell you about it."

"*If* she gets that chance," Pritchard mumbled under his breath.

Blossom locked eyes with him in the rearview mirror. "Don't underestimate the power of prayer, son. Your mama needs your strength right now. Let her know you're pulling for her."

Pritchard felt as though his Sunday school teacher had scolded him. "Yes, ma'am."

Mayhem greeted them at the hospital. A harried female doctor clad in blue scrubs shooed them from the examining area to the waiting room. "We'll find you once we know what we're dealing with."

The waiting room was packed with patients of all ages, some nursing wounds and others moaning in pain. Blossom secured seats for them in the far corner of the room by a window and headed off to the cafeteria for refreshments. She returned a few minutes later with coffee for everyone and a basket of homemade nibbles she could not have found in the cafeteria.

Shelby slipped away, and Pritchard assumed she was going to the restroom. But when she returned, she handed him her phone. "My mom wants to talk to you."

Pritchard took the phone and walked toward the exit. "Hey, Kate. I was waiting to call you until we found out more about Mom's condition."

"I need to be there. I'm looking at flights now. I'll fly as far as possible and drive the rest of the way. I'll text you when I figure out my itinerary."

Pritchard felt a rush of relief. "Good! I'd rather not have to cope with this alone. Safe travels."

An hour later, Kate texted Pritchard from the Austin airport. Her flight was scheduled to arrive in Charlotte around ten fifteen. She would rent a car for the three-and-a-half-hour drive to the Lowcountry. Based on Pritchard's estimation, she would get to the hospital around two in the morning.

A few minutes past eight, Dr. Lydia Becker, the same harried doctor they'd met earlier, finally arrived with an update. "A CT scan revealed that Isabelle had an ischemic stroke due to a blood clot in the right hemisphere of her brain. We have commenced thrombolytic therapy to dissolve the blood clot. Now we wait. It's going to be a long night."

"Is surgery a possibility?" Savannah asked.

"We will reassess if the thrombolytics don't have the desired effect," Dr. Becker responded.

"Are you confident in the care she'll receive here, or should we consider transferring her to MUSC in Charleston?" Pritchard asked.

"She's receiving the necessary care here. I'll recommend it immediately if there's any need for a transfer to a more specialized facility. Now, if you'll excuse me, I need to get back to the patient," the doctor said and disappeared through the double doors to the treatment area.

Pritchard turned to his family. "You heard the doctor. We're in for a long night. There's no reason for all of us to stay."

Harper glanced over at Cody. "Do you mind giving me a ride home? I have to be at work early in the morning."

"Not at all." Cody checked his watch." I need to head out as well. I should check in at the station."

Harper kissed Pritchard's cheek. "Text me with updates, no matter the time."

"Of course." Pritchard then looked at Blossom and Shelby. "What about you two? Savannah and I can hold down the fort if you need to get back to Magnolia Shores."

"I'm not leaving until Mom gets here." Shelby clutched her phone. "I've been texting with Silas. He's got everything under control. But Blossom, you don't need to stay on my account. I'm sure you need to check on Jolene."

Blossom shook her head. "I go where you go, baby girl. Silas is keeping an eye on Jolene for me."

"Then I guess we wait," Savannah said, pulling Pritchard down to the seat beside her.

Minutes clicked off the wall clock at an excruciatingly slow pace. The waiting room emptied one by one as patients were called back for treatment. When Pritchard noticed Shelby sitting by the window, staring into the dark parking lot, he moved to the chair beside her. "Tell me about your conversation with Izzy last night."

"I was hard on her when she told me what happened with Savannah and your baby. I said some harsh things. Do you think I gave her a stroke?" Shelby sobbed, bringing her balled fist to her mouth.

Pritchard put an arm around her, drawing her close. "No, sweetheart. You did not give her a stroke. If anything, Izzy gave herself a stroke. She was apologizing when she passed out. A long overdue apology, I might add. We're all ready to put this ugly business behind us and focus on the future. I hope we get a chance to be a family."

"I hope so too." A smile tugged at the corner of Shelby's lips. "She was more like her old self last night, not the mean Izzy who's been making everyone's lives miserable lately. She seemed to like the idea of being the grand mistress of Magnolia Shores. I suggested she could take guests on nature walks and host afternoon teas. She could have fun meeting new people and sharing the property's history."

Pritchard and Shelby discussed their ideas for the resort for over an hour. For someone so young and inexperienced, he was impressed with her insight. He assured her she would play a vital role in managing The Sanctuary.

When they finally looked up, Pritchard saw that both Savannah and Blossom had fallen asleep. Savannah's head rested on Blossom's shoulder, while Blossom's was tilted back, her face to the ceiling, as she snored softly.

Pritchard and Shelby soon dozed off and were awakened by the doctor around two o'clock. But before she could provide an update, a haggard-looking Kate trudged into the emergency room. After introductions and greetings, the doctor said, "I have nothing new to report. We'll do another scan in the morning to determine if our treatment is working. As soon as a bed opens up, she'll be moved to intensive care."

"What's the prognosis, Doctor?" Kate asked.

"I'm sorry, ma'am. It's a little too early to make that judgment."

thirty-three

. . .

Shelby waited until the doctor left before collapsing into her mother's arms. "I'm glad you're here."

"Me too, sweetheart. I've missed you. Let me get a good look at you." Kate drew away, pressing her palms to Shelby's cheeks. "You look healthy. The salt air and sunshine agree with you."

"I have so much to tell you. Unfortunately, I need to get some sleep. With Izzy in the hospital, I'll have to get up early to serve breakfast to our guests. I can get Blossom to drive me home if you want to stay."

"You go ahead. I want to talk to Pritchard, and I'm hoping the doctor will let me see Izzy. Besides, I'm too wired from the trip to sleep. We'll catch up later."

Shelby followed Blossom outside to the bus, and they rode back to Water's Edge in silence. When they arrived at Magnolia Shores, Blossom said, "I'll cover for you if you decide to sleep in tomorrow."

"No way! I've got this. Although, if you happen to be awake, I wouldn't mind a little help."

"You've got it. I'll meet you in the kitchen at seven," Blossom said, and they parted with a hug in the courtyard.

Despite being exhausted, Shelby was too worried about her

grandmother to sleep. When six o'clock rolled around, she gave up trying and headed to the kitchen.

Pearl and Hilda were distraught to hear about Izzy's stroke. "She was such a nice lady," Pearl said.

Shelby's jaw dropped. "Are we talking about the same woman?"

"Yes! She was set in her ways and had high expectations, but she was always kind to us."

"She's not dead yet," Shelby snapped. "Stop talking about her in the past tense."

Blossom and Shelby served the guests a simple breakfast of warmed croissants, fresh fruit, and sausage links. Most of the guests had seen the ambulance and asked with genuine concern about Izzy's health.

Once everyone had been served, Shelby left Hilda and Pearl to clean up and took a large tumbler of coffee outside. She walked down to the beach and around to the tip of Sandy Island, where the ocean met the inlet. She needed to be alone with her thoughts. As the world came alive around her, she sat in the sand and stared at the ocean. Her mind drifted back to childhood mornings on the beach. Izzy had often snuck a rambunctious Grace and Shelby out of the house so their parents could sleep in. They watched porpoises dive and sea turtles leaving their nests. They built sandcastles, swam in the ocean, and searched for shells. Her grandfather and his yellow lab, Honey, often joined them. The sweet old dog loved to race up and down the beach, chasing flocks of seagulls. Her grandparents were knowledgeable about wildlife, making every excursion a learning experience.

Shelby was so lost in thought that she didn't hear the rumble of a boat engine, and the loud ringing of her phone startled her. She had set the ringtone on high to avoid missing calls about Izzy. But the call wasn't from her mother or Pritchard. It was Matt.

"Good morning, sunshine. What're you doing sitting on the beach alone?"

Shelby looked up to see Matt waving at her from his boat. She waved back. "Thinking about my grandmother. Izzy had a stroke."

Matt's breath hitched. "I'm sorry, Shelby. When did this happen?"

"Last night, right after you left. She's still unconscious. We don't know the extent of the damage yet or if she's even going to make it." Shelby stood up and brushed the sand off her shorts. "What're you doing?"

"Getting minnows to fish with later. Wanna go for a ride?"

"As long as we don't leave the cell service area. I'm waiting to hear from my mom about Izzy."

"No worries. I'll stay near the shore."

Shelby waded knee-deep into the water, and Matt nosed the boat close enough for her to climb onto the bow. He cast his net a few times, filling his live bait well with minnows, and they took off at a slow speed up the coast with Shelby sitting beside him on the leaning post.

"So, how was your date last night?" she asked with a smirk.

"It was a disaster. I agreed to have drinks with her as a favor to my sister. The girl was my youngest sister's friend, but she was painfully shy. By the time I got home, I was exhausted from carrying the conversation."

Shelby laughed. "Poor girl."

Matt leaned into Shelby. "I'm not interested in other girls. A certain freckled face, strawberry-blonde has gotten under my skin. I'm willing to give us another go if you are?"

Shelby raised an eyebrow. "Are you suddenly okay with dating a *kiddo*?"

Matt chuckled. "If you're okay with dating a lowly carpenter."

"I've learned the hard way that money doesn't matter."

His smile faded. "I hear a *but* in your tone."

She looked away from him, staring out over the bow. "A *but* that has nothing to do with you, Matt. Now that I've finally gotten Luke out of my system, I need to focus on myself for a change, to decide what I want to do with my life. But I enjoy hanging out with you, and I could really use a friend."

He chucked her chin. "I can be that friend. I won't pressure you. I'm willing to wait as long as it takes for you to come around."

"Do you really like my freckles?"

"I'm crazy about your freckles." He touched the tip of her nose. "Can I play connect the dots on your face?"

Shelby laughed out loud. "Many people have said that to me. You're the first person who's made me laugh."

Her phone rang, and she dug it out of her pocket. "This is my mom." Accepting the call, Shelby blurted, "How's Izzy?"

"The same. She hasn't woken up yet. They've moved her to intensive care. Where are you? Is that a boat motor I hear in the background?"

"Yep. I'm taking a ride with a friend," Shelby said, shoulder-bumping Matt. "Where are you?"

"On the way home. I'm crossing the Merriweather Bridge now. I need to shower and eat before heading back to the hospital."

"I'll get my friend to bring me back. I'll see you in a few."

Matt was already turning the boat around when she ended the call. "I know you're worried about your grandmother, Shelby. And I'm here for you. Whatever you need—a shoulder to cry on, boat rides, fish, if we catch any this afternoon."

She rested her head on his shoulder. "Thank you. For now, just being my friend is enough."

"Where should I sleep?" Kate asked as she lifted her rolling suitcase out of the trunk of her rental car.

Shelby mentally ran down the list of their current guests. "Most of the rooms in the garden and pool houses are occupied. Do you mind staying in the caretaker's cottage?"

"But isn't that where you're staying?" Kate asked, slamming the trunk closed.

"Izzy and I were cramping each other's style, so I moved to a tiny room in the pool house."

"Good. You should have your own space. I guess it's the cottage for me, then." Kate cast one last longing look at the main house before wheeling her suitcase in the opposite direction.

Shelby followed her inside the cottage.

"This place is depressing," Kate said about the outdated interior. "I can't believe Mom agreed to stay here."

"She didn't have a choice," Shelby muttered.

Kate parked her suitcase in the middle of the room and lifted back the heavy drapes to let in light. "We should spruce it up before she comes home from the hospital."

"That's a great idea! She'll be spending a lot of time here while she recovers. Harper can help. She owns an interior design firm."

Kate's face registered surprise. "She does? I didn't realize that. Good for her." She turned back toward Shelby. "Darling, I've missed you so much. I want to hear about everything going on in your life. Give me a few minutes to get settled and cleaned up, and we'll meet in the kitchen for an early lunch."

"Sounds good. I need to shower and change as well."

Twenty minutes later, Shelby entered the kitchen, dressed in white jeans and a blue linen top, her hair still damp from the shower. Blossom was at the table, sipping sweet tea and thumbing through one of her grandmother's recipe books.

Jolene greeted her at the door with tail wagging. "I'm happy to see you too," Shelby said, leaning over and rubbing the dog behind the ears.

"Mom's here," Shelby reported to Blossom. "She says Izzy is still unconscious."

Blossom looked up, concern etched in the lines on her pretty caramel face. "I'm sorry to hear that. Have they done another scan?"

Shelby straightened. "I'm not sure. She didn't say." She went to the refrigerator. "Do we have any sandwich meat?"

"I don't believe so. If you'd like a BLT, there's plenty of bacon and beautiful summer tomatoes. I'll go to the market this afternoon."

Blossom got up from the table and rummaged through the junk drawer for a notepad. While Shelby microwaved bacon, Blossom made out a list of groceries. When Kate arrived, Blossom helped Shelby toast bread and put the sandwiches together, adding a scoop of potato salad and a deviled egg to each plate.

The threesome sat down at the table together for lunch. Kate appeared refreshed in a green summer dress with her beautiful auburn mane tied back in a low ponytail, but dark circles rimmed her emerald eyes, and lines creased her forehead. Yesterday had been a long day for her mother. Shelby wondered if she'd gotten any sleep at the hospital.

"I'm going to cook dinner for your family tonight," Blossom announced, still working on her grocery list. "You'll need a break from the hospital, and you have to eat. You should all be together at a time like this."

Kate offered her a weary smile. "Thank you, Blossom. That's very kind of you."

Blossom set down her pen and bit into her sandwich. "It's the least I can do. Staying busy keeps me from worrying so much."

Kate checked her watch. "I should get back to the hospital soon. I want to be there when they do the second CAT scan."

"How long are you staying?" Shelby asked. "I'd like to see Izzy, but I shouldn't be gone for too long with guests in the house."

Kate shrugged. "Then we'll take separate cars. I doubt I'll come home until dinner."

Shelby cut her eyes at her mother. "I'm not allowed to drive, Mom. Remember?"

Recognition crossed Kate's face. "Oh, right. I forgot about that. I talked to Pritchard for a long time after you left the hospital last night. He raved about your performance, your capability, and how well you carry yourself."

Shelby beamed. "Wow! I'm glad he thinks so. I've been trying really hard."

"And it shows," Blossom said, jabbing a forkful of potato salad at Shelby.

Kate smiled. "I agree. You can drive Izzy's car until we figure out how to get yours to South Carolina." She paused, staring up at the ceiling in thought. "Although logistically, it might be easier to sell that car and find you something here."

Shelby would be happy driving a golf cart if it got her where she needed to go. "Thanks, Mom. Izzy's car is fine for now."

After finishing her sandwich, Blossom excused herself to take Jolene outside to potty, giving Kate and Shelby a moment alone.

Kate wiped her lips and dropped her napkin on her empty plate. "I'm glad to hear you're making new friends. Who were you boat riding with this morning?"

"His name is Matt. He's a super nice guy. I like him a lot, but he's older than me. We've agreed to be just friends for now."

"Mm-hmm. The look on your face tells me otherwise. How much older is he?"

"Thirty-one." Shelby held her breath, waiting for her mother to freak out. But her response surprised her.

"That's only seven years. I know couples who are ten years apart. Age doesn't matter much when you reach a certain point in life."

"We'll see. Maybe something will come of our relationship. But for now, I need some time to myself." Shelby took one last bite of her sandwich and dropped the crust on her plate. "Luke came to see me this week," she said and told her mother about his visit.

Kate appeared horrified. "Why that rotten little . . . I have in mind to call his mother."

Shelby laughed out loud. "Don't, Mom. He's not worth it. Believe it or not, I'm finally over him."

Kate narrowed her eyes as she looked closely at Shelby. "I think you mean it."

"I do. And I'm tired of talking about him. How's Dad?"

Kate stiffened. "I'd rather not talk about him either."

Shelby's skin prickled. "Why? What's wrong, Mom?"

"There's nothing for you to worry about, sweetheart. I'm sorry I brought it up. Your father and I are going through a rough patch. But we'll be fine. We always are."

Shelby watched her mom rinse her plate and place it in the dishwasher. Kate seemed down, and Shelby sensed it was more than her concern over Izzy. Were the problems in their marriage worse than her mom was admitting?

thirty-four

. . .

Pritchard remained at the hospital for a long time after Kate left on Saturday afternoon. He'd barely slept in the past thirty-six hours, only dozing occasionally in the chair beside his mother's bed. The antiseptic smells and constant beeping of the monitors wore on his frazzled nerves, but Blossom's words played repeatedly in his head. *Don't underestimate the power of prayer, son. Your mama needs your strength right now. Let her know you're pulling for her.* He needed to be as close as possible to Izzy so that she could feel his strength.

Truthfully, he'd forgiven his mother long ago for interfering in his relationship with Savannah. He'd been so young, and she'd been adamant he wasn't ready to be a father. He might have reacted the same way if he'd been in her shoes. But he'd been disappointed in the unfair way she'd been treating Savannah and Harper since they came back into his life. She'd been trying to apologize when she had the stroke. He prayed she lived so they could finally be a family.

Around six o'clock, he was debating whether to bail on the family dinner when Dr. Becker stopped by with the results of Izzy's recent brain scan. "I have good news. The thrombolytic therapy is working. The blood clot is dissolving."

Pritchard ran his fingers through his disheveled hair. "That's wonderful, Doctor. Are you concerned that she hasn't woken up?"

"Not yet. She needs rest to heal." A frown crept across Dr. Becker's face as she took a closer look at Pritchard. "I am concerned about *you*, however. You look awful. Have you been here this entire time?"

"Yes, but I'm leaving soon to grab dinner with my family."

"Excellent! And don't come back! You need a good night's sleep. Your mother has a long road of recovery ahead of her. You'll need all the energy and patience you can muster to help her through it."

"But what if she wakes up and I'm not here? I don't want her to be afraid."

The doctor's expression softened. "You're a good son. Your mother is lucky to have you. Leave your number at the nurses' station. They will call you if she regains consciousness."

Pritchard watched the doctor leave before turning back to Izzy. "You heard the woman. The doctor ordered me to get some rest. I admit, I'm pretty worn out." He kissed her forehead. "I love you, Mom. You're going to be okay."

Savannah and Harper had dropped off his car at the hospital earlier, and by the time he got to Magnolia Shores around seven, the others were having cocktails on the terrace. They gathered around him while he updated them on Izzy's condition, breathing a collective sigh of relief when he told them her treatment was working.

"That's awesome news," Shelby said. "I've been so worried. Mom suggested we give the cottage a facelift to boost Izzy's spirits when she comes home." She glanced over at Harper. "Do you have time to take on this minor project?"

"Of course! We'll brighten it up with cheerful colors while keeping it cozy." Everyone laughed when Harper removed her paint wheel from her bag and began flipping through the colors.

Savannah suggested they talk to her brother. "Since Will

already has a paint crew working on the main house, they may be able to knock out the cottage while they're here."

Prichard smiled. "Great idea. I'll call him tomorrow."

"We can throw that awful plaid furniture in the construction dumpster," Kate said.

Shelby smiled. "Yes! Let's! I bet Harper has a suitable replacement in her storage unit."

Harper nodded. "I'm certain of it."

When Blossom called them to dinner, they continued discussing ideas for the cottage renovation as they migrated to the table. Blossom had recruited Pearl to help with the dinner. They'd set the rectangular table with candles in hurricane globes and small bouquets of wildflowers.

Pritchard sat at one end of the table and Savannah at the other, with Harper and Cody to Pritchard's right, and Shelby and Kate to his left. He bowed his head and offered the blessing, asking the good Lord to take extra special care of Izzy. When he finished, he lifted his wine glass. "Despite our reason for being here, having my family together means the world to me. We've been through some difficult times together, but I hope tonight will mark the beginning of happier days."

Shelby wasn't surprised to see tears in Pritchard's eyes. His sentimental nature endeared him to her and deepened her respect for him. Unlike her father, who rarely showed emotion, she appreciated a man who wasn't afraid to express his feelings. Although she didn't know Matt all that well yet, she sensed he was an honorable Southern gentleman like her uncle.

While the others chatted around them, Shelby turned to her mom. "How long are you staying?"

Kate forked at her lettuce. "I'd originally planned to go home once Izzy regained consciousness, but I have plenty of vacation time built up, and I've decided to stay a few days, maybe a week.

Once Mom wakes up, the doctor will have to assess the damage from the stroke. And I'll need to line up caregivers for when she comes home. I can help Harper refresh the cottage and spend time with my girl," she said, winking at Shelby.

"Can we go shopping for cars?" Shelby asked, her butt coming out of her chair.

Kate laughed out loud. "Why do I have a feeling you already know what you want?"

"I do! I want a Jeep Wrangler. I bet we can find a used one in good shape. I'd like to custom paint it sky blue like Blossom's bus."

"That's a tall order, Shelby. But we'll see what we can find."

Shelby grew serious. "Thank you for sending me here, Mom. I was furious at first, but I really needed this change. And I love the Lowcountry. Would you be upset if I stayed permanently? I very much want to play a role in the development of The Sanctuary."

Kate reached for her hand. "Not at all, sweetheart. The new resort sounds fascinating. I will miss you terribly, but you living here will give me reason to visit more often."

"I would like that." Shelby relished the idea of having her mother all to herself, away from her overbearing sister. The past weeks had been turbulent, but she envisioned calmer days on the horizon.

Izzy floated toward the soft light. The warmth enveloped her like a cocoon, offering a sense of peace she'd never experienced. Her husband appeared in front of her. "Turn around, Izzy. It isn't your time yet."

"Why, Edward? I yearn to be with you." She stretched her arms, desperately trying to bridge the gap between them, but an unseen barrier held her back. "I've apologized to Savannah, Harper, and Pritchard. My purpose here is fulfilled. I'm prepared for what lies beyond this world."

"Your work is far from complete, Izzy, my dear. You said the words. Now you must show them you mean them."

A flashing light caused Izzy to blink her eyes open. Her vision cleared, and her eyes traveled the room. She saw the bag of clear liquid dripping into her veins, the darkened window, and the open door through which she could see two nurses talking in hushed voices in the hallway. Someone was sleeping in the chair beside her bed. Squinting, she realized that someone was Savannah. She tried speaking, but her tongue was heavy, and she felt like her mouth was filled with cotton. She couldn't lift her left hand, but she could pat the bed with her right.

The soft sound woke Savannah, and she sat up straight in her chair. "You're awake! Thank God! I'll get the nurse," she said, slowly rising.

Izzy moaned and slowly shook her head.

"No? Okay." Savannah moved to the side of the bed. "You gave us a terrible scare, Izzy. Pritchard wanted to be here when you woke up, but he was exhausted and I insisted he get some sleep. I woke up during the night to go to the bathroom. I started worrying about you, and I knew I couldn't go back to sleep, so I decided to come check on you."

Izzy attempted to speak again, managing a garbled "Sor-ry."

Savannah stroked her blanketed leg. "I know you are. Pritchard loves you so much. For his sake, I'm willing to try and put this ugly mess behind us. We have much to be grateful for. Harper is back in our lives. The future of Magnolia Shores is bright. I respect the close bond you share with Pritchard, and I would never intentionally interfere in your relationship, but one day, I would very much like for you and me to be friends."

A pained smile tugged at one corner of Izzy's mouth. She'd been misguided about so many aspects of her life, and she didn't deserve Savannah's forgiveness. But she'd apologized to Pritchard, Savannah, and Harper, thereby taking the first step toward a new beginning—a loving and kind relationship with her family.

The journey ahead showed promise.

I hope you've enjoyed *Southern Discomfort,* the first installment in the Sandy Island series. Blossom returns in *Beyond the Carolina Sun* to help Kate through her marriage crisis. If you want to read more about Savannah and her family, be sure to check out the Marsh Point trilogy. You might also enjoy my other family drama series: Palmetto Island, Hope Springs, and Virginia Vineyards.

Use the QR code below to access my online store where you'll find bundled series and receive early access to my new releases. Buying direct means you are supporting the artist instead of big business. I appreciate you. Ashley Farley Books

Also available at Barnes and Noble, Kobo, Apple Books, Amazon, and many other online book sellers.

acknowledgments

I'm forever indebted to the many people who help bring a project to fruition. My editor, Pat Peters. My cover designer, the hardworking folks at Damonza.com. My beta readers: Alison Fauls, Anne Wolters, Laura Glenn, Jan Klein, Lisa Hudson, Lori Walton, Kathy Sinclair, Rachel Story, and Amy Connolley. Last, but certainly not least, are my select group of advanced readers who are diligent about sharing their advanced reviews prior to releases.

I'm blessed to have many supportive people in my life who offer the encouragement I need to continue my pursuit of writing. Love and thanks to my family—my mother, Joanne; my husband, Ted; and my amazing children, Cameron and Ned.

Most of all, I'm grateful to my wonderful readers for their love of women's fiction. I love hearing from you. Feel free to shoot me an email at ashleyhfarley@gmail.com or stop by my website at ashleyfarley.com for more information about my characters and upcoming releases. Don't forget to sign up for my newsletter. Your subscription will grant you exclusive content, sneak previews, and special giveaways.

about the author

Ashley Farley writes books about women for women. Her characters are mothers, daughters, sisters, and wives facing real-life issues. Her bestselling Sweeney Sisters series has touched the lives of many.

Ashley is a wife and mother of two young adult children. While she's lived in Richmond, Virginia, for the past twenty-one years, a piece of her heart remains in the salty marshes of the South Carolina Lowcountry, where she still calls home. Through the eyes of her characters, she captures the moss-draped trees, delectable cuisine, and kindhearted folk with lazy drawls that make the area so unique.

Ashley loves to hear from her readers. Visit her website @ ashleyfarley.com or online bookstore @ ashleyfarleybooks.com. Join the fun and engaged with like-minded readers in her exclusive Facebook group Georgia's Porch

Get free exclusive content by signing up for her newsletter @ ashleyfarley.com/newsletter-signup/

Made in United States
Troutdale, OR
08/09/2024

21893333R00147